Washington's Providence

A Timeless Arts Novel

Chris LaFata

First Printing, November 2013

www.chrislafata.com

Cover Art by Tamara Smith
www.tamarasmithdesigns.com

ISBN 9781492900719

This book is dedicated to my wife, Molly, and my daughters, Madeline and Grace.

New York City

April 30th, 1789

One thing about the past: I will never get used to the smell. Even the outskirts of the city were filled with the stench of horse manure and urine.

We entered the city from the north, an hour and a half's walk from our arrival point. It was just after dawn and blisters had already formed where my toes rubbed against the insides of my boots. A few wagons passed, but no one acknowledged us.

Our clothing reflected the period well enough, but I couldn't shake the feeling of being out of place. Like maybe we were too clean, too pristine for the dirt and grime surrounding us. I kept waiting for someone to point and say, "They don't belong here," but we remained anonymous and blended with the rest of the inhabitants of New York.

The unpaved streets were rough, marked by dirt, rocks, and patches of mud created by the contents of chamber pots tossed from windows in the early morning. Mark led the way with a purposeful stride across the narrow, stone sidewalks.

I stopped and inspected one of the two-story buildings. Divergent shades of red and brown bricks formed the exterior. Situated on either side of a simple white-washed door were two, large glass windows, not much of a deterrent to anyone motivated to get inside.

Here I was with a firsthand perspective of the eighteenth century, and I'm focused on why there aren't bars over the pedestrian-level windows. Twenty-first century cynicism, I guess.

Mark tugged at my arm. "Come on John. Let's get moving."

I started walking and turned my attention back to our task of locating Federal Hall where we would later see President Washington. There would be plenty of time to explore. I wanted to see the harbor. How weird would it be with no Statue of Liberty? It was already strange not seeing the sea of yellow taxis flowing through the city. No Empire State Building. No Times Square. No Central Park. No Grand Central Station. No hotdog vendors. No pizza. No fake Rolex watches.

Instead we faced narrow streets, tiny buildings, mud, and horse shit—*good God*—it was everywhere. This wasn't just an early version of New York City. It was another world. If Mark wasn't so positive our location was correct, this place could easily be mistaken for any early-American city. You can read about early American life, but until you experience it, you're not prepared. Not really. I would have to prepare future clients for this sensation.

And where were the American flags? I saw none displayed. The people seemed to be going about their business like it was an ordinary Thursday, not the inauguration of the first president of the United States.

My stomach had that tight, nervous feeling it got when something was wrong.

"I thought there would've been more activity today," I said, passing the marker for Division Street. "Everything I've read said church bells rang all morning in celebration. How come we don't hear anything?"

"It's probably still too early," said Mark. "It's not even seven yet."

"Something just feels...off."

"It's natural," he assured me. "I had the same anxiety my first time scouting. You'll see."

Maybe he was right. At this hour, only a handful of wagons ambled amongst the sparse pedestrians. Still, this was New York: the city that never sleeps. Or would that name come later?

I pulled my hand-drawn map of the city out of my pocket to see where we were. "You're probably right. Here's Queen Street. We need to go this way."

The streets deeper in the city were paved with brick cobblestones not yet worn down from years of use and we had room to walk side by side. More signs of life were visible as residents emerged from their homes and began mulling about. There was no morning chatter. People kept their heads down and their business to themselves. *Definitely New York,* I thought.

My initial fear of discovery for being out of place was unfounded. No one even noticed our existence.

As if on cue, a man hobbled toward us with a slight limp and his head down. Unwashed straggly hair dangled from under his battered tricorne hat. We parted to let him pass and he finally noticed us and looked up. He muttered something unintelligible and went on his way, the pungent smell of rye whiskey accompanied his wake.

Mark shrugged and kept moving. The reassuring view of white sails from the docks alleviated some of my stress. At least those felt right and were supposed to be here.

We followed Queen Street until we reached the corner where a brick post identified Wall Street. To the left, a clear view of the docks on the East River. We turned right and started toward

Federal Hall, which could be seen in the distance.

Mark looked back. "After we locate a good spot to hear the speech, let's sample some of the local delicacies. I'm starving."

I wasn't sure I could eat. The unsettled feeling in my stomach was still there. I would relax after we got back. Mark had been on enough trips to the past where this wasn't such a big deal, but this was still pretty new to me, and my first experience hadn't gone all that smooth.

"Yeah," I responded. "We have a few hours to kill. Maybe we can check out the docks later—"

I stopped and instinctively grabbed Mark's shoulder. Federal Hall was proudly flying the Union Jack—the British flag.

What the hell?

The butterflies in my stomach transformed into birds clamoring to get out. I fought back a wave of nausea.

I pointed at the flag. "Something's wrong with the calculations. We're a few years early." My temperature rose as blood rushed to my head.

"I don't think so," Mark pulled his glasses down, looking over the rims. "It's not as simple as picking a date. We have to consider the rotation of the Earth *and* the universe for spatial calculations. We're at the right place at the right time."

"There's no way they'd fly the Union Jack on the day of Washington's inauguration. We *have* to be early. Maybe you input the wrong date or something."

"Not a chance," he insisted, his attention redirected to a man walking by.

I held a hand up. "Excuse me, sir. Do you know where we could locate President Washington?"

The man looked up, perplexed. "Haven't heard of 'im." I couldn't tell if he was more startled by the question or by being spoken to. He hurried away with his hands in his pockets and his head hunched.

"I guess that answers our question," I said. "Let's get back to Donna and go home. We'll see what happened from—" Mark's shoulders had sagged. "What?"

"We can't," said Mark. "We're stranded."

PART 1

"…. physicists believe the separation between past, present, and future is only an illusion, although a convincing one."

Albert Einstein

ONE

Present Day

"How would you like to come to the desert for the job of your dreams?"

Mark Shippen's question intrigued me enough to fly to Las Vegas to interview for a position I knew nothing about. Normal people probably wouldn't consider boarding a plane without more details, but Mark was my oldest friend. I trusted him. Oh, and he said it paid seven figures.

According to my math: *Job of my dreams* recommended by my oldest friend plus *seven figures* equaled *me sitting on a plane* to interview for a mystery job.

After grabbing my bag from baggage claim, I headed for the limousine lane where Mark told me a driver would be waiting. Expecting some guy standing next to a black limo, I was surprised to see an attractive blonde holding a sign with my name on it leaning against a red Jeep Wrangler.

Nice work, Mark.

She was tall, about five-nine, and wore a military-green tank top revealing well-defined arms. Her hair was pulled into a tight ponytail tucked under a green baseball cap with the words, *Timeless Arts* stenciled in yellow. Mirrored aviator sunglasses concealed her eyes.

"I'm John Curry," I said offering my hand.

"Hello, professor," she replied with a firm handshake. "Lillian Campbell. Welcome to Nevada. We've got a long drive so hop in."

I flinched at being referred to as professor. I had taught college for most of my adult life, but my last contract had expired, leaving me in a career no man's land. Add one more element to Mark's job opportunity: I needed a job.

Without opening my door, she walked around the front of the Jeep and got in the driver's side. I climbed in the passenger seat and threw my bag into the back. "I could get used to being chauffeured around." I presented my most charming smile.

She forced a smile and gripped the steering wheel with both hands. "Sorry to disappoint you, but I'm not your driver. I'm doing this as a favor."

I sat in silence for a moment feeling foolish. She pulled out of the loading area leaving the protection of the covered airport garage and into the intense Nevada sun. I silently berated myself for forgetting sunglasses, picturing them sitting in the console of my parked car at my apartment.

Lillian stepped on the accelerator, changed lanes without warning, braked hard, accelerated, and braked again as she navigated the endless stream of Las Vegas taxis. Feeling a wave of nausea, I cracked my window. Mistake. Hot air blasted me like a hair dryer aimed at my face. I closed the window and redirected the air vents.

A billboard advertising the latest-greatest Cirque du Soleil show caught my attention. "Do you catch many shows?"

"No, it's too far of a drive from the facility." Her attention remained focused on the road. At least she paid attention while driving like a maniac. "Besides, we're much too busy." Traffic thinned the further we moved away from the airport lessening the sudden lurches caused by her spastic driving. It was a welcome relief to my stomach.

"What do you do?"

"I'm a guide too." Lillian exited the highway and headed north.

A guide?

Mark hadn't told me much about the position other than the company needed a historian. Technically, I wasn't even a historian. "So you teach history too?"

"No, my doctorate is in Historical Musicology."

"Oh." I had never heard of that major.

Disappointment washed over me. Mark's Ph.D. was in Physics. Lillian had hers in Historical Musicology—whatever that was. Interviewing for a position where the other employees held terminal degrees was intimidating. A career in community colleges never necessitated me going down that path, nor did I ever want to. What kind of guide needs a doctorate anyway?

From the way she was talking, she must've thought I knew more than I did. Because what kind of idiot would fly to Nevada for a job he knows nothing about?

Me.

"I don't know much about the position. What does a guide actually do?" *And why would it pay seven figures?*

She shot me an incredulous look and cocked her head. "Mark said you didn't have a lot of details, but you really don't know why you're here?"

"He needed a historian." *No, I don't.*

"I don't know why he'd bring you all this way and not tell you. You should probably wait and hear it from him." Her lips pursed together in a tight grimace, obviously frustrated.

I thought it better not to press. Lillian seemed easily irritated and I couldn't tell if it was due me or something else. I didn't know how much longer we had to drive and wasn't looking to aggravate her more. "Fair enough."

She didn't say another word so we drove in silence. She didn't even turn the radio on. I stared out the window at the desert landscape and watched the horizon where hazy mountains butted up against a crisp-blue sky.

"So," I finally managed. "Historical Musicology. I guess you're really into music."

"My passion has always been music," she said. "I'm even named after the famous opera singer, Lillian Russell. Have you heard of her?"

"No. Sorry."

"It's okay, most people haven't. My parents were both symphony musicians so I guess it was inevitable that I'd follow in their footsteps. I started studying piano and voice when I was six, majored in music in college and ended up with my Ph.D."

"It was inevitable," I grinned. "What do you listen to now? Any favorite bands?"

"Probably none you'd recognize. I never really got into popular music. To me, comparing classical music to pop music is like comparing the Sistine Chapel to a four-year old's finger painting."

"That's kind of a simplistic view. It's not all that bad." It bugged me how a music lover could dismiss popular music so matter-of-factly. "Isn't classical music really just the popular music of its day?"

"Maybe. I guess it's just how I look at it," she said, stiffening.

We rode in silence for a few more miles. The desert terrain became more mountainous. We passed a sign announcing our entry to the Pahranagat National Wildlife Refuge.

"How do you feel about classical music?" she asked.

"I guess I never took the time to appreciate it. Other than making music soundtracks, what's the point?" *Let's see how you like it.*

"Now who has the simplistic view?"

"Touché," I said, smiling.

Both hands gripped the steering wheel hard enough to reveal the whites of her knuckles. "So you teach history at a university?"

"Taught. Community college, actually." I felt a little ashamed for not teaching at a big school. I never felt that way before. It was something about the way she asked the question. "I took the position so I could be closer to my daughter, but she moved with her mom to Colorado a few months ago. My contract ran out so I'm officially unemployed." That was the abbreviated version of the story. Up until a month ago, I had been under the impression I would be offered tenure, not an expired contract and a pat on the back.

"I'm sorry to hear that."

"It's okay. Things usually have a way of working themselves out. How about you? Any family?"

"No." She kept her eyes on the road, her face partially concealed by the visor on her cap. "I never made the time. I came close to getting married once, but it didn't work out."

"What happened?"

"I'd rather not talk about it."

Must have been her sparkling personality.

I gave up any more attempts at conversation. The combination of my flight and the bright sunlight coupled with the long car ride made my eyes heavy. Lillian didn't speak and I found myself dozing off.

A sudden deceleration woke me from my brief slumber. We

had turned off the interstate, and were heading up a dirt road. A sign proclaimed the town of Delamar twelve miles further. Now, I understood why Lillian showed up in a Jeep rather than a limo. The four-wheel drive was a necessity for navigating the terrain. I looked in the side mirror and saw a cloud of beige smoke following our trail.

What type of place this remote would need historians, music Ph.D.s, and physicists?

After half an hour of the rugged sound of tires traversing desert clay and stones, we entered the town of Delamar. There wasn't much to see other than broken remains of stone buildings and partially washed away foundations.

Lillian broke the silence. "I didn't realize you were awake. We're almost there. Welcome to Delamar."

As if anyone could sleep through that stretch of road. "Nice place. I'll bet the rent's cheap."

Lillian smiled. "You'd be surprised. It's hard to imagine this place used to have fifteen-hundred residents."

"What were they mining?"

"Gold, mostly, but something in the process of extracting the gold produced a dust that killed a lot of the miners. The town's nickname was the 'Widow Maker.'"

There was little evidence of a thriving population. It looked as if Mother Nature had decided to reclaim her landscape with a vengeance. Even the buildings further into the town were little more than solitary walls. The dry-rotted remains of mine entrances dotted the mountain landscape. We passed the rusted-out hulk of a seventies-era Dodge peppered with bullet holes and surrounded by crushed beer cans.

"How long has it been abandoned?"

"Since the thirties, I think."

We started up a short incline off the main street and approached what must have been one of the mine entrances, guarded by a massive steel door looking like it was plucked from the NORAD military base at Cheyenne Mountain.

Lillian pulled up to a steel post, swiped an access card through a reader and pressed her thumb against a black pad. Slowly, the doors parted and she pulled the Jeep forward.

"Pretty hi-tech. What *is* this place?"

Lillian ignored my question and drove through the steel doors. We emerged into an enormous, well-lit hangar-sized cavern. Parked were four more Jeeps and two huge, forty-foot RVs.

The bright, modern-looking parking lot contrasted completely with the worn, barren openness of Delamar.

I pointed to the RVs. "How the hell did they navigate those through the dirt road?"

Lillian shrugged.

She parked on the far-left side of the hangar, near an elevator wall set into the side of the cave. We got out of the Jeep, and I took a moment to stretch my legs after the long, bumpy ride. The door began to swing shut and my heart started racing. In a matter of minutes, I would finally be able to learn what this was all about. The entrance closed with a resounding thud.

Lillian led us to the elevator and swiped her access card through the reader next to the doors and pressed her thumb to the sensor. The doors opened and we stepped inside.

The ride down took more than a minute and my ears started to pop. I estimated we were going down more than a hundred feet.

"It's 280 feet down," she offered, as if reading my mind.

When the doors opened, Mark was waiting to greet me.

TWO

Mark Shippen's features looked the same as they had in high school. He still had long dark brown hair pulled back in a ponytail. Given his dark goatee and black-rimmed glasses, he looked like he should be working in tech support or maybe behind the cash register at a comic book store. A white lab coat, one size too large, draped over his wiry frame. His smile was wide and warm, and he gave me a bear hug the way he always did after not seeing me for a while.

"Thanks for coming. Sorry for all of the cloak and dagger stuff," he said. "This isn't like any project I've ever worked on and we're trying to be as discreet as possible. You'll soon see why we're not ready to go public."

We stepped into a small reception area. Lillian said goodbye and exited through a metal door on the opposite wall.

His eyes gleamed over a wide smile. I had only seen him this enthusiastic twice in my life. Once, after his first kiss with Pam Baliss, whom I'd mockingly nicknamed Pam *Bliss*. The other when he got his acceptance to MIT. "There's so much to tell you and I'm not sure where to start."

"I'm intrigued." I looked around the room, a small waiting area decorated only with a flat-screen television and leather sofa. "What's up?"

"You've heard of particle accelerators, right?"

"You mean like that thing in Switzerland?"

"Yeah," Mark said smiling. "That *thing in Switzerland* is the Large Hadron Collider."

"And..."

"Come on, let me show you."

I followed Mark through the metal door.

"We've taken particle acceleration to a whole new level." He hurried down a flight of stairs.

The steps led down into an open room even larger than the hanger where we had parked the Jeep. People in lab coats sat at two rows of computer stations facing each other.

A glistening gunmetal-gray sphere, about fifteen feet in diameter, dominated the room. It was positioned in a recess on a small, yellow platform, flanked on either side by steel rings embedded into the wall.

Mark grabbed my arm and pointed, "Yes, that's why you're here!"

"So you created a giant disco ball?" I asked.

"No, not a disco ball, Professor Curry," a man's voice said from behind me. "It's much more than that."

I turned to see a man wearing a white lab coat that matched Mark's. He looked to be mid-50s, with dark hair starting to gray at the temples. A tuft of hair stuck up on his head giving him the appearance of having just crawled out of bed.

Mark introduced us. "John, this is Dr. Lawrence Cistern. He's the head scientist here at Timeless Arts."

I shook his hand, unable to take my attention off the sphere.

"Nice to meet you Dr. Cistern," I said, finally meeting his gray, contemplative eyes. "Mark—I mean *Dr. Shippen*—mentioned something about particle accelerators when we were upstairs.

That's what this is, right?"

He nodded his head. "Call me Lawrence. We like to consider ourselves a little less formal than our counterparts at the universities. And thank you for coming on such short notice. Mark's been raving about how you'd be a great fit for our team."

"He will," said Mark patting my back.

"Thank you," I said. "He didn't give me much choice anyway. So what does it do?"

"Basically," answered Mark. "It allows us to take particles and send them around in circles really, really fast until we smash them into each other."

"Why don't we go upstairs to my office so we can talk?" suggested Lawrence.

"I was hoping I would have time to change and freshen up before the interview," I said. "I wouldn't normally wear jeans. I left my bag upstairs. I can go change—"

"It's okay," assured Mark. "Just be yourself. This is more of a formality than interview—to make sure we're all in agreement. We'll forgive you for your jeans."

Formality? For a seven-figure salary? They were either desperate or I was in way over my head.

We followed Lawrence up another metal staircase to an office with a picture window overlooking the sphere in its niche below. A large mahogany desk polished to a reflective shine was topped only by a sleek silver laptop and a pewter business card holder. There were no personal items, family pictures or even a pen holder. I got the impression Lawrence was a neat freak—at least in aspects of his life outside of personal grooming.

An oil painting hung on the right side of the room. The wall behind the desk held a large, flat-screen TV. Each of us sat down in an ergonomic, mesh office chair.

"Before we start," Lawrence said, "we'll need you to sign a confidentiality agreement stating that nothing you learn here will leave the facility. Mark has assured me personally that you are upstanding and can be trusted, but for legal purposes, I have to ask you to read and sign this before we can continue."

I scanned the document, signed it and handed it back. It seemed pretty straightforward.

"Thank you, John," he said smiling as he opened a drawer, placed the document inside and closed it. "Now, what do you know about time travel?"

Time travel?

The kid in me wanted to shout out and jump for joy. The cynic in me felt like I was the butt of an elaborate hoax conceived by my friend. *Okay, I'll play along.*

"I know that if you fly around the Earth really fast, you can reverse its rotation and turn back the clock." I smiled.

Mark gave me a hard look. We had both called bullshit when we'd seen Superman use that technique to save Lois Lane in the movie.

"Most people consider time travel science fiction," he said, ignoring my jest. "Something that *seems* plausible, but only enough for us to enjoy the premise of a book or movie. Einstein believed time travel was possible if it was into the future, and until recently, no physicist would argue with that. But when the Large Hadron Collider was turned on for the first time, everything changed."

I took a short breath. "Wait, you're serious? This *is* a *time-travel* operation?" Maybe I wasn't catching on to what he was trying to explain.

"Yes, it's serious," said Mark.

Lawrence agreed. "You're correct. We are a full-service time-travel company. At least that's what we're planning."

I had just flown to Las Vegas, driven through the desert for three hours with a Historical Musicology *snob*, and now I was being told the job I'd invested so much hope in was for a *freaking* time-travel company. Maybe I could get paid in Monopoly money too. I'd had enough of the joke. I turned to Mark. "You outdid yourself this time. You had me going for a while, but you didn't have to go through all this trouble—"

"Just hear us out," said Mark holding up a hand. "I can tell you think this is crazy. I'm not messing with you—not this time." He stared at me, eyebrows raised.

I didn't answer. Could he be telling the truth? Anxiety swirled through me, starting in my stomach and branching out to my extremities.

Lawrence continued, "We've developed a short video for clients and potential clients to explain what we do. How about we show it to you and then we can answer any questions you have?"

"Okay," I said in a calm voice. "I'm sorry. I was a little thrown off. I'd like to see it." I reassured Mark with a subtle nod. His body relaxed, and he settled back into his chair. My jaw unclenched.

Lawrence hit a few keys on the laptop and the video began to play on the flat screen. The Timeless Arts logo appeared, accompanied by a familiar piece of classical music. A rich, deep voice began to narrate and images appeared as he spoke.

> "Have you ever wondered what it must have been like to sit in the audience and watch a play in the presence of William Shakespeare? Listen to an opera conducted by Mozart? Or share the wonder of Parisian attendees by entering the 1889 World's Fair through the entrance under the yet unfinished Eiffel Tower? Maybe your tastes are

more contemporary and you've always wanted to see the Beatles perform at an intimate setting like the Cavern Club. A breakthrough in science has made it possible to experience these events firsthand. We now have the ability to literally walk in the shoes of our ancestors, to experience the thrill of a Beethoven symphony or hear the roar of the crowd when Babe Ruth steps to the plate to call his shot.

"Timeless Arts is the world's first full-service time-travel experience. Time travel was made possible when scientists discovered a way to create and control passageways, called Wormholes, from one time and place to another time and place of their choosing. Think of them as conduits that act as shortcuts to our past."

The camera zoomed to a section of the accordion-shaped peaks and valleys and showed an elbow-macaroni shape connecting two valleys.

On the screen a picture of a rotating galaxy appeared. It looked like a wispy, oval-shaped cloud superimposed on the night sky. The galaxy began rotating in a counterclockwise motion.

"As you can see, our universe is in constant rotation, much like our Earth. Initially, you see the universe as a large, flat rotating object."

The camera angle zoomed in on a cross section of the galaxy revealing an accordion-like topography showing peaks and valleys throughout.

"Closer inspection reveals the depth that equates to our three-dimension understanding of the universe."

"The most complicated concept for most people to grasp is the fourth dimension—time. As Einstein noted, *'The separation between past, present, and future is only an illusion, although it is a convincing one.*' The reality of our universe is that it is not constrained by a linear, one-way timeline. Time and space can move forward, backward, up, or down. Stabilized wormholes allow us to access mankind's history—to send us through a loop to the past and bring us back again."

The view once again focused on macaroni-shaped wormholes connecting two valleys of the universe's topography. The image faded out and was replaced by paintings and portraits of people from different historical periods: Elaborate Elizabethan dresses with puffy sleeves and necklines, colonial waistcoats and breeches with stark-white stockings, and Victorian men in top hats accompanied by women in frilly dresses and flower-lined hats.

"We will help you prepare for your experience by giving you firm grounding in the history of the event, providing you with appropriate period clothing, and teach you what you need in order to communicate with the locals who you will encounter on your trip. You will be accompanied at all times by an experienced and professional guide who will lead you through your adventure to ensure that your experience is as rich and authentic as historically possible.

"At Timeless Arts, our only goal is to observe the splendor of the human experience as illustrated through its art. We are not here to evaluate history. We are here to *appreciate* history, to answer questions that have confounded historians, and to strengthen our own understanding of the world in which we live."

The video faded and Lawrence closed the laptop. He didn't

say anything and just looked at me.

"What do you think?" asked Mark, breaking the silence.

I looked at him and then at Lawrence. "You really figured out a way to travel to the past?"

"Yes, and we want you to be one of our guides," Mark replied.

I was stunned, trying to wrap my mind around it. The need for a historian made sense now. I still wasn't sure I was qualified, but, yes, I knew I could do it.

"How'd you do it?"

Lawrence spoke, "Before CERN turned on the Large Hadron Collider, there was a media outcry that we were going to destroy the world. Articles were written predicting that the LHC was going to create a black hole that was going to suck the Earth into it and destroy our entire solar system. Of course, those theories were completely unfounded. The smartest people in the world generally don't try to get together to destroy the planet. When the LHC was turned on, it didn't produce a black hole, but the unexpected *did* happen. It created a passageway called a wormhole."

"Like what was mentioned in the video," I said.

Lawrence smiled and Mark began to speak. "Yes, a wormhole is a bridge—a kind of a shortcut through space and time. Most people understand that we live in a three-dimensional world. If we lived in a two-dimensional world, everything would be flat—like this business card." He grabbed one of the cards from the holder.

"Because we live in a three-dimensional world, we can walk across the card." He held it in the palm of his hand so it rested flat.

"Let's assume that from one end of this business card to the other is a timeline. Now, take this card and roll it so that its two opposite ends touch at the same place. Imagine we take a paper-clip and poke it through the card so that it goes through one side and touches the card on the other side. The paperclip is now touching two different points on the timeline at the same time. It would be doing what the wormhole does. And since the paper is rolled, we would have created a *loop* within the timeline and successfully entered our past."

I nodded my head in agreement.

"It's actually a little more complicated than that," added Lawrence, "but essentially, we've harnessed the ability to travel through the fourth dimension—time."

"How come no one in the media ever declared that time travel was invented?"

Lawrence spoke. "Because it wasn't at the time. When we developed the LHC, it was designed to fire protons at high speeds and then crash them into each other, or *collide* them. We were trying to re-create conditions right after the Big Bang, but on a smaller scale.

"In order to speed up the particles, we sent electrical and magnetic pulses to keep the protons moving, similar to a booster station for electrical lines. We found that the faster and more violent the collisions, the more anomalies appeared in our data—eventually causing damage to the facility. I correctly speculated that we were seeing a precursor to the formation of wormholes, but testing was suspended until the scientists could analyze the data and *agree* with what was happening. I never got the opportunity to prove my hypothesis. A decision was made at the highest levels that our experiments would not resume at the current pace, and the press was told that some damage had occurred to the machinery during testing, so the project was put on hold.

"Some of our associates were afraid that if we continued down this path of research, governments could use it to destroy political enemies or do something that could modify human history. Two of my colleagues even wrote a paper saying that the LHC was damaged *on purpose* by someone from the future in an attempt to avoid some kind of catastrophic paradox."

I leaned forward. "I'm not sure I follow. How do you know they aren't right?"

"They're wrong and they should have known better." His tone sounded smug. "Think about what a paradox is—something that is true cannot also be false, right?"

"I guess."

"Consider one of the classic time-travel clichés." He leaned back in his chair, relaxed. "Let's say someone wanted to travel back in time and assassinate Adolf Hitler before he rose to power. World War II would have been avoided—*But that never happened*—not in our world. Our history *is* the way we know it to have happened. If someone went back to change that history, he would create a new timeline putting him into an alternate dimension or parallel universe." He held his hands out, palms facing about two inches apart.

"If you traveled back in time and altered your history," The heels of his hands touched creating a v-shape. "You would seamlessly transition into an alternate reality where your revision of history would become the *only* history—at least to you—"

"And you'd become part of that history because you'd be stranded there," added Mark.

"That makes sense, I guess."

Mark touched my shoulder. "All you need to know is you can't mess with the past. If you make any dramatic changes, you cut off your way home."

The idea of getting stranded somewhere in the past was alarming. I pictured myself trapped, living on the muddy streets of Elizabethan England, watching Shakespeare's plays and praying I wouldn't say something that would land me in the Tower of London. The entire concept of time-traveling to historic events, as awesome as it sounded, seemed almost too dangerous to risk those kinds of consequences. "How do I know what a *dramatic change* is?"

"Just don't modify the history as you know it. Don't cause a scene. Don't kill anyone. Don't father any children."

I waited for Mark to smile, but his face remained serious.

Lawrence spoke. "Rest assured, John. The last thing we want is to lose an associate or—God forbid—a client. We have strict safeguards in place to ensure every precaution has been considered. We are merely observers."

"But why? I mean, I *love* the idea of traveling back in time. I do, but is it worth the risk?"

"For art," replied Lawrence. "We're not trying to change the world. We're trying to enhance our understanding of it—to understand humanity. The reality is people will be lined up in order to take the risk to visit the past. I have to admit some of us wanted to do this just to see if we *could* accomplish it, but that takes resources and money—*a lot* of money. Fortunately, we have a benefactor who has both money and a vision."

"Harrison Meade," answered Mark. "*That* Harrison Meade."

Harrison Meade was a world-famous billionaire playboy and philanthropist. I had just seen his picture on the cover of a celebrity-gossip magazine at the airport.

"So money's no object then."

"That's real," said Mark referring to the painting on the wall.

I took another look at the painting. Two figures stood in a grass field surrounded by red flowers. Trees stood along the horizon.

"It's a Monet. A gift for our first successful trip to the past."

"Mr. Meade's been an outstanding supporter of our work," said Lawrence. "His love of the arts is renowned. When I first approached him about privately funding our research I had no idea that he would be so eager to jump on board. It was his idea to create this company. I tried to explain to him that the science was most-likely decades—or even centuries—away from being able to do something like that, but he didn't care. He gave us everything we asked for and more."

"This is incredible," I said, "Almost too incredible to believe. You've had so many breakthroughs in just a few years time."

Mark leaned closer. "You have no idea."

"I still don't understand what job I could possibly be qualified to do. Lillian mentioned tour guide. I'm assuming you want me to travel back in time."

"It's every history lover's dream job."

"Yeah, but you said you do this for art. I don't know anything about art—about *Beethoven*. I mean—I could learn, but I'm no expert."

Mark shifted in his chair. "You will be. Didn't you always say, if you really want to learn something, teach it? That's what you'll be doing—leading clients on Observations and teaching them how to behave and interact with the past."

"Observations are what we call our trips to the past." Lawrence's gray eyes bore into me. He was probably a fantastic poker player. "How would you like to experience one for yourself?"

"Just like that?"

"Just like that—no strings attached. If you're convinced it's too dangerous, or if you just aren't interested, you're free to walk away."

An offer to be one of the first people to time travel was not to be taken lightly. I would really have to think it over.

Nah. Of course I would do it.

"Where to?"

"How would you like to see Mozart? In the flesh?" His face remained serious.

"Mozart?" I laughed. "Come on—"

"We're serious," said Mark. "It really *is* Mozart."

"Okay," I said thinking out-loud, "But why *me*? Why the hard sell? I don't even teach at a *university*."

"Because Mark recommended you—"

"I trust you," added Mark. "And *he* trusts you."

"Who's *he*?"

I looked at Mark and he raised his eyebrows.

Lawrence said, "Mr. Meade made one request of us when we started this company—to be present for the inauguration of George Washington—a great hero of his."

Lawrence folded his hands together atop his desk. "Harrison Meade has requested that *you* be his guide."

THREE

I shifted uncomfortably in my chair. "How does Harrison Meade know who I am?" Harrison Meade was the kind of guy celebrities hoped to meet, the cream of the A-list. The idea that he even knew who I was unnerved me.

"We came up with a list of historians who would be suitable candidates to scout out Washington's inauguration," said Mark. "Mr. Meade had his team research the list and came to the conclusion that he preferred someone who was a personal friend of someone on our team."

"How did I even get on this list?"

"I added you."

"Mr. Meade wanted us to brainstorm," added Lawrence. "We were instructed to list all possibilities so we could rate them based on their knowledge, abilities, and willingness to participate."

"This is unbelievable," I said, "but I'm going to need some time to think about this."

"Of course," said Lawrence. "Stay here for a few days if you like. Get a feel for the facility. Think about going to see Mozart. Or, if you like, you can catch a flight home tomorrow. It's your call."

I stood and shook hands with Lawrence. Mark led me out of the office back down to the main room that housed the time machine. I stopped and stared at it.

Could this thing really transport people to the past?

It didn't look like any of the time machines I'd seen in movies —just simple and round.

"Mark, this whole idea sounds impossible," I said. "Aren't there people much more qualified than I am to do this?"

"Of course. *Most* people are more qualified than you," he answered with a quick laugh, "But we already asked all the *real* historians, and they all politely declined. Well, some of them weren't all that polite."

"So I wasn't Meade's first choice then?"

"No, but you made the top three. Don't sell yourself short. Just because you don't teach at a university doesn't mean you're not a bright guy."

"Thanks. I just get the feeling this is too good to be true."

He smiled. "I felt the same way. The first time I climbed into Donna, I wasn't sure—"

"Sounds dirty."

He laughed. "The *time machine*. We call it Donna—you know, because it looks like a disco ball. *Donna Summer.* Get it?"

I rolled my eyes.

"Give me a break. I didn't come up with it."

"So where'd you go?"

We walked back toward the stairs.

"Mozart. It's the first Observation we've fully developed. It's why we brought Lillian in. She's our lead."

I guess that's what a Historical Musicology degree does.

"So what was it like? Did you meet Mozart?" I thought of how cool it would be to encounter someone famous like Mozart. We wouldn't be able to understand each other. Did Mozart speak English? But still, Mozart.

And George Washington. Wow.

"No, we're strictly there to observe. Remember, no dramatic changes? We don't take any unnecessary risks." His eyes widened and his face broke into a grin. "We've been dreaming about this kind of stuff our whole lives. It's why I wanted you here."

Mark led the way up the stairs, paused and turned around. "The other reason is I'm going with you as the technical expert for the machine, and I know I can trust you."

"Trust me?" I asked. "You said that upstairs. What did you mean by that?"

"We're going to eighteenth century New York City. We have some knowledge about it from books and letters, but no one has actually been there for over two hundred years. If I'm going there to scope the place out, I want to go with someone I can trust with my life. I happen to like the twenty-first century and would like to come back. I don't want to miss any Joss Whedon movies."

We trudged up the stairs back to the elevator and went back up to the cave where the parking lot was located.

"Your quarters are up here," he said, motioning me to one of the trailers. "We're working on more permanent accommodations to use for guests. Right now, we only have room for the full-timers down below. Anyway, these are way nicer than what I'm living in."

The door to the trailer opened into the main room that housed a modern kitchen and living space. It also featured a full-sized refrigerator and microwave, but I wasn't anticipating taking any meals here. The living room had a flat-screen television on the same wall as the kitchen sink. Opposite the television sat two plush recliners. Smooth jazz played through speakers in the ceiling.

Three steps led up from the kitchen past a small bathroom into a tastefully decorated bedroom with another flat-screen television.

On the nightstand was a stack of books on which rested a green pamphlet that read, *Souvenir and Official Programme of the Centennial Celebration of George Washington's Inauguration As First President of the United States*. The books under the pamphlet were biographies on George Washington.

"We figured you might want to brush up on your history before the big trip," Mark said as I looked at the stack.

"I still haven't said yes," I pointed out as we walked back to the main room of the trailer. I noticed that my overnight bag had been set on the floor next to the dining room table. I realized I hadn't grabbed it when I arrived in the Jeep.

"You're at least going to see Mozart?"

I raised my eyebrows. I didn't know what my hesitation was. I wanted to do this, but something in my gut wasn't right. "Lillian's kind of a snob."

"Lill's not so bad once you get to know her. Look, if this doesn't convince you, nothing will. Besides, you won't have to pony up the half million that our clients will have to pay." Mark cocked his head and frowned. "I mean—what the hell? You'd pass up the opportunity of a lifetime because someone's a snob?"

He was right. Lillian wasn't the reason for my hesitation. I was scared. What if I never came back? What if I never saw my daughter, Tabby, again?

He continued, "Cut the crap. You *want* to believe. What's your problem? I thought you'd jump at the chance."

"Sorry. This just seems a little too much for me to process. My life's just been thrown for a loop. The contract on a teaching job I was sure was going to be long term expired, and now I'm being asked to be a time traveler. Do you know how crazy that sounds? I was expecting—I don't know what I was expecting."

"This is *real*. That's what I've been trying to tell you. Do you think I'd be here if it wasn't? I've worked too hard on this—we all have. I know it sounds like fantasy, but it's not."

He paused for a moment. "You'd get a million-dollar salary with a two-hundred thousand dollar bonus for every successful scouting trip."

The thought of that much money sent a jolt through my body. I felt my blood pressure pick up. It *would* be life-changing. I'd never have to worry about money again and Tabby would be set for life too.

Mark exhaled an exasperated sigh. "I told you it was over seven figures, but I didn't want you taking the job just because of the money. Don't be an idiot. Go see *Don Giovanni* with Lillian. If you're not convinced within the first ten seconds, stay in the machine and come back. I promise you—you won't. We'll even pay you for your trouble."

What did I have to lose? Maybe some disappointment if it didn't work, but I was being pursued for this—not the other way around. I could hang out for the weekend, think about their offer. If I decided it was bullshit or dangerous, I would just go home. No harm done.

And if it was real. If it really worked the way they were saying…

"All right, all right." I raised my hand in submission.

Mark grinned smugly, "I knew you'd come around. It'll be just like the old days. Hanging out."

"I know, but you didn't have to call me an idiot."

* * *

I agreed to meet Mark for dinner on the main level at seven. He gave me an electronic access card like the one Lillian had used to open the elevator door. He said we could get my biometric thumb scan later. I took my time showering and freshening up. It's amazing how dirty you feel after riding in an open Jeep through the desert air.

Back at the elevator, I swiped my access card. The reader turned green, the elevator doors opened and I stepped inside. The panel listed three options: Main, Residence, and Science. I swiped for Main, and the elevator started to descend.

The door opened to a small reception room that looked a lot like the one on the science level. A door on the opposite wall opened into a long, well-lit hallway. I followed the hallway for about fifty feet until it turned a corner and opened into a cafeteria that was about the size of the one in my high school. People sat at tables beside a huge buffet that looked like it belonged in Las Vegas. Glass-doored coolers lined a ten-foot section of the wall like the beverage section of a convenience store.

Mark motioned me to his table. He wore jeans and a blue hoodie that read *"Everyone is born right-handed. Only the gifted overcome it."*

"Lill will be down in a *minute,*" he said. "Have a seat."

She appeared wearing jeans with a red sweater, and for the first time I got a good look at her.

She's kinda hot, I thought as she approached. Light blue eyes and high cheekbones highlighted her heart-shaped face. Her blond hair fell just past the shoulders.

"Hello, gentlemen. Shall we grab dinner?"

The buffet choices ranged from prime rib to chicken soup. Lillian chose a salad with grilled chicken and Mark grabbed two slices of pizza loaded with everything. I decided on salmon with a side salad because I wanted to appear to be at least somewhat health conscious—especially in front of Lillian. I grabbed a bottle of water from the cooler.

Mark did most of the talking, describing our long friendship to Lillian and how we managed to keep in touch over the years. Lillian told us more about herself, and I was impressed to learn she was fluent in Italian, French and German—including a few regional dialects of each language.

"So John, Mark tells me you're going to come with me to Prague." Lillian said.

"Prague? I thought Mozart lived in Vienna."

"He did." Her lips formed a tight, forced smile. "But he was commissioned to write an opera to be performed in Prague because the *Marriage of Figaro* was such a hit."

"Prague is a sister city to Vienna in many ways," Mark added. "A lot of the movie about Mozart was filmed there because the city was never modernized to the extent that Vienna was. Chalk one up for the Cold War."

"If you saw the movie, *Amadeus*, you've actually seen the theater we'll be attending," said Lillian. "It's the same one. The filmmakers used it to add authenticity. It's the only theater where Mozart performed that's still standing."

"I've seen the movie," I said. "But I've never been to an opera before. How cool is it that my first opera will be one actually conducted by Mozart?"

"Very cool," said Mark.

"You're very fortunate." Lillian's body stiffened.

I couldn't understand why I irritated her. It couldn't have been the chauffeur comment when we'd first met. "Well, thank you for agreeing to let me tag along. When do we go?"

"I have scheduled a trip for Monday morning at ten."

"The nice thing," said Mark, "is that we're not tied to a strict schedule. We can go whenever we want. We'll need time to brief you on what to say, how to act, what to wear. Since we've done this a few times, the prep will go pretty fast."

"Just remember," added Lillian. "We are strictly observers. We don't take anything with us from our modern world, and we don't bring anything back. Careful attention is paid so that our dress is completely authentic as to the materials, methods of construction and the fashion of the time. Do you know anything about *Don Giovanni*?"

"Honestly—nothing at all," I answered, embarrassed. "Like I said, I haven't ever been to an opera. I was never interested enough, I guess."

She handed me a manila envelope labeled *Don Giovanni Observation*. "I figured as much. The performance is in Italian so you won't understand the language, so here's a synopsis. It's about Don Juan."

"Yeah, the womanizer!" Mark landed a playful punch on my arm. "You can relate, huh, *John*?"

Thanks, Mark. Give the ice queen another reason to hate me.

"Yeah, whatever. Who else is going?" I browsed the contents. Behind the summary was an itinerary of the day's events.

"It'll just be the two of us. I've designed this Observation to have only one guest with me, so as long as I can *trust* you—being a *womanizer* and all—I think it'll work out fine. In the meantime, you can start your prep work for the inauguration."

I shot Mark an evil glare, and he gave me a big smile. I looked back at the information.

Something in the itinerary caught my attention. "If we arrive north of the city, how come we're leaving through the west gates? Isn't it the wrong direction?"

"Mark, do you want to answer him?"

Mark turned to me. "Donna is sort of like a time-travel taxi.

She drops you off and picks you up from predetermined locations—all controlled from here—at least after we identify good entrance and exit points. When we go to New York to scout our Observation, we'll control her ourselves."

"Okay," I said. "I'll look at this closer later. Now what? What do you guys do around here for fun?"

"We get to bed early and start researching what we're getting paid to do," answered Mark. "You're not on vacation, *amigo*. Besides, Dr. Cohen will want you well-versed before he lets you go."

"Who's Dr. Cohen?"

"The lead historian here at Timeless Arts," said Lillian. "Brilliant man—and quite a stickler for the details. You have your work cut out for you."

"Yeah," added Mark. "If you really want to impress him, show off your knowledge of some detail of the event that the average person wouldn't know."

I already knew more than the average person, but I interpreted Mark's comment as a challenge. I'd show Dr. Cohen I could be as prepared as any of the Ph.D.s around here, and then maybe Lillian would finally chill out when she understood I was qualified.

FOUR

"Pull your shit together." Mark startled me as he slammed down in a chair at my table. We were seated in the cafeteria. It was mid-morning and the place was empty.

I looked up from the book I was studying. The rest of the books from my nightstand were scattered across the cafeteria table.

"What are you talking about?"

"Lawrence wants to pull you from the Observation. Says you're too apathetic about everything and he needs someone more engaged."

My body tensed and I felt the adrenaline pulse through my extremities.

An employee with a lab coat had entered the cafeteria and headed for the beverage section. I kept my voice to a whisper. "Are you kidding? What do you think I've been doing for the past two days? This isn't light reading." I gestured toward the books.

Mark's jaw clenched and he ran a hand through his hair. His voice strained. "I don't know, but Lillian doesn't think you're going to work out either. Apparently, she voiced her concern to Lawrence and confirmed his own reservations about you."

"What the hell. I haven't said two words to that uptight bi—"

Mark stood up. "He wants to meet with you at eleven in his

office. I put my own ass on the line to get you here. Don't make me look bad." He turned and walked toward the door.

I jumped from my seat and followed him. "Hey, you brought me here, remember? I didn't ask for this. I was perfectly content."

He stopped and faced me. "Maybe that's the problem. Maybe you're too content. People would kill for this opportunity. Show some fire." He spun and stomped away. "Stop floating through life."

I stood, red-faced. The lab coat passed me with an apprehensive gait and hurried out.

I returned to the table and flopped into the chair. *Screw this place,* I thought. Just because I hadn't been giddy with excitement, I was apathetic? I wasn't floating through life.

I looked at the clock. Forty-five minutes until I had to face Lawrence. My body felt heavy, defeated.

I grabbed the manila envelope Lillian had handed me the day before: *Don Giovanni Observation,* then tossed it back to the table.

Was I blowing it? I had read Lillian's itinerary. I had been measured for my opera clothing. I thought I was going with the flow, taking it all in. I scanned the books on the table. I was doing what I was supposed to be doing.

Floating.

* * *

I arrived at precisely eleven and knocked on the outside of the door, even though it was open.

"Come in," said Lawrence. He wore horn-rimmed glasses.

Seated across from him was Mark. Neither spoke, but I felt the tension in the room. An empty chair waited for me.

I stood, directing my attention to Lawrence. "Please, I'll do everything you ask. I may have come across as lazy or indifferent, but that's not the case. I've already read the itinerary for the opera and would be prepared to lead the Observation for Washington's inauguration today if necessary."

"I'm glad to hear that. Please sit down."

I sat next to Mark and he gave me a subtle nod, his earlier anger gone. "I'm getting mixed signals," I said. "When I got here, you told me to think about it for a few days and take the trip to Prague. What happened?"

Lawrence thumbed through the packet. "You attended three colleges before finishing your bachelor's degree. You've changed jobs every two to three years, most recently finishing a two-year contract without being renewed. I'm beginning to see a pattern."

"Is my whole life in there?" Anger flared up again. I felt my sweat glands open. "Why didn't you do a background check before you brought me here? I changed positions because that's what I had to do. Contracts ran out. Needs changed. I've never been fired from anything in my life."

Lawrence placed the paper on the desk and looked at me. His voice remained calm. "We've done our due diligence." He folded his hands, resting them on the paper. "John, what we do is very precise and the reverberations of our work can have greater consequences than anything you've dealt with. We need our associates completely focused on details because even the slightest deviation can cause peril to both the associate and our clients."

"I'm aware."

"Our team works toward our objectives with absolute resolve because we have to. There's no room for failure and there's no room for doubt. Tell me, are you positive you believe in what's going on here?"

I shifted in my chair, feeling everyone's eyes on me. "At first?

No. The idea of time travel took me by surprise, but after spending a few days here, I think you're on to something great. I mean, you've got incredible power, and you're using it for *art*. That's amazing to me. I admire what you're doing."

Lawrence's face was emotionless. "Tell me what you know about the *Don Giovanni Observation*."

I hoped I had remembered enough of Lillian's itinerary. "We'll arrive north of Prague at 6:30 AM the day of the opera and hire a carriage to travel into the city where we'll meet our contact. Our contact—it wasn't clear who—will give us a tour of the city and escort us to the opera. Afterwards, we'll leave the city through the western gate, locate the time machine—Donna—and return home."

Lawrence remained passive. "Our clients travel under assumed names during observations. Why?"

"It wasn't entirely clear, but I'm guessing we're trying to stay out of the history books in case we interact with someone and they write it down." I didn't understand why I was getting the pop quiz. Was it some kind of test to make sure I was studying? "Can I ask a question?"

"Of course."

"What did I do wrong? I've done everything you've asked."

"Nothing. Your conduct has been appropriate. It's a perception. You're approach has been—nonchalant."

"John's always been even tempered," Mark said. "That isn't necessarily a bad thing."

"At any rate, it's out of my hands." Lawrence removed his glasses and rubbed his eyes.

"So I'm still going?" I raised hopeful eyebrows.

"Mr. Meade has invited you to meet for dinner tomorrow." He looked at Mark. "He'd like you there too."

Relief overcame my anger, but my mind raced. Why would Harrison Meade invite me to dinner? Was it a final test? Maybe he would reprimand Mark for nepotism and wasting everyone's time in bringing me here. That didn't make sense. Why waste his time? Dinner had to be a good sign.

FIVE

I was invited to meet Harrison Meade for dinner outside the facility at 6:00. I stepped out the front entrance ten minutes early, grateful for the fresh air. I hadn't made time to see the sun in the three days I'd been there.

I found Meade standing over a small charcoal grill next to a sun-faded picnic table. He was telling a joke to a statuesque blonde seated at the table. Meade was the kind of guy celebrities and heads of state pined for: rich, influential, generous. The beat up picnic table and desert backdrop didn't fit my preconceived notions of what to expect.

What did I expect? We were in the desert out in the middle of nowhere. Was there supposed to be a sixty-foot yacht floating in a crystal blue Mediterranean seaport?

"John Curry, welcome," said Meade, smiling. His handshake was firm and he touched my elbow with his left hand—the classic politician greeting. A flush of adrenaline rushed through me. He was the first A-list celebrity I had ever met.

His jet-black hair was naturally wavy and he scrutinized me with dark brown eyes. He had the striking features and countenance women would have fawned over even if he wasn't one of the richest men on the planet. Specks of gray peeked through his tanned, unshaven face.

Some guys have it all, but hey, at least I was taller.

"I thought I'd show off my famous barbecue for you." He flashed the practiced smile I had seen hundreds of times on television and in magazines. "Please, have a seat."

I didn't want to appear starstruck or a sycophant. "Fantastic. When I was invited to dinner with a billionaire, I expected lobster and caviar."

He laughed. "Not with this view. I think something earthy is more suitable, don't you think?" He looked over the desert vista, the ruins of Delamar completely hidden behind hills and rocks. "John, this is Anja."

Anja put down the magazine she was skimming and stood up. She had to have been at least six feet, complete with Barbie-doll proportions. "Pleased to meet you," she said with an Eastern European accent.

Anja was stunning—had to be a model—high cheek bones, pouty lips. She looked familiar, but I didn't want to embarrass myself by asking where I'd seen her. Her beauty was distracting. My dinner companions were from a different stratosphere. What could I possibly talk to them about? I wanted to be confident, but felt suddenly insignificant.

I realized I was standing there not saying anything. "So world-famous barbecue, huh?"

"When I turned eleven, I spent the summer with my aunt in New Orleans." He flipped the chicken. "She taught me to cook, and the result was my barbecue rub." He smiled as if remembering an inside joke.

I was about to have dinner with one of the world's richest and most famous men. I didn't want to waste time talking about barbecue rub. He didn't give any indication I was being let go. I wanted to know why he had specifically requested me to be his guide on the George Washington Observation. "Thank you for inviting me—not just to dinner. All of this. Timeless Arts. It's incredible. But why me?"

"You're the ideal candidate," he said, looking up from the grill. "I wanted someone real, not just an academic who's spent his entire life with his head inside a book. It helped that we had inside information on you."

"But yesterday, I thought Lawrence was going to let me go. He seemed pretty angry."

"Don't worry about Lawrence," he said. "He sometimes forgets how important relationships are to success, and would any of us be here without good relationships?" Meade raised his arms and surveyed our surroundings.

"I guess not." I couldn't tell if Meade was referring to his relationship with Lawrence or my relationship with Mark.

"Right on time, as usual." He looked behind me.

I turned to see Mark.

"Hello Mr. Meade," he said. His eyes fluttered when he spotted Anja. The movement was subtle, and I'm sure mine did the same thing. Maybe it wasn't so subtle.

"I was just telling John why he's the perfect escort for my trip to Washington's inauguration."

Mark's mouth formed a relieved smile and he gave me a thumbs up while Meade turned his attention back to the grill.

The chicken was a superb blend of sweet and spicy, complemented by the cold beer waiting for us in a cooler next to the table.

Who knew billionaires drank domestic?

"Excellent, Mr. Meade." I said. "You'll have to give me the recipe."

"Please, call me Harrison. We're friends now." He took a swig from his bottle. "I'm going to give you the same advice my aunt gave me: '*Variety isn't the spice of life. Taking chances is.*' Go make your own recipe. It'll mean much more to you."

I looked at his girlfriend, "Anja, you're going to have to coax it out of him when he is in an *especially* good mood."

That brought laughs from all around.

"How's your research going?" Meade asked.

"It's going well. We'll need to arrive early to find a good spot. Washington wasn't known for his public speaking skills." I glanced at Anja, unsure if she was allowed to hear our conversation. I didn't know if any of this was top secret.

"It's okay," Meade assured, reading my concern. "You have no idea how much I'm looking forward to this. Ever since Lawrence approached me with the time-travel concept, I knew *this* is what I wanted to do."

Mark spoke up. "For his first trip, John is going to see Mozart."

"Outstanding," replied Meade. "I think you'll find it inspiring as well as eye opening. I hope you enjoy coffee." He gave me a wry smile and then moved on to another topic. "Listen," he said. "I brought you guys presents for your trip to New York." He reached down next to the table and handed each of us a duffel bag.

I opened mine and examined the contents: a white vest with straps that covered the shoulders and straps that wrapped around the waist. "Why would we need bullet proof vests?"

"They're not only bulletproof, but stab-proof as well," he said.

Mark examined his. "We haven't had any close calls yet, but I guess it's better to be safe than sorry."

I looked up from my vest. "What about the whole idea that we can't take anything modern to the past?"

"It's good you were paying attention," said Meade. "I don't hold Lawrence's concern for altering the past by taking a few hidden precautions. I want you to keep this under wraps. Can you do that?"

"I guess—sure," I said, looking at Mark. He nodded. I was a little thrown by the scheming. Weren't we all on the same team?

"Look," said Meade. "I get that we have a pretty good idea of what's going to happen during the trip—especially after it's been scoped out, but I don't want to show up somewhere five minutes later than anticipated and cross paths with some eighteenth-century armed robber. All I want is to make sure that we're all safe and can return to our own time in one piece."

Mark held up his vest. "I think these can be concealed pretty well under our clothing."

Apparently, Mark didn't hold Lawrence's concern for taking modern technology to the past either.

"They're covert models," said Meade. "Designed to be discreet. I own one myself. These should be able to withstand any weapon fired at you, either on purpose or by mistake. They're rated to withstand bullets fired from a .44 Magnum. To give you some perspective, a .44's firepower is about forty-percent more powerful than an eighteenth-century musket."

"Is this really necessary? If we're going somewhere dangerous, I'd rather not go."

Mark answered, "It is just a precaution. Believe me, I don't want to be shot at either, but the reality is that we don't know exactly what we're getting into when we travel to New York. Making the first trip to a location in the past is a bit like fumbling around in the dark until you can find the light switch. I feel safer knowing we have at least some protection if we encounter any kind of unstable situation."

"Okay," I said, positive no battles were fought on the day of Washington's inauguration."What's the worst that can happen?"

Harrison looked at me but didn't say anything.

"It will look good on you," offered Anja. "It will cover up your paunch."

"I hope you're talking to him," I said, pointing to Mark.

"Excellent," said Harrison clapping his hands. "Try it tomorrow when you go to Prague. See how it feels. This observation has been conducted enough times where we know there's no danger." His piercing eyes bore into me. "Just remember to be discreet."

I nodded, but still felt uneasy about deceiving everyone and wearing a modern vest under my clothing. Meade had the ultimate say on whether I would be a part of Timeless Arts, and I needed to stay on his good side. I was willing to bend the rules if it meant I could be involved, and besides, Mark didn't seem worried.

"Okay, who wants another beer?"

* * *

After an early-morning run, I stopped by the fitting room to grab the silk suit I would be wearing to the opera. I said hello to Lawrence as I walked back toward the elevators.

"Are you ready for your trip?" he asked.

"Definitely," I responded, nodding toward the machine. "I can't wait."

He forced a smile. If it were up to him, I wouldn't be going. I was sure of it.

"Listen, Lawrence," I said. "I'm on board one hundred percent."

"Stay with Lillian, and do as she instructs, and it will be the most incredible day of your life."

"I will."

I returned to my room, showered and started to get dressed. I had been fitted earlier in the week, but now I got to experience dressing for an eighteenth-century opera.

My underwear consisted of linen breeches that went down to my knees, secured with garters just like a woman of the time would wear. Timeless Art's policy was to be as authentic as possible. I visualized myself swinging and dangling all day before the opera. Screw it, if I was going to wear a Kevlar vest, it wouldn't hurt anyone if I wore real underwear too.

The Kevlar vest was comfortable enough and didn't restrict my movement. I placed my long-sleeve undershirt over the top and tucked it into a pair of dark-brown outer breeches. They were button-flied and tighter than I would have liked, but I could survive. The breeches went down to my knees where they were secured by small brass buckles. I pulled up my white stockings and fastened the buckles.

I pulled an already-tied white linen cravat over my head and tucked it into my shirt. I completed my ensemble with a matching waistcoat, buttoned all the way up to the cravat, and a complimentary frock coat.

Surprisingly, the most comfortable parts of my outfit were the shoes. I had assumed that twenty-first century shoe technology provided more comfort, but the soft black leather and short heels felt as good as any pair of wingtips I ever owned. Interestingly enough, there wasn't a left shoe and right shoe, just two identical shoes of with the same shape.

A simple brown wig, arranged in a ponytail, completed my outfit. When I looked into the mirror, I thought I looked like Sam Adams on the beer bottle—but better dressed. I was an eighteenth-century American gentleman. The clothing was modeled after Benjamin Franklin's simple ensemble that wooed French society during his stint as American Ambassador.

I felt like I belonged on the set of a period film—at least until I swiped my access card and stepped into the elevator. Strangely enough, I didn't feel ridiculous. I felt the same as I did when dressed in a tuxedo or any formal wear. I stood a bit straighter and felt more confident, silly, considering I wore silk knickers.

The Science level bustled with excitement. Scientists manned all of the computers, and the time machine was opened on a hinge, like a plastic Easter egg. Red chairs circled a control panel in the center.

Lillian was dressed in a simple, gold dress with white ruffles extending from each sleeve. The low cut, square neckline showed off a little cleavage. Around her neck hung a gold necklace with a round black pendant. The dress plumed out and dragged across the floor. A round straw hat balanced delicately on top of a curly, blonde wig. She looked good.

Too bad the interior doesn't match the exterior. Our interaction the past few days had been minimal and we'd only spoken briefly when she gave me a manila envelope containing our itinerary. I didn't know when she went to Lawrence to tell him I wasn't qualified. Or why.

Since I had to spend the entire day with her, I thought it might be a good idea to ease the tension. I strutted across the room toward her and used my best English accent, "My dear lady. You look magnificent."

"Thank you, sir," she said, tilting her head while curtsying in response. She didn't smile.

No surprise there.

Lawrence and Mark approached, wearing lab coats.

"How are you feeling?" asked Mark. "Are you ready for your long day? Did you get enough to eat?"

"Yes, mom, I'm fine." I glanced toward the machine again and my heart pumped faster—partly due to the potential danger, but mostly because of anticipation. Was I really on my way to witness the premiere of one of Mozart's greatest masterpieces?

Lawrence shook my hand. "Everything is set. You can leave whenever you're ready." His eyes darted to the stairs.

Meade and Anja headed down toward us. He wore jeans and a black leather jacket over a white t-shirt. Anja strode behind him in form-fitting white slacks and a loose linen shirt.

"I'm just coming to wish you well before you leave," he said, giving me a hard slap on the back.

"Thank you." I shook his hand. "I guess we're all set."

Lillian climbed into the machine via a small ladder attached to the side. It took her a moment to collect all the fabric from her dress and pile it in with her. After she was seated, one of the scientists handed her a large leather bag embroidered with red trim. I climbed up next and sat across from her.

The inside seemed smaller than it looked. Six red leather seats circled a center console, each equipped with a five-part harness. A touch-screen control panel faced Lillian's seat.

As I clipped my seatbelt, Mark climbed into the machine and touched the screen. Excitement welled up. I wondered if the first travelers on passenger jets felt the same way. Beads of sweat emerged around the crown of my head.

"I'm double-checking your coordinates," he said. "We've done this enough where we don't anticipate any problems, but it's always good to triple check everything. Lillian knows the drill. After the opera, you can wait for Donna to bring you back or simply hit this Home button, and she'll return right away. Good luck."

He shook my hand and climbed out. One of the technicians lifted the ladder and rotated it so that it flipped into the time machine.

"Have a good time," Meade yelled. "Tell Giacomo I said hi!"

I gave him an inquisitive look and looked at Lillian.

"Our contact in Prague," she said.

The machine swung shut, and I felt like I was sitting in a giant clam shell. Our only light came from the touch screen. It was claustrophobic, and the air was stifling. The harness felt tight.

A muffled whirring noise from outside our shell seized my attention.

"That's the accelerator getting started," Lillian said.

I remained silent, but my heart still raced. The anticipation felt like I was climbing up a tall roller coaster for the first time.

The whirring grew louder.

Lilian looked at me. She took three deliberate, controlled breaths.

The resonance increased, no longer a whir—more like a sustained note—and loud.

"Hang on tight. Here it comes."

SIX

Just outside of Prague

October 29th, 1787

The whirring continued to build and then, abruptly, stopped.

"What happened?" I asked. "Did something go wrong?"

"We're here," said Lillian. "Pretty cool, huh?"

"It's kind of anticlimactic. I was expecting a big explosion or something—maybe some whizzing through hyperspace."

"There aren't any windows."

Give me a break. I'm having a moment.

She pressed a button on the screen and the machine's shell began to open. Through the darkness, I could make out a small clearing near a thicket of oak and maple trees.

"Holy shit! It worked!"

Lillian smiled and unbuckled her harness.

I did the same. "I can't believe it. I mean, I *wanted* to believe—but up until now, I had it in my mind that Mark could have been playing some kind of trick on me. We're actually here?"

"We're here," repeated Lillian, sounding a little annoyed. "There's a hill behind those trees. Beyond that, we'll catch our carriage into the city. Let's get moving before the time machine is recalled."

I rotated the ladder to the ground and climbed out. My feet landed on soft grass, wet from morning dew. It was slightly overcast and a chill ran through me.

I grabbed Lillian's bag and helped her down the ladder. I was glad to be wearing all of my layers of clothing. The temperature was probably in the mid-thirties, quite a contrast from the desert climate in Nevada.

Lillian took her bag from me and reached inside. She pulled out a small leather pouch and handed it to me.

"This is money for our incidentals while we're here," she said. "It's important that you be the one to pay since you're the man. You can use the pocket on the inside of your waist coat."

I thanked her and put the pouch inside my jacket. She retrieved a white shawl and wrapped it around her shoulders.

"What else do you have in the bag?" I asked.

"A change of clothing and a fresh wig. You couldn't expect me to go to the opera in this could you?"

"Actually, it's pretty flattering," I said. In the low light, I couldn't tell if she was blushing.

I carried her bag, and we headed toward the grouping of trees. I turned and stared at the giant orb.

Amazing.

Minutes ago, I was standing in one of the world's most high-tech facilities. Now, I stood halfway around the world and over two hundred years earlier. Even if the time-travel part was removed, this was the way to reach a destination. No lines. No airport frisking. No jet lag.

"Come on," said Lillian, leading us up the hill.

Light had begun to creep over the horizon revealing rolling hills and a forest blanketed in mist. The dawn chorus of birds announced the coming day. A loud whoosh reverberated, followed by a momentary breeze.

"What was that?"

"The time machine returning. That sound was the air rushing together and filling the space that was just vacated."

We reached the top of the hill and I spotted a small white-washed building below us, a trickle of smoke disseminating from the chimney. Next to it stood a stable.

"There's the inn where we'll catch the carriage to the city. From now on, you should refer to me as Marguerite." She started down the hill.

"Why are we traveling under assumed names? I understand we don't want our names to end up in history books, but can't our assumed names end up there just as easy?"

"These observations are recurring, and it's simpler to have a standard set of names used each time."

"I don't get it."

"We don't just show up for the opera. I have to prepare for this observation by traveling earlier to meet our contact and let him know who will be accompanying me to the opera. We settled on *John* if I am traveling with a man because it was popular at the time. When Mark escorted me, he was *John*. When Mr. Meade was with, *he* was John. It's only coincidence that you're actually named John. Congratulations. Your name was popular two hundred fifty years ago."

"So what happens if you're traveling with a man and a woman?" I switched Lillian's bag to my other hand. It was starting to get heavy.

"Then I have to prep the observation by making an earlier trip —three days earlier than now—to tell my contact that *John and Elizabeth* will be accompanying me. Doing it this way will allow us to schedule observations more efficiently when we start bringing back clients on a regular basis."

"So if you have three guys scheduled to attend the opera separately, you only have to make one prep trip for three observations." It finally made sense.

"You're very sharp."

The inn was situated on the opposite side of a dirt road. A squat, wooden bench welcomed us in front of the inn and we sat, greeted by the pleasant smell of burning beechwood from the fireplace. The bench was damp from morning dew, but I didn't care.

"What's the plan, Marguerite?"

"The carriage will pass through in the next fifteen minutes. I will speak to the driver. When I ask you, you pull out your money and pay our fare. Let me see your money pouch."

I handed her the pouch, and she counted out some coins and handed them to me. I eyed the silver coins. Each had an image of a woman pressed into it, along with an inscription that read: *M. Theresa D.G.*

"There will be two travelers inside the carriage. Let me do the talking. They don't speak English anyway."

We sat and waited. A rooster crowed from behind the building. We could hear people stirring inside the inn. A door opened and an old man popped his head out and looked at us. He just frowned and closed the door.

"Friendly," I said.

"He does that like clockwork," said Lillian. "I'm not even sure how he knows anyone is out here."

We heard the rumble of wheels approach and observed two horses pulling a carriage. It stopped in front of us. Lillian walked up and said something to the driver in German. A boy of about twelve emerged from the inn and attended to the horses.

The driver stepped down from his perch, opened the passenger door and unfolded some steps. Lillian instructed me to pay him, and I did. He took our money without a word, turned and went inside the inn.

"The driver's going in to get his breakfast," she said.

I peeked inside. The space was small and cramped, covered in dark wood. Windows curved along two sides, but the shades were drawn. The seat upholstery was a deep maroon.

The attendant exchanged the horses and two travelers appeared from the inn. The first was as an older man, dressed in black with matching hat and gloves. His companion was much younger, in his late teens or early twenties. He wore a light blue silk suit with gold embroidery. His blonde hair was pulled into a ponytail. He noticed Lillian and his tight lips transformed into a bright smile. When he saw me, he frowned.

Why do I keep getting that from everyone?

The older man walked past us and stepped into the carriage, barely even acknowledging our presence. The young man sidled up to Lillian and whispered something to her in French. Lillian laughed as he grabbed her hand and kissed it.

My insides alerted me that I disliked the young man. He climbed into the carriage and turned to help Lillian up. I climbed in last.

Lillian sat across from me already engaged in conversation with the young Frenchman. I still held her bag and she made no attempt to retrieve it, so I placed it on my lap and shifted my weight in an attempt to get comfortable on the thin velvet-covered cushion.

That proved a bit tough to do, as the old man sitting next to me glared with death in his eyes.

Did I do something wrong, or is this guy just rude?

I tried to ignore him by studying the rest of the carriage. The dark wood absorbed most of the early-morning light that managed to trickle through the drawn shades, but I couldn't get past the feeling of being watched. His gaze warmed my face as if I sat next to a heat lamp.

The carriage lunged forward a few minutes later as we started off toward Prague.

Lillian and the young man spoke in French. I couldn't understand the language, but I understood flirtation. The young man was laying it on thick. He made a joke and laughed, his arms raised and face animated. His hand came down and rested on Lillian's lap. She laughed playfully and removed his hand.

And it pissed me off.

Why does this even bother me? I don't even like her.

Do I?

The ride was bumpy and I fought back a wave of nausea. I opened the shade to look outside and the young Frenchman admonished me. He indicated that I should close the shade.

"Sorry," I said, ignoring his command. The shade was staying open.

"John," said Lillian. "This is Monsieur Claude Phillipe Durand."

I looked at the young man. He bowed his head. Then he looked at the shade and back at me. He raised his chin indicating that I should close the shades.

Again, I ignored him.

Fuck him. I'm not sitting here in the dark so he can try to fondle Lillian.

Lillian continued, "Claude is traveling with his tutor, Monsieur Gisçard. They are also traveling to Prague for the opening of the opera."

I turned to Gisçard. He was studying me. His brow furled.

I reached out to shake his hand, but he remained motionless, simply staring.

What is wrong with this guy?

I directed my attention to Claude, but he ignored me and looked at Lillian.

Well, that was rude.

"Did I do something wrong?"

Lillian gave me a stern look. "John, they don't speak English."

I smiled. "What did I do to these two? I'm just trying to be nice. I guess the French *really are* assholes." I didn't try to hide the contempt in my voice.

"I don't know. Don't embarrass me."

"All I did was sit here."

I spent most of the trip staring out the window. Occasionally, I would glance at Lillian only to catch Claude trying to place a hand on her leg. She would politely smile and remove it, but after a few minutes, his hand would creep its way back to her thigh. No wonder he was traveling to see a play about *Don Juan*.

I made no attempt to look at Gisçard. The old man creeped me out. I returned my attention to the window but sensed him staring.

Finally, I turned to him. "Do I know you?"

He held his glare but did not speak.

"John!" scolded Lillian.

"It's okay," I said, looking back to the old man. I wasn't planning on punching him, but I needed to understand why I was getting the stare down.

He ignored me. His face was tanned and leathery, hardly the pasty complexion I was used to in academic types. His steel-gray eyes were punctuated by a bushy unibrow that formed a V shape between his eyes giving his face a perpetual frown. A scar ran from the top of his right eye and disappeared under his hat.

His eyes studied me as if he was looking for something and then looked up and to the left as if he was trying to recall the answer to a problem.

"*Mon Dieu,*" he said with a raspy, smoker's voice. His frown morphed into a perplexed look. "*C'est vous.*"

"He thinks you're someone he knows," said Lillian.

She spoke to the old man in French, trying to explain that it would not be possible for him to know me. I had just arrived from America and had never traveled to France.

The old man considered what Lillian told him and simply repeated, "America," while nodding.

The next hour felt like the longest in my life. Claude continued to flirt with Lillian in French. Every few minutes, she would remove his hand from her leg or hand, but she didn't appear annoyed. Gone was the standoffish persona. She was almost playful now, laughing and going along with Claude's coquetry.

Lillian asked me for her bag and I handed it to her, hoping she would pull out a can of mace. Instead, she produced a book and handed it to Claude. He calmed down long enough to inspect it before resuming his flirtations. I tried to read its title, but couldn't make it out in the subdued light.

We traveled into Prague from the North on the main passage between Prague and Dresden. A huge stone wall guarded the city. We passed through a gate unhindered and stopped a few minutes later.

"We have to get out here," said Lillian. "It's time to go through customs."

We stepped out of the carriage and this time I was able to hold Lillian's hand and help her down. Claude rolled his eyes. When

Lillian reached the ground, she took her bag from me.

Two customs agents walked over to us and addressed us in German. Lillian smiled, reached into her bag and pulled out a leather wallet. She opened up the two folded sheets of paper contained inside and handed them to one of the agents. He looked at the paper, and his eyes widened. He smiled and said something to Lillian, then turned his attention toward Claude and his tutor.

I looked at Claude. He was yelling at the other customs agent who rifled through his bag. The agent found the book Lillian had given Claude and showed it to his partner. Claude resumed yelling at the customs agents in French while his tutor held his arm firm.

"Let's go," she said grabbing my arm and leading me away.

I glanced back and caught Gisçard staring at me. He mouthed something under his breath. I'm no lip reader, but it seemed like the same word he said earlier.

America.

"I'm sorry about that ride," she said. "They've never acted like that before."

"Who did he think I was?"

"I don't know. Someone he met in America, I guess. I told him it wasn't possible. Thank you for not losing your cool."

"I'm unflappable," I said, remembering how she had gone to Lawrence with reservations about me. "It was just a little uncomfortable. How come we didn't get hassled like they did? What was on those papers?"

"Two letters of introduction from His Imperial Majesty, the Holy Roman Emperor Joseph II of Austria," she said, smiling. "It's amazing how good we are at counterfeiting things in the twenty-first century. We used his actual seal."

"What was the book you gave to *wandering hands* back there?"

"Just a copy of *Night Thoughts,* by Edward Young. Nothing that'll get Claude into trouble. You'll see him again tonight."

"Really? *He's* our contact? He was kind of annoying. I mean, it's obvious he likes you, but can't you see through him? I think I saw him try to hump the tree he was peeing on during our restroom stop."

"No," she said. "I meant you'll be able to see him from our seats at the opera. Believe me, I have no interest in *him*."

She smiled again and locked her arm around mine. "Shall we?"

"What's happened to you?" I asked. "You're like a different person now."

"What do you mean?"

"You've acted like the ice queen toward me ever since we met. Now, we get here, and— you're giddy."

She laughed and looked up at me. "I'm sorry if I made you feel uncomfortable. I wasn't even aware I was doing anything. Look around. Can you believe we're here?" She smiled, and my tension dissolved. "Come on," she said, tugging on my arm. "Let me show you Prague."

SEVEN

As we meandered through the cobblestone streets, I looked behind us and saw an immense castle dominating the skyline. I was ashamed at myself for not noticing it as we approached the city.

Merchants and traders peddled their wares from carts. The stench of stale urine permeated the air.

Geez, the eighteenth century smells like the back alley behind my middle school. The citizens of the city didn't seem to notice, but it definitely had my attention.

"We're in Lesser Town," explained Lillian. Her expression regained its intensity. "Our contact is in Old Town, so we'll need to cross the river."

I was too busy admiring the architecture. "All the buildings look important." Other than a red-tiled roof, each building had its own unique style. About the size of a three-story townhouse, the one we passed was yellow with even-spaced windows and ornate archways. The next, baby blue, trimmed with white and gold. The neighboring house, salmon, then yellow, green and orange.

Sprinkled throughout the cityscape were medieval churches, their spires seen in all directions above the roof line. Colorful tenements nestled against the ancient stone buildings beautifully contrasting the old and new.

I was in love with the city.

The bustling cobbled streets led to two square, gothic towers. One looked about twenty-feet taller than the other connected by a stone rampart. People passed through an archway underneath.

The archway led to a stone bridge that spanned the river. It was about ten yards wide and the length of five or six football fields. Small buildings dotted both sides, filled with merchants who used them as storefronts. Spaced evenly along the edges were statues, mostly depicting Catholic saints.

"It's amazing to see the originals," said Lillian. "If we came back in our own time, we'd only see copies."

My eyes felt like they were bulging out of my head trying to take in every detail. I managed to mumble an affirmative noise, but couldn't think of anything that put what I was experiencing into words.

We continued across. When we reached the halfway point, she grabbed my arm and pulled me to the North side.

"Here," she said. "This is St. John of Nepomuk. It's said that if you touch this part of the bridge, it'll bring you good luck and you'll someday return to Prague."

The statue depicted a bearded priest wearing a Cardinal's headpiece and holding a miniature carving of Jesus on the cross. A ring of five stars encircled his tilted head.

She continued, "He was the court priest here until King Wenceslas killed him for refusing to divulge the queen's confessions."

"*Good* King Wenceslas, from the Christmas song?" I asked.

"No, Wenceslas the Fourth is the one that threw him off the bridge. The legend is that when John's body hit the water, five stars appeared above the water and hovered there all night—"

"Hence the ring around his head."

I reached out and touched the statue. Being thrown in the river to drown was an awful way to die. In fact, I couldn't think of a worse way.

A disheveled man walked up next to us and began relieving himself over the side of the bridge into the river. Seeing me staring, he flashed a toothless grin. Lillian observed my shock and intertwined her arm with mine, leading me away.

We continued our walk across the bridge, trying to avoid the persistent locals who pushed their trinkets at us. A single tower guarded the far end.

"We're passing into Old Town now," said Lillian as we walked under the archway.

We followed the cobblestone street for about a block and came upon a three-story red building with white-trimmed windows. To the right of the second story window was a black plaque with a gold coiled snake. A sign next to the door read: *U ZLATÉHO HADA.*

"We're here," said Lillian, enthusiastically.

"This is a coffee shop?"

"It's the first coffee house in Prague," replied Lillian. "It opened almost seventy-five years ago—from today." She pointed to the plaque. "It reads: *The Golden Snake House.*"

We entered under an ornate white archway containing a coiled-snake keystone matching the plaque and entered the café. Earthy, yellow walls led up to a series of domed ceilings. The welcoming aroma of coffee, chocolate and fresh-baked bread greeted us. People crowded the tables, their language was excited, their expressions animated.

"He's here," she said excitedly and rushed across the room. At a corner table, a man looked up from a newspaper. When he saw Lillian, he stood to greet her. They embraced for a long moment as I made my way to them.

He had to be our contact. Lillian ran to him as if he was her long-lost relative, but the hug lingered more than a casual greeting.

Interesting.

Lillian spoke to the man in Italian. I was able to make out *John Hall*, my identity during this Observation to the opera.

The man smiled warmly and bowed. His gray hair was powdered and pulled back, held by a gold ribbon.

"John," said Lillian. "I present to you Giacomo Girolamo Casanova de Seingalt."

"*Buongiorno*," said the man. He waved his hand in a *no-no* gesture, and in heavily-accented English said, "No title. Giacomo or Casanova."

* * *

He was in his sixties, tall and lean with compact shoulders. A tailored black velvet jacket and matching vest embroidered with gold hung over a flounced shirt giving him the appearance of being overdressed compared to the other patrons. His olive complexion was dominated by a beaked Roman nose and bushy eyebrows. Lines around his eyes testified his propensity to smile.

"Casanova?" I said, surprised and suddenly awestruck. I smiled and held out my hand to shake his, not sure what to do, but he smiled and pulled me toward him and hugged me tight. As if we had met before, he finished off the hug and kissed my cheek.

He spoke in Italian, and Lillian translated, "He is happy that you have heard of him and apologizes for not addressing you in English. His grasp of your language is very limited and he never bothered to learn it. He asks how you know of him since you are from America. Have you heard of his famous escape from prison in Venice?"

"Of course I've heard of him," I said, not taking my eyes off the man. "He's probably the most famous lover ever."

Lillian said something to Casanova as we seated ourselves at the table. She turned to me, "Most people won't know of his sexual prowess until after his memoirs are published. He's working on them now. I told him that you have indeed heard of his famous escape."

Casanova turned to me and asked me a question. I looked to Lillian for the translation.

"He wants to recount the details of his escape. Would you like to hear about it? He has just put it to paper and plans to publish it."

"Yes, yes. Of course," I responded. I couldn't contain my enthusiasm.

Unbelievable. I had to confess. I wasn't even positive Casanova was a real person, more like an idea or legend loosely based on fact. The proof stood in front of me and I was already charmed, whether by my own expectations or by the man himself, I didn't know.

He was visibly pleased by my remark and clapped his hands. Lillian explained that Casanova wanted to narrate his tale properly, but first, we needed refreshment.

He stood and excused himself to get us coffee, which he pronounced *Kaff-ee*, emphasizing the first syllable.

"Holy shit! That's Casanova," I said, leaning closer to Lillian.

"Isn't he wonderful?" asked Lillian, as he got out of ear's reach. "In his eyes, we've only met twice before, but I've been able to see him about a dozen times now. It's amazing how our conversation can be fresh and different each time we meet. He's able to adapt gracefully to whomever I bring. He was especially impressed by Mr. Meade who spoke fluent Italian."

"God, I feel like a douche-bag American for not knowing any languages other than English," I said, frustrated. "How many languages do you speak? It seems you can talk to anyone that we run into."

"Just the important ones: French, Italian, German—some Russian. Remember, I've been studying music my entire life. Language is part of the process. You pick things up."

"I'm learning a new language—as soon as I get back."

"You should. It'll make your job much easier." She leaned in closer and lowered her voice. "He's never told me this story before. I've only read about it. His escape from the Venetian prison helped make him famous in most of the royal courts of Europe. He was known to take two to three hours to give his account. I'm not sure what you said, but it triggered something in him. You know what? You're not so bad, John Curry."

I didn't think I was bad at all.

Casanova returned shortly. His movements were graceful for his age, and he had a flair for the dramatic—even for the simple task of pulling his chair out and sitting down. His motions controlled and deliberate, I wanted to listen to everything he had to say.

I'm having coffee with Casanova.

He began speaking in Italian and then switched to French. Lillian explained that he felt his tale sounded better in the French language because it rolled off the tongue better. I smiled and nodded. Why should I care what language he was speaking when I couldn't understand either? I got the impression that he was trying to impress us—or maybe just Lillian—with his command of both languages.

A waiter arrived and brought us three coffees and three glasses of water. One of the cups contained espresso for Casanova. Lillian and I each received a coffee mixed with milk. He also placed a piece of dark chocolate in front of each of us.

Casanova began his tale in French, allowing time for Lillian to translate.

"It happened in 1755, when he was a young man of thirty."

For over two hours, I sat captivated, learning about his escape from "an inescapable prison."

EIGHT

Casanova's smile revealed he was satisfied, and the tale had ended. Lillian beamed with admiration and clapped. I smiled and nodded. Once again, he spoke in Italian.

"He says that he has not had an audience for the tale in a long time and is grateful for our attention," translated Lillian.

"Tell him I want to know what happens next. It would make a great movie—well, you know what I mean."

There were probably dozens of movies made about Casanova. Maybe there *was* a movie about his escape. I had just never heard of one. Was he the first hero to escape from an inescapable prison? Probably not, but it was better than hearing about his frolicking around with women—although I'd like to hear that too. There was so much more to this guy.

She relayed my message, and the old adventurer nodded appreciatively.

Casanova suggested we stroll through the city and see the building where the opera would take place. He pointed out structures and chronicled their history as we passed. It dawned on me that this city had been around for almost a thousand years.

How many people have walked these streets? How many others had a personal tour from a famous local?

We came upon what Casanova referred to as the Town Square.

On the southern end stood a gothic tower, and Casanova directed us to get a closer look. The stone building looked like many of the churches throughout the city, but this one housed a large astronomical clock consisting of a smaller gold ring rotating inside a larger sphere. With no hands, it reminded me more of the Spirograph drawing toy I had as a kid than a clock. The background of the sphere depicted the Earth and sun surrounded by twenty-four Roman numerals. Situated on either side were carved sculptures representing vanity, greed, death, and consequences.

Casanova referred to the clock as the *Orloj*. Built before Copernicus, when Europeans still believed the sun and moon revolved around the Earth, the clockmaker was blinded by the town council so he would never be able to reproduce a similar or better clock for a different city. Exacting revenge, the clockmaker snuck into the tower and damaged the clock's internal mechanism to such an extent that it remained in disrepair for another hundred years. For the past hundred years, the clock worked off and on, and it was almost sold for scrap two years ago. Although he had never seen it function, Casanova hoped that it would be restored. A local watchmaker was currently attempting to repair it.

"I hope they find a way to get it running again," I remarked. "I would really like to see it."

"Maybe you should check YouTube when you get home," said Lillian. A knowing smile spread across her face.

I returned her smile and made a mental note to search for the clock when I returned home.

Step one: learn a new language.

Step two: read Casanova's biography.

Step three: YouTube.

Got it.

A short walk found us standing in front of the opera house.

The large, three-story building looked as I had expected. Cream-colored stone formed the lowest level and housed the main entrance and box office entered by walking under one of three archways. The upper two levels were light green and adorned with evenly-spaced windows trimmed in the same cream color. Four corinthian columns spanning the second and third levels called attention to the magnificence of the building. The building could have been plucked from ancient Rome or Greece and I'd have been none the wiser. Modern buildings had nothing on the artistic flair of the Prague opera house.

Casanova pointed to the building and spoke in Italian.

"He says that this is Count Nostitz's Theater," Lillian translated. "It only opened a few years ago and the locals are very proud of it. They are also pleased to have Mozart premiering one of his operas here tonight. We are very fortunate to be here." She paused and looked away before meeting my eyes. "Casanova has offered me a private tour of the city and I've accepted. Why don't you do some sightseeing and meet us back here around six? It will be very crowded, so don't be late."

"Excuse me?" I said. "You can't leave me here. I don't speak the language. What am I going to do? I don't even know what time it is."

"You'll be fine. Besides, how many historians get the opportunity that you are getting? Take advantage. *Carpe diem.* Seize the day, John."

The old man tilted his head and smiled. Off they walked, arm in arm.

I had just been ditched.

Carpe diem, indeed.

I stood, gut-punched and thought, *What the hell is wrong with me?* What was it about Lillian that turned me into a fourteen-year old boy, especially in the carriage with Claude? I did have an opportunity none of my colleagues could even fathom. To waste it fawning over some girl was ridiculous—and it was *freaking Casanova* who she walked off with.

Not knowing what to do, I headed back toward the Town Square, confident I could find my way back at six. It had been hours since I had eaten, and all of the coffee from earlier had made me jittery.

I found a sign with a picture of a frothy beer mug, but more importantly, I smelled food. The opened door led to a passageway leading down a flight of stairs. Housed under a stone-arched hallway, entering the tavern felt more like walking into an underground vault than restaurant. Hanging from the ceiling were candlelit, circular chandeliers, around four-feet in diameter. Long tables ran lengthwise on either side occupied by a variety patrons producing a cacophony of voices speaking German, French and possibly Bohemian dialects—none of which I understood. The lack of windows and flickering candles gave the restaurant a macabre feel, but it was interesting and welcoming.

I didn't see any open tables, but spotted an opening next to a group of well-dressed men raising beer steins and toasting each other in loud German. I decided to immerse myself.

Carpe diem.

I motioned to the open space on the bench, and one of the men gestured it was okay to sit. He wore a long frock coat and had his hair held back by a ribbon, matching the dress of his six companions.

A barmaid approached, and I pointed to a half-eaten plate of pork and potatoes in front of one of the men and said the word, *bier*. She nodded and walked away. When she returned, I opened my money pouch and produced a coin. From the wide eyes she made, I assumed it was pretty valuable. I observed that two of the men at my table also took notice. I held up my beer and made a circular motion with my hand, signaling I was buying a round for the table. The men cheered me and raised their half-empty steins in approval.

The man to my right asked me a question in German. I indicated I didn't understand.

"English?" asked another. He was older, probably in his mid-to-late forties.

"American," I said.

"Ah, thank you, American. I am Lukas," he said. His hair was sandy blonde, and he had a large, bulbous nose and arched eyebrows. He introduced his companions: "This is Frederich, Wilhelm, Bernard, Rudolf and Karl. We are traveling from Vienna."

His German accent was thick, but understandable. "What brings you to Prague all the way from America?"

"The opera," I said.

Hearing this, they all raised their glasses and called out, "*Prost!*"

"We are also here for the opera. We would not miss the opening of Herr Mozart's newest masterpiece. Were you here for the Marriage of Figaro?"

I shook my head. "This will be my first opera."

"You will enjoy it. The Nostiz is one of the finest opera houses in Europe. What brings an American such as yourself to Europe?"

"Mozart," I proclaimed, raising my glass.

"Herr Mozart. *Prost!*" they all said and cheered once again.

When my food arrived, Lukas let me eat and resumed his conversation with his companions. The herb-roasted pork was overdone, but still edible. *Better safe than trichinosis.* The pilsner was warm, not the way I was used to drinking it, but quite good.

The Viennese travelers bought the next three rounds, and a happy alcohol buzz spread through me.

None of the other men spoke English, so in between toasts, I conversed with Lukas. As a boy, he traveled with his father and spent time in London, where he picked up the language. He'd also seen Germany, Switzerland, and Italy on his Grand Tour. He recounted his travels with pride, and it dawned on me that Lukas's generation was one of the first to have the ability to see the world. Most people from his era never wandered further than a twenty-mile radius from where they were born. He would one day like to see America but didn't know if his wife could bear the long journey across the Atlantic. She wasn't as adventurous.

He asked how long it took me to reach Europe from America.

Oh, about forty-five seconds.

I blurted out "six weeks," and he nodded his head in approval.

"Well, friend, it is time to collect the wives and prepare for the opera." Lukas and his companions stood up.

I had completely lost track of time and was quite inebriated. I followed them up the stairs taking slow, deliberate steps. The crisp air outside was a welcome relief from the stale smoky air downstairs.

The temperature had dropped considerably during my time in the tavern. The sun was setting and clouds blocked any remnants of the day's warmth. I made my way back toward the theater, trying to shake off the effects of the alcohol while silently cursing myself for wasting the opportunity to explore the city. On the plus side, I had just experienced an inside look at eighteenth-century life that no one from my time ever had, and concluded the bonds of friendship can be struck up at any time and any place over a beer.

Three cheers for alcohol. Prost!

As I got closer to the theater, I sensed excitement in the air. People of all classes packed the streets, hoping to obtain tickets to the show. A long line had formed in front of the box office, and I was suddenly worried I wouldn't be able to locate Lillian and Casanova in time to get in myself.

What time is it?

A horse-drawn carriage forced its way through the mass of bodies and halted in front of me. The chauffeur hopped down and hurried to open the door. A buxom woman spilled out of the coach, her red gown adorned with a gold floral pattern. Her red-faced husband followed donning a powdered wig and girthy midsection. He stood at least six inches shorter.

I chuckled and scanned the crowd looking for Lillian.

Nothing. The mass of people pressed toward the opera house.

I walked around the corner to see if they were waiting at a different location, maybe a less crowded area.

Nothing.

Would she ditch me here? How am I going to get home if I can't find her? I should never have let them leave my sight.

I returned to the initial rendezvous point and waited. My pulse raced, and my muscles tightened. Panic threatened to overtake me.

What am I going to do? I don't even know where the pickup point is.

"John!"

I turned toward the sound and recognized Lillian across the street.

I sighed with relief and realized I was trembling. I calmed myself by taking a few deep breaths. My happy buzz was completely gone.

I need another drink.

They approached arm in arm, and I fought back a hint of jealousy.

Lillian's gold dress had been replaced by a blue gown with cream stripes, aligned with a pattern of red roses. She wore a red choker around her neck and a blue feather in her powdered wig. A white ruffle highlighted her low-cut neckline.

Casanova had changed clothing too. His brown overcoat and matching breeches were embroidered with a gold floral pattern, and his bluish-green waistcoat contained the same pattern of red roses as Lillian's gown.

"Change of clothing?" I asked as they got closer. I projected calm and collected, but my heart still pounded.

"Yes, Giacomo had it made for me as a surprise," replied Lillian. "Isn't it wonderful?" She twirled around and performed a slight curtsy.

"Yeah, wonderful."

Casanova greeted me with a bow and said, "*Buonasera.*"

He led us to the side of the theater and up a flight of stairs. Lillian informed me that we could get into the theater through the performer's entrance. He knocked and a doorman promptly opened the door. The man greeted Casanova with a jovial laugh and let us in.

The hallway's walls were white, but my eye was immediately drawn to the ornate ceiling murals spanning the entire area. Red velvet chairs sat on either side of the doorways. An intricate pattern of black, white and gold gave the floor a regal impression.

Casanova led us up a staircase and down a small hallway carpeted in crimson. An usher greeted us and escorted our group to a door and opened it. Our theater box was on the second level, third from stage left. Scarlet paper adorned the walls and matching red dividers separated the seating areas. Three red velvet chairs waited for us. Positioned in the back corner sat a large, porcelain pot shaped like a coffee cup.

I whispered to Lillian, "Is that what I think it is?"

"Yes," she said, "And don't think of using it in front of me."

My bladder forewarned me I would have to make a decision on whether to use the chamber pot in front of her and Casanova soon enough.

Great.

The inside of the theater looked like how I remembered it from the movie *Amadeus*. Four balconies wrapped around the opera house, each level painted red and trimmed with elaborate gold designs. There were two box levels above us and one below, identical except for the ones in the back of the room built wider to seat more people. Candles mounted on the front of each box provided light for the audience.

A large chandelier lit by an innumerable number of candles hung from the center of the ceiling. Three smaller, candle-lit chandeliers stepped down on either side providing sufficient light for the theater, but smoke from the candles formed a haze that hovered above. It amazed me that this theater still stood in my own time. The chances of it burning down had to be considerable.

People circulated below greeting each other, and the energy heightened my anticipation. The main seating area on the floor was small, and I counted sixteen rows. People began filling the boxes around us.

A brisk knock on the door diverted my attention. Our usher had returned holding a tray with three glasses of red wine. Casanova handed the man a few coins, and the usher closed the door as he left the box.

Casanova handed us each a glass. My eyes drifted from the wine to the chamber pot. I didn't want to be rude and not drink it, but I wasn't ready to rush my decision about whether to use the chamber pot either. I took a small sip and rested the glass on my lap.

Casanova once again spoke in Italian.

"Mozart also premiered The Marriage of Figaro in this opera house and was quite fond of Prague," offered Lillian. "The Viennese were a more fickle audience and Mozart preferred the praise heaped on him by the Bohemians. Giacomo also says that he helped his friend, Da Ponte, with some of the lyrics."

She reached over, placed her hand in Casanova's and continued. "Lorenzo Da Ponte was Mozart's lyricist for three of Mozart's operas and was considered the greatest librettist of the day—"

Casanova interrupted her, rattling off vigorous Italian while holding up two fingers.

"He says that Da Ponte has only collaborated on *two* operas with Mozart," said Lillian.

I thought Casanova didn't speak English. Did he understand more than he led on?

Lillian asked Casanova a question in Italian, and he nodded and stood to leave.

After he left the box, Lillian explained, "Da Ponte *did* work with Mozart on three operas. The third one will be finished three years from now."

"You didn't have to make him leave. He *was* right you know," I said.

"No, I didn't send him away because of that. I thought you deserved a souvenir for being a good sport today," she replied. "He's going to pick up the playbill for tonight's performance. You'll own a copy of something that doesn't exist in our time."

"Are we allowed to do that?"

"We can't bring things from the future to the past. There's

nothing wrong with taking home a memento."

"Whoa, I'm pretty sure we were expressly told *not* to take anything. Won't that create one of those time-travel contradictions I keep getting warned about? What'll happen when you bring the next person to the past...? Wait, are you testing me?"

Lillian's cheeks flushed red. "Well," she sighed. "We haven't really tried bringing back anything yet. This'll be the first."

I realized what was going on. "You're trying to bribe me to keep quiet because you *abandoned* me for a few hours so you could prance around with *monsieur bonjourno.*"

I immediately regretted the remark.

I should really think before speaking.

"Don't judge me," she snapped, her hands balled into tight fists. "You need to get off of this male-machismo horse you've been on since we started this trip. We've known each other for what—two days? So don't assume there's anything between us—there's not. I was trying to be nice. You shouldn't even *be* here. I have no idea why Lawrence was so eager to hire you—*because you're Mark's friend?* You're a *community college professor*. You're not even qualified to be here. It wouldn't have worked that way for the rest of us."

I sat in silence. Shocked.

Finally, I understood the reason for her coolness toward me.

And it pissed me off.

I felt my own face redden. "*They* recruited *me.*"

"Answer this: would you even think twice if you had the chance to sleep with Cleopatra or the Mata Hari or Marilyn Monroe? No, you wouldn't because you're a *man,* and it's perfectly okay for you."

"You forgot Amelia Earhart."

"Fuck you." She turned her body away from me, arms folded.

This wasn't about me after all. Lillian felt guilty for abandoning me to spend the day with Casanova and the reality of getting ratted out scared her. Plus, she had a point.

"Maybe you're right," I said, "I probably *would* jump at the chance to hook up with Marilyn, but I'd have to be pretty drunk to go for Amelia."

"You brought her up."

"Look, I won't judge you. I was just a little miffed that you'd ditch me like that. I wasn't prepared. Even though I'm only a *community college professor*, I survived. No harm done."

She turned toward me, her eyes filled with tears of anger.

"I'm sorry. I was out of line. I'm frustrated with myself. I shouldn't have abandoned you like that. We should have been trying to scout a closer entrance point. Instead, I jumped at his invitation."

"I might have done the same thing."

"No, you wouldn't have abandoned me. I know that."

Probably not.

"Are you going to tell Lawrence when we get back?"

"No, but you can't ditch me again." I put a hand on her shoulder. "Let's just leave the souvenir here so we don't mess anything up. I want to get home when this is over."

"I'm an old soul—always have been," she murmured. "He knows music and literature. He understands me more than anyone I've ever met. He cares about what I say and asks me what I think. I don't think you can understand how refreshing that is. Most of the academics I've been around have rarely even *talked* to girls, so they're bumbling idiots around me. I mean, look at me—"

The door opened, and Casanova returned with three playbills. The usher followed with more wine. Casanova saw Lillian's face and shot me an angry look. He sat next to her and caressed her cheek. She leaned in toward his embrace.

She whispered something to him in French, and he turned to me and thrust the playbill toward my hand. It was bound in gold paper.

"It's the libretto for the opera," she said composing herself. "It has all of the lyrics so the audience can follow along."

"Merci," I said and looked at the libretto. It read: *Il Dissoluto Punito osia, Il Don Giovanni. Dramma giocoso in due atti.*

Since I couldn't read Italian, the libretto was useless, but it was not lost on me that I was holding a priceless piece of history in my hands.

Maybe I should accept the gift and take this home. I wonder what it would be worth...

Ummm—no.

Members of the orchestra took their seats in front of the stage and started tuning up. I looked out over the balcony. What seemed to be a thousand people crammed into the theater. The weight of the moment, or maybe the effects of the alcohol, overwhelmed me. I felt dizzy and exhilarated all at once.

Still, I couldn't get over the feeling that I was being watched. I turned to Lillian.

"Where's your boy, Claude?"

"He's not my boy," she corrected. "Middle section on the floor. Far left."

I scanned the crowd. Sure enough, I spotted Claude. He was engaged in an eager discussion with a female opera-goer. To his left was Gisçard, who stared up at me.

I returned his gaze, hoping he would turn away, but he did not.

A large cheer pulsed through the crowd and Mozart himself walked to his position in front of the orchestra and bowed toward the crowd. All thoughts of Gisçard melted away and my eyes began to tear up. I'm not sure I can put into words the emotions of seeing Wolfgang Amadeus Mozart alive and in the flesh. I tend to get choked up when I hear the Star Spangled Banner performed. This was the same feeling—except magnified by ten times. It was heady, unbelievable, and I wanted to drink in every detail.

Mozart was small with a slender build. He wore a gold silk overcoat with white ruffles sticking out of the end of each sleeve. His reddish brown hair was tied back and held by a ribbon. His smiling eyes were large and round and full of mischief. He flashed a wide, toothy smile and bowed.

The crowd gave two more cheers, and the opera began.

NINE

Don Giovanni

The overture began with a thundering, ominous symphony of sound. My eyes flooded with tears, and I had to stop myself from sobbing aloud. I was transfixed on Mozart as his arms directed the orchestra.

Lillian leaned over and whispered in my ear, "Mozart just finished writing the overture a few hours ago. The copyists didn't have time to create copies for everyone in the orchestra. This performance was supposed to start a half hour ago."

I nodded and directed my eyes to the stage as the curtains opened. The set looked like the courtyard of a noble, complete with stone pillars and stairs. A few moments after the overture, a man appeared and began singing in Italian.

I surveyed the crowd. Many watched, but some of the audience had their backs to the stage and talked to each other. A few minutes into the performance, I was having trouble hearing the singers above the murmurs of conversation..

"What's happened?" I whispered to Lillian. "Why is everyone talking during the show?"

"The opera is a social scene. People attend to be seen and to socialize. Watch what happens once the sword fight begins."

On cue, the performers acted and sang out a scene in which

Don Giovanni, the main character, tried to seduce and ravish a girl. She called for help and a man, her father the Commendatore, appeared and challenged Don Giovanni to a duel with swords while the daughter ran to get help. After a brief confrontation, Don Giovanni struck the Commendatore down.

Some of the audience shouted comments toward the stage, prompting laughter from other spectators. It was the type of response I'd expect from a crowd watching professional wrestling, not an opera. Not in front of Mozart. Here I was having an emotional experience and these people were making catcalls toward the female performers.

The lead female could not have been much older than nineteen or twenty, with a well-proportioned figure and pointed nose. The actor playing Don Giovanni appeared to be in his early twenties and sang with a rich baritone voice.

"The singers are much younger than I expected," I said to Lillian.

She nodded. Casanova sat, focused on the performance.

At one point in the opera, one of the characters pulled out a book and showed it to one of the female singers. Lillian pointed out to me that the book contained the names of all of Don Giovanni's conquests, eighteen hundred in total. She translated what she said to me for Casanova. He smiled and shrugged.

At the end of the first act, the crowd dispersed to seek refreshment and probably a place to relieve themselves. Casanova walked over to the chamber pot in the corner and began emptying his bladder—right in front of us. Lillian and I sat uncomfortably facing the theater to avoid having to watch and trying not to listen. Men in boxes all around the theater relieved themselves with little regard.

When he finished, Casanova motioned me to take my turn. I

politely declined.

As awe-inspiring as it was to see Mozart perform, I still sat in a building with no air conditioning filled with over a thousand people—most of whom did not bathe that day, or possibly that week. Casanova's interaction with the chamber pot reminded me of my own needs in that arena, but I couldn't bring myself to use the chamber pot in front of Lillian or Casanova.

"I'm going to get some fresh air," I announced as I headed toward the door.

"You have about twenty minutes," said Lillian. "Don't be late."

I made my way outside through the theater's side door, confident I could find my way back to the box. The crisp October air was a welcome relief from the stale odor of the unventilated opera house.

Opera goers milled around and I noticed a few faces staring at walls as men peed on the sides of buildings and into the street. I didn't judge them, having done the same thing during my happy hour with Lukas and his German friends. After finishing my own business in a secluded area of the street, I returned to the side door, knocking the same way Casanova had done earlier and waited. No answer.

Unsuccessfully, I tried the handle, but the door didn't budge. I repeated my knock. Nothing.

Swearing under my breath, I made my way to the front of the theater and walked under the covered archways to the entrance. A burly usher refused my entrance. He said something to me in the local dialect which I didn't understand, but the message was clear: *No ticket, no entrance*. Since I had entered through the side door with Casanova, I never had an actual ticket to the performance.

I decided to return to the side entrance to try my luck again.

As I rounded the corner, I observed Claude across the street talking to a young girl who was also dressed for the opera. It seemed as though the young Frenchman couldn't help himself whenever a female was present. Two boys stood behind him, watching and smiling. The girl didn't mind the attention. Claude laughed and she giggled as he stroked her cheek. A man brushed past me in haste and made his way toward the seduction. As Claude moved in for a kiss, the man arrived and shoved him away with a strong arm.

Daddy to the rescue.

The father yelled at Claude and his friends in German, shaking a threatening fist, and Claude put up his hands and backed off with an innocent expression. The man dragged his daughter toward the front entrance scolding her every step of the way.

After the father was out of earshot, Claude made a remark triggering juvenile laughter from his friends. He turned his attention back toward the theater, and our eyes met. His smile morphed into anger. He said something to his two friends, and they approached me.

I turned to walk away, but decided I didn't want to look like a coward.

Sometimes, I make dumb decisions like that.

"*Vous et votre putain a essayé de me faire arrêté,*" he yelled as he approached. His friends followed. One was my height, but big, like a corn-fed Midwestern farm boy. He had a long, brown overcoat on and muddy boots. The other was smaller, about Claude's size, and dressed in a green-silk frock coat, probably nobility.

"Hi Claude," I replied. "I have no idea what you are saying."

"He says you and your whore almost got him arrested today," said the well-dressed friend. His accent was noticeably French, but easy to understand. The bigger one moved behind me to block my escape.

Great. Now what did I get myself into? I didn't have much experience fighting and never felt the need to prove my point by exchanging blows with someone. Apparently, Claude didn't feel the same way. At any rate, I'd had enough of the French pretty boy.

"Tell him it wasn't my idea, but if he hadn't acted like such a half-witted, French *douche bag,* Marguerite wouldn't have given him the book." I felt my muscles tighten.

The friend stared at me blankly for a second, trying to comprehend what I said so he could translate. Claude didn't seem to care and yelled something to the big friend.

The bigger guy moved in to grab me, and I turned to clock him with a right hook. He ducked under my punch and drove his body into me, shoving me hard against the wall. *Shit.* All the air left my lungs, and I felt a momentary wave of panic as I tried to catch my breath. He clutched my left arm and moved behind me holding me in place. Claude's better dressed friend advanced to grab my other arm, but I held him back by trying to kick him.

"John!" I heard a familiar voice call. Lukas and his two friends ran toward me. The big guy let me go, and Claude and the smaller one backed off as well.

"We thought we lost you," He grabbed my arm and pulled me toward the front entrance. "No more running off on your own."

When we were safely away, Claude yelled something at me in French, and his two friends taunted me.

"I thought you were good at making friends," joked Lukas as we headed toward the front entrance. "You should have bought the boys beer."

"I think he'd prefer a nice Chardonnay," I said, trying to catch my breath. "He's from Paris."

"Oh, the *French,*" laughed Lukas.

Karl and Wilhelm joined in.

"I don't have my ticket," I said as we approached the entrance, unoccupied except for a few stragglers late returning from intermission.

"Don't worry," replied Lukas, pulling out two tickets. "You can use my wife's to get inside."

We entered with no hassle from the usher. Music filled the lobby. The opera had resumed. Violins accompanied a duet between a soprano and baritone voices. We headed up the stairs to the balcony levels.

"We saw you from our seats across the theater," said Lukas. "You have a fine-looking woman with you."

"She's my cousin," I said, still smarting from the fact that she was *Casanova's* fine-looking woman tonight.

"You have handsome looks in America. I *really* have to visit now."

"Wait until you experience Spring Break."

Lukas tilted his head, not understanding.

"Thank you," I said, not bothering to explain.

"Farewell, friend," Lukas clasped my hand with both hands. "The next time we meet you will have to explain to me what *douche bag* means."

* * *

When I opened the door to our box, Lillian looked up, clearly relieved to see me.

"What happened?" she whispered as I returned to my seat. On the stage, Don Giovanni and his servant were singing to a woman on a balcony.

"I had a run-in with your friend, Claude." I said. "He and two of his friends tried to jump me outside for almost getting him arrested."

"Claude? Really? Are you okay?"

"Yes, a few of *my* friends showed up and rescued me."

Lillian's head flinched and her eyes narrowed. "Your friends? Who?"

"You're not the only one with friends here in Prague." I sat back in my chair. "I met some Germans while you were off with Casanova."

Casanova eyed us thoughtfully.

I turned toward him. "I got into a fight." I held up two fists and made a punching motion.

Casanova smiled and clapped his hands together. I got the feeling he had been in a couple of scuffles in his day.

"We can talk about this later," said Lillian and put her hand on mine. "I'm glad you're okay." She turned back to the performance.

Surprisingly, the rest of the opera held my attention. I didn't think I would be able to understand it or enjoy it since I didn't know what was being sung. The music held me in rapture. Part of it was undoubtedly because Mozart himself was conducting, almost literally within reach.

The highlight was the finale when the statue of the murdered Commendatore appeared and bellowed, "Don Giovanni." Gossip ceased, and the audience watched, rapt, as the ghost attempted to give Don Giovanni one last chance to repent. Holding true to character, Don Giovanni declined and was led to Hell, disappearing from the stage in a plume of smoke. Although portrayed as a villain, I admired Giovanni's fearlessness and refusal to repent in the face of judgement.

Having nothing modern to compare the performance to, I was impressed by the stage design and the ability of the singers. The orchestra was outstanding, but would Mozart have any less?

After the performance, the audience once again gave Mozart three cheers. He waved happily and looked around. For a moment, our eyes met and I found myself cheering at the top of my lungs. He bowed and exited the pit.

I had just had a moment with Mozart.

Would the same thing happen when I observed Washington's inauguration?

This job is pretty sweet.

"That was fantastic," I said, forgetting all my frustrations from the day. "Thank you, thank you." I grabbed both of Casanova's hands and shook them. Then I grabbed him and hugged him which prompted a laugh.

He led us toward the door, and Lillian let us know that she needed a moment alone. I guess she wasn't opposed to using the chamber pot. Casanova and I waited outside in the hall together.

He said something to me in Italian and handed me a small, folded piece of paper. I tried to open it and read it, but he grabbed my hand, indicating he did not want me to read it.

"Più tardi," he said, smiling.

I placed the paper in a pocket in my vest. My heart raced. What could Casanova possibly want to say to me? I raised my eyebrows, questioning the gesture, but he remained silent.

Lillian appeared shortly, and we exited through the side door where we came in.

Casanova asked something that Lillian translated as, "Would you like to attend the after-party?" but we declined. We had a time machine to catch.

Lillian asked me to wait ahead so she could say her goodbye. I watched as she walked toward Casanova, shoulders slumped, until she found his embrace.

Not wanting to intrude, I walked toward the front of the theater and watched the opera-goers exit the building. A few were quite drunk by the way they were staggering and I snickered to myself.

I pulled Casanova's folded note from my pocket and stepped under a street lantern for light. The short message was written in French, and I scanned the note for Lillian's name, Marguerite, but didn't see it. Since I didn't know the implications of bringing something like this home, Lillian would have to translate it before we left. Hopefully, the message wasn't embarrassing. I folded the note and returned it to my pocket.

Lillian caught up a few minutes later visibly distressed. She wiped tears from her eyes with a silk handkerchief and we walked in silence. I carried her bag as we headed in the opposite direction from where we entered the city.

"It's okay," I said after a few minutes. "You'll see him again."

"Not like this." Her voice strained as if holding back a sob. "I'm sorry I abandoned you. Really. I hadn't planned on anything like this happening, and I got caught up in the moment. Please forgive me."

"I'm okay," I assured her. "After what I just experienced, I'd be okay even if I was beat up by a few Frenchmen." I smiled to try to lighten the mood.

Lillian didn't notice. "I had to do some maneuvering to obtain the entrance to the opera. I've always been used to the advances of men. It comes with the territory. I know that. It just gets hard when I finally meet someone who's passionate about the same things that I am. Plus, it's the stories. Countless books have been written about the people he's met. He could be a poster boy for the Enlightenment."

"I get it," I said. "He's a charming guy. I'd have loved to have hung out with him and talked to him more. The first thing I'm doing when we get back is invest in French lessons. I feel like a complete idiot for not being able to talk to anyone or understand what is happening."

"Don't feel like an idiot," she said. "You'll get the hang of it." She grabbed my hand.

"How far is our rendezvous point?" I asked after a few more minutes of walking.

"Not too far. Once we exit the gates, it's about a five minute walk."

We arrived at the gate and found it had been closed for the night. The guards gave us strange looks, wondering why two people on foot would want to leave the city at such a late hour. Lillian said something to them in German and produced some coins to bribe the guards into lowering the door, which was actually a drawbridge. At first, the head guard declined the bribe, but relented when Lillian produced one more coin that raised both of the guards' eyebrows.

We crossed over the moat and when we were safely across, they raised the drawbridge behind us.

"Let's hurry," said Lillian. "We only have fifteen minutes."

"How long will it take to get there?"

"Just a few minutes, but we have to move."

We walked briskly, diverting from the main road toward the trees in the distance. My attention turned to the note in my pocket. Lillian would have enough time to read and translate the note for me. I could discard it before we left.

My thoughts were interrupted by a loud, creaking noise coming from behind us. I turned to see the drawbridge being lowered again. I could make out the silhouettes of three people. Two small figures and one large figure came bounding toward us.

Fucking Claude.

"Claude," I said. "What should we do?"

"He can't see the time machine. We need to get out of here. Run!" We took off toward the trees in the distance.

I turned and spotted Claude and his friends giving chase.

We were probably about seventy-five yards ahead of them, but Lillian's opera gown slowed us. Had she been dressed properly, we easily could have lost them.

"It's no use," I said. "We're going to have to stop and see what they want. We're not going to be able to make it to the machine unnoticed."

Lillian relented and we turned to wait for them. We were at least fifty yards away from the trees.

"Hand me my bag," she said, and I handed it over.

"You don't by any chance have a taser in there, do you?"

"No, just some pepper spray. I don't know what use it will be against three though."

"Keep it handy. Hopefully, we won't need it," I said. "Maybe Claude will be reasonable."

He won't.

She cupped it discreetly in her hand, hiding it from view. They arrived a few seconds later. The large one trailed behind, huffing and puffing.

Claude said something in French. His expression was smug, and I didn't like the way he was eyeing Lillian.

Lillian ignored him. "He asks where we're off to."

"Ask him how he's going to get back into the city."

"We can get back in. We have money," the small friend said.

"What do you guys want?" I asked.

"To finish what we started," said the small one. "A girl like this is too beautiful for you to have all to yourself."

The big one once again moved to try to get behind us. I sidestepped, blocking his path. "Not this time, *Mongo*."

He tried to shove me out of the way. I grabbed his arms, and Lillian stepped forward and pepper-sprayed him in the eyes. Immediately, he let out a high-pitched scream. Covering his eyes with his hands, he sank to the ground and rolled around, still screaming.

One down, two to go.

Claude and the smaller one moved in to grab Lillian. She stepped back to avoid their advance, but tripped over her gown and lost her balance. She went sprawling on the ground, and they moved toward her. I ran at them and swung at the smaller friend with full force. He saw me and tried to dodge, but I connected enough for him to lose his balance. I gave him a quick kick, and he landed on the ground.

Almost immediately, he sprang to his feet and lunged at me. I saw the blade in his hand glance off of my chest. I was startled for a second, but the adrenaline kicked in and I punched him as hard as I could in his ear. He dropped the knife and fell to the ground. I took a quick step toward him to give him a kick, but he was already up, sprinting back toward town.

Claude was on top of Lillian. He struck her and cocked his fist to hit her again. She shifted her weight and flung him off of her. She rolled toward her bag and reached in to grab something, but Claude jumped on top of her again.

I ran toward them. "Hey, Claude. You French dandy piece of shit."

He looked at me for a second and decided that he had enough time to at least give Lillian a black eye for his troubles. He was too late. Lillian smashed something across the side of his head, hard. It sounded like a dish breaking. Claude grunted and fell over next to her. Lillian stood and kicked him in the side.

It was dark, but I could see that the side of Claude's face was covered in blood.

I stood over Claude and cocked my foot, contemplating whether to kick him while he was down. He would have done it to me, but I held myself back.

Lillian's shoe sat on the ground. Covered with blue silk, it had a three-inch wooden heel—hard to believe she had run in these at all. I picked it up, approached her and knelt down. "You lost your shoe."

I reached for her foot and slipped it on. The fit was perfect, just like in the fairy tale.

"Thank you." Her wig had fallen off and her hair was a mess, sticking up and pasted to her face by sweat. She was beautiful.

"*Assez!*" yelled an angry, raspy voice. Gisçard stepped toward us. He held a pistol in his left hand. It was pointed at me.

"What is it with you?" I asked.

He held up his right hand. The glove he had worn earlier in the day was gone revealing a white, mangled hand. It looked like he was giving me the shaka sign from surf culture, as if to say, *Hang loose, dude,* but I realized he only had his pinky and thumb. The other fingers were gone.

"America," he said. He squinted and aimed the pistol toward my head. "You."

What the hell is this guy talking about?

"No," said another voice.

Casanova. Thank God.

He had a pistol of his own and it rested on the nape of Gisçard's neck. The old man hesitated, then lowered his hand and dropped the pistol on the ground.

"*Laisser,*" said Casanova, indicating that we should leave.

Claude and his big friend lay on the ground. The big one was still whimpering. At least he was no longer screaming. Gisçard stood with his head down, dejected.

Casanova smiled and bowed—one last exploit for the old adventurer.

"Let's go," said Lillian. "We're late."

She ran over to Casanova and kissed him on the cheek.

Gisçard focused on me. His eyes radiated hatred. It was hard to take someone with such a thick unibrow serious, even if I had come pretty close to being killed by him.

Maybe it was relief, or maybe it was nervousness. I made a face and stuck out my tongue.

He let out a scream and charged me. His left hand reached inside his jacket and pulled out a dagger. I backed up and moved to my right, anticipating his lunge.

He moved fast for an old man, but not fast enough. His thrust missed and I timed my punch perfect, landing square on his nose. I felt the cartilage break as he crumpled to the ground.

Casanova stood holding the pistol at his side. "*Lassier*," he repeated.

Lillian grabbed me and we hurried toward the thicket.

"Are you okay?" I asked.

"I think so," she said. "Come on."

I regarded Casanova one last time. "Thank you."

He nodded and looked once again at Gisçard, now crumpled in a defeated ball on the ground. I turned and headed for the trees.

Donna sat just ahead in a small clearing. It was the most beautiful sight I'd ever seen. The hatch stood open and we ran over. I threw Lillian's bag inside and dropped the ladder. She climbed up, and I followed her in. When we were both inside, she pressed a button and the hatch closed. We buckled our seat belts, and I noticed that she had a red mark under her right eye.

"He got you. Are you okay?"

"I'll be okay," she said. Her shoulders slumped. "What was that all about?"

"I have no idea. I guess I shouldn't have stuck my tongue out at him." I pictured Gisçard holding up his mangled hand, pointing his pistol at my head. *America. You.* What the hell did that mean?

Lillian stared blankly. I wanted to tell her that she lost her wig, but the whirring began to build and I decided to shut up.

TEN

The hatch opened slowly, revealing the group who'd seen us off waiting for us. It was an odd feeling knowing that only moments ago, I was staring down the barrel of a pistol held by an eighteenth-century French noble after being knifed by one of his thugs. I made a note to thank Harrison Meade for the vest the first chance I got.

Lawrence saw our disheveled appearance and his face turned to one of horror.

"What happened?" he yelled, rushing over.

Lillian climbed down the ladder first. She didn't say a word.

"We got jumped by some French opera-goers," I said.

"That's never happened before." Lawrence's face turned bright red, his eyes narrowed with distress. "Did they see the machine?" The tuft of Lawrence's hair stuck up like the crest of a bird's head.

"No," I answered.

"How did this happen? This is unacceptable. What did you do?"

"It's okay, Lawrence," said Lillian. "We didn't alter history."

"*Didn't alter history?* How could you know? I need a full report. We can't run the risk of having our clients getting attacked. What changed? What did you do different?"

"It was my fault," I said. "I went outside during intermission and saw a Frenchman trying to fondle some girl in the street. He saw me and came after me. I didn't even try to intervene."

Lawrence turned on Lillian. "Why did you let him outside?"

"It wasn't John's fault. It was mine," she said. "I got caught up in a conversation with Casanova."

"It was me. I should've stayed inside. It's just—the smell. All those people and the smoke from the candles. It was making my eyes water. I had to get out of there. It won't happen again."

Lillian shot me a relieved glance. Her eyes seemed to say, *Thank you.*

Lawrence stepped toward me, nostrils flared. "You're right it won't happen again. I didn't want you on this in the first place. We've never had a problem with this observation—"

"Lawrence, please," pleaded Lillian. "We're okay. He didn't do anything wrong other than step outside for air. Please, we're tired and need some rest. It's been a long day."

"He was your responsibility."

Taking the brunt of the blame made my body feel heavy. I went through the events of the day and tried to make sense of what happened. Did I do something wrong? What could I have done to avoid the showdown with Claude and Gisçard?

"Lawrence," I said. "I don't know what transpired, but I'll fill you in on everything. If you think it's something I did—I don't want to jeopardize what you're doing here." A wave of fatigue settled over me making my legs feel like spaghetti. I couldn't recall a time I had been as tired.

Mark approached me. "You look like Hell."

Lawrence took a step back and sighed. "Get some rest. We'll talk in the morning." He looked at Lillian and back to me. "We'll talk when we have clear heads. Nine a.m. in my office."

"Are you okay?" asked Mark.

"Yeah, I just need some sleep. I'll fill you in later."

That was enough for Mark and he turned his attention to Lillian.

I went up the elevator alone and walked across to my trailer. Harrison's car was gone. I climbed the stairs and walked inside.

I noticed a four-inch tear through my vest and my undershirt from the knife. I removed my clothing and was reassured to see that the vest was completely intact. I dropped the clothing on the floor and jumped in the shower.

Afterward, I collapsed on the bed and slept.

* * *

For the first time since college, I slept through my alarm clock. A frantic banging at the door brought me out of a deep sleep. The alarm buzzed angrily.

What time is it? 9:04.

Mark yelled, "Are you in there? Are you up? John, wake up!"

I flung my legs off the side of the bed and wobbled over to the front door. I felt hungover. Drinking alcohol all day and then fighting for your life will do that.

Ugh. I'm not even old yet. Why do I hurt like this? Imagine what Casanova feels getting up in the morning. Or that bastard, Gisçard.

You. America.

"I'm up," I said. "Just stop the banging." I opened the door.

"They're all waiting," he said, eyes creased with worry lines. "Lawrence wants his report from the Observation."

"Okay, okay. Give me a minute."

"Hurry."

This couldn't be good. My chest tightened, anticipating another tongue lashing from Lawrence. I didn't want to get fired for what happened in Prague.

I showered and dressed in jeans and a button down shirt. By 9:13, I walked up the stairs to Lawrence's office, my hair still wet.

Already seated were Lawrence, Lillian, Harrison, and an unfamiliar man in a wheelchair. He looked to be in his mid-fifties, skinny. His sparse black hair was combed over the top of his head.

"Good morning, John," said Lawrence. "I take it you're well-rested." His anger had subsided, but his tone warned me it was still there.

"Sorry," I answered, sitting in the open chair. "I slept right through the alarm."

"Yes, enhanced fatigue is a small side-effect of time travel," said the man in the wheelchair. "We haven't been able to identify why yet, but hope to have an answer soon."

Lawrence fidgeted with a paperclip. "John, I'd like you to meet Dr. Elias Cohen. He's our chief historian at Timeless Arts."

"Sorry I can't rise to shake your hand. You'll have to come to me," he said, offering his hand with an amiable smile.

How'd they get the wheel chair up here?

"Pleased to meet you, doctor," I said, gripping his hand.

"I'm sorry I wasn't here to greet you when you arrived," he continued. "I was in New York doing some research. I hope the books I left found you safely."

"They did. Thank you."

Being introduced to Dr. Cohen was a relief. It meant I wasn't being fired—at least that was my hope. The tightness in my chest loosened.

Lawrence began, "Dr. Cohen has been working on a few entrance points for the inauguration and will share some information shortly, but first, we need to hear your statement as to what happened in Prague. We need to make sure that all safeguards are in place before we open this Observation up to the public. I fear yesterday's events have set us back considerably."

"Sure, Lillian would you like to begin?" I asked. She looked tired. Her hair was pulled back in a tight ponytail and she wore no makeup. The spot under her eye was swollen and red. She looked like hell.

"Lillian has already given her statement. We'd like to hear what you have to say," said Lawrence.

"Of course," I said, confident my only mistake was stepping outside for air during the intermission. "We arrived before dawn and located the tavern where we caught the carriage to Prague. We met Claude and his tutor, and Claude spent the trip trying to be frisky with Lillian. She gave him the book, and when we reached customs, the authorities detained Claude and his tutor, allowing us to enter the city unhindered."

Lillian interjected, "For the record, I've given Claude the same book during the previous two trips."

"You know," I continued, "The tutor, Gisçard, acted hostile toward me the entire carriage ride—"

"I'd never even heard him speak before." Lillian leaned forward in her chair. "He acted like he knew John from somewhere and that John killed his dog or something. It was very strange."

Lawrence and Dr. Cohen exchanged looks of confusion. Harrison was unreadable.

"Please, continue," said Dr. Cohen.

"After entering Prague, we crossed the bridge and met Casanova at the coffee house where we probably sat for three hours. Casanova told us the story of his escape from the Venetian prison while Lillian translated so I could understand. Afterward, we toured the city together, Casanova gave Lillian some new clothes as a surprise and we went to the opera around 6:30."

When Lillian realized I was covering for her, her shoulders relaxed.

"I would have loved to hear Casanova tell the story of his escape," said Dr. Cohen. "He was famous for telling the story all over Europe. Oh, to hear him tell the tale." His smile grew as he contemplated.

"Maybe we could record it sometime," I said, trying to lighten the mood.

Lawrence shifted impatiently. "Please continue, John."

"The opera was amazing. Seeing Mozart—just incredible. During the second intermission, I decided to go outside for air. I saw Claude and two of his friends flirting with a girl, but her father intervened. When Claude saw me, he and his friends tried to pick a fight. I never said a word to provoke him, didn't try to stop them from talking to the girl or anything. Luckily, a few locals came to my rescue. I realized I'd made a mistake and decided not to leave Lillian's side again—and I didn't. After the opera, Claude, his tutor, and his friends followed us outside the city gate and attacked us. Lillian pepper-sprayed one of the attackers, and I chased off another. Claude jumped on top of Lillian and hit her once before she brained him with something. What did you hit him with, anyway?"

"My chamber pot," Lillian answered.

There was a collective, *Eeew* at the thought of having a chamber pot smashed over someone's head.

"We were about to leave when Gisçard pulled a pistol on us. Luckily, Casanova intervened and pulled his own pistol on Gisçard—allowing us to leave."

Lawrence looked horrified. Dr. Cohen and Meade sat straight-faced. Lillian stared at floor.

I continued, "Claude and his friends were okay when we left. No one was seriously hurt—except for a few egos maybe. I don't think anyone ran back to the city to spread the word that three boys had been bested by me and a girl in an opera gown. We got into the time machine unmolested, and I didn't see anyone try to follow when we left."

I purposely left out the part about being stabbed with a knife. Hearing it would have made Lawrence blow a gasket.

"Casanova intervened? Do you have any idea what the repercussions are?"

Meade spoke up. "Did he write about it? Is there anything about the incident in the historical record?"

"No," answered Dr. Cohen. "If Casanova did decide to write about the incident, he never got around to it."

"Then everything's okay, Lawrence," said Meade.

"That still doesn't explain *Icosameron*."

"What's *Icosameron*?" I asked.

"A novel written by Casanova," answered Dr. Cohen. "It's a work of science fiction, but it describes a utopian society that has technology such as the television, airplanes and cars."

"Really?" I looked at Lillian.

"I don't know. I never brought anything like that up during our discussions, and neither did he."

Dr. Cohen waved his hand dismissively. "Is it such a stretch to transform the idea of flying horses into airplanes? Can we please move on?"

Lawrence sat for a moment, apparently collecting his thoughts. "Where did you get the pepper spray? You know that anything from our present is against policy."

"I told her to carry it," said Harrison. "I've been telling you we need to take precautions when we go back in time. I realize we can't alter the past, but we need to consider the safety of our clients and ourselves. Ninety-nine percent of the time, we're not going to have to worry, but as you can tell, things can go awry."

Lawrence opened his mouth to speak and then decided to remain silent.

"I think Harrison's right," said Dr. Cohen. "The world is a dangerous place, but it was even worse two hundred years ago. Desperate people will do desperate things. They might decide just because John is clean and well-groomed that he's wealthy, which can provoke some kind of altercation."

Lawrence scanned the room. "Okay," he said, "but nothing large. Pepper spray is okay, but no guns, electronics, tasers, or anything like that. If someone feels they need to bring in something from the present, it must be cleared by me or I pull the plug. This is not up for debate. Is that clear?"

I almost asked about bulletproof vests, but decided if Harrison wasn't speaking up, neither was I.

Everyone nodded.

"Okay, well I'm glad you made it back safe," said Lawrence, his demeanor back to that of affable scientist. He turned toward Lillian. "In the future, no one leaves your side. We can't risk something like this happening again. You can leave now if you like. We need to begin discussions on our newest Observation to New York. Of course, Mr. Meade you're welcome to stay."

Harrison made no move to leave.

I let out a slow exhale, relieved I was officially on board to go to New York, despite the misgivings Lawrence had about me.

Lillian excused herself, brushing my shoulder with her hand as she left. I heard Mark pass her on the stairs. Lawrence handed Dr. Cohen a keyboard and mouse and got up to dim the lights.

Mark entered the room and sat down in Lillian's chair. After he was settled, Dr. Cohen began.

The screen behind the desk revealed a map of New York in 1789.

"I think it's best to enter the city from the north here," Dr. Cohen pointed to one of the areas north of the city that looked to be farmland. Two groupings of trees converged around a small lake. "If possible, we should try to avoid water travel. If you enter early in the morning, you should be able to get in undetected. It should also give you ample time to enter the city and witness the President's procession, which will begin just before noon. My only concern is hiding the machine during the day. The metamaterial can cloak the machine fairly well when activated, but in the right sunlight, it's possible someone could see it."

"So we're not just getting dropped off?" I asked.

"Not on a preliminary survey," said Lawrence. "We need to be one hundred percent sure we can enter and exit the observation without being detected. If we miscalculate and infiltrate the past in an area where the machine can be seen, we need to have the flexibility to change our strategy on the fly—something that can't be controlled from this end."

"Those trees should provide some cover," said Mark. "Besides, won't most of the city be converging on the inauguration to get a glimpse of Washington?"

"Good point," Harrison said.

Dr. Cohen nodded. "The inauguration will take place here at the Federal Hall at the corner of Nassau and Wall streets," he pointed to the location on the map. "I don't think you should linger much after the inauguration is over. Don't try to shake hands or meet anyone famous. As tempting as it is, this first trip is to scout out a vantage point, nothing more."

Lawrence agreed. "Does anyone have any questions?" he

asked.

"What about money?" I asked.

"I'll see to it that we can get you some cash for the trip," said Harrison. "Spanish money, doctor?"

Dr. Cohen nodded. "Tavern keepers won't be too keen on taking British pounds on the day of the inauguration. Continentals would still be worthless. Spanish pieces-of-eight should suffice."

"You'll both have spending money," Harrison said.

"Just remember, *no souvenirs,*" Lawrence added. "We can't risk disrupting the time continuum."

"We know," answered Mark.

"Of course," I agreed, suddenly glad that I refused the libretto from Lillian when we were at the opera.

Casanova's note.

Panic gripped my chest. I had forgotten about it. I never had time to ask Lillian to translate, and then the fight... Did the note even survive the trip back? Did it simply fade away during the trip to the present or crumble to dust, the victim of accelerated aging? How did taking souvenirs from the past work? I sure as hell wasn't going to speak up and ask now. I needed to get back to my room.

"As far as clothing goes," continued Dr. Cohen, "The clothing you wore at the opera will be acceptable. We should get you fitted for some boots since the streets of New York aren't all paved, and you'll be entering the city through farmland. Mark, you can wear your contacts, but you might want to take your glasses as well."

"I will," answered Mark, "but I hate those glasses."

"Anything else?" asked Lawrence.

"Yes," said Dr. Cohen. "Try to get as close as possible to the speech. It will be difficult. Legend holds that at the end of Washington's oath, he uttered, *'So help me God,'* and that has remained a tradition for American presidents."

"Though if I remember correctly," I interrupted, "the *'So help me God'* quote didn't show up in history books for another sixty years or something like that."

"That's correct—just like the whole Parson Weems *cherry tree* fabrication that was made up after Washington died," said Dr. Cohen. "Unfortunately, even if we know the truth, we won't be able to go public. It's a personal interest of mine."

I nodded. I wanted to know too. "If we arrive early enough, I'm pretty sure I can get us a spot close enough to hear. History is on our side, right? What about the church service at St. Paul's? Should we plan on attending?"

"I hadn't planned on you going to the service, but it is an important part of the day," said Dr. Cohen. "What do you think, Lawrence?"

"I don't have any objections. Mr. Meade? This Observation is being put together at your request. Would you want this as part of your experience?"

Harrison paused for a moment. "I would like to attend the service. See what you can do to get us in."

"Perfect," I said. Excitement crept into my voice. Instead of reading about the inauguration, I was actually planning on witnessing it. "When can we do this?"

"You can leave whenever you like, but I would suggest Thursday or Friday to give you adequate time to prepare," said Lawrence, "You are the resident expert on this Observation and you need to be prepared for everything."

"Wait," I said. "Thursday or Friday? Isn't that kind of soon? Doesn't something like this take months of planning?"

Lawrence gave a yielding glance to Harrison.

"It's for my aunt," he said. "The one I told you about. She has terminal lung cancer. I want to present her with one final gift while she's still strong enough to make the trip."

I looked around at everyone. All eyes were on me, but no one said a word. The decision was in my hands. "If you think we can prepare properly, I'm okay with it. Friday it is."

* * *

After our meeting, Harrison rode up the elevator with me.

"Thank you for being discreet about the vest," he said.

"I told you I'd keep it a secret. You saved my life, you know. I didn't mention that during the assault one of the attackers had a knife. He would have stuck it right in my heart if you hadn't insisted I wear the vest. Thank you."

Harrison nodded. "Lillian told me she thought you'd been stabbed. She noticed your vest was cut."

I hadn't even thought about what Lillian saw.

"How's she doing?" I asked. "She didn't look good today, and I haven't had a chance to talk to her since we got back."

"She's a bit unsettled," he said. "She's holding herself responsible for what happened. She'll be okay."

The doors opened to our hanger, and we walked out.

"See to it that Lawrence doesn't learn about the knife attack. He's a good man, but he's been maniacal about not taking anything modern to the past. Let's keep the Kevlar a secret until I can convince him of the necessity. I'm not traveling without it."

I agreed and went into my trailer. When I closed the door, I found Lillian waiting for me.

ELEVEN

"Thank you for covering for me," said Lillian. "I was sure you were going to tell them about Casanova. Lawrence would have fired me on the spot."

"Hey, don't worry. I told you I wouldn't tell him. We can't change what happened. We can learn from it and move on. Besides, you got the war wound, not me." I gestured to the swollen lump under her eye. "You can fix the situation the next time you go back."

"I brought you something," she said reaching into a briefcase. She pulled out a pamphlet bound in gold paper.

"The libretto?" I asked, taking it in my hand. My pulse jumped. After all the talk about not bringing back souvenirs—I held it gingerly, afraid it might explode in my hand.

"Now we know it works," she said. "I'm not sure what would happen if we tried to bring another one back during a different Observation, but you can bet I won't even attempt it. It's my way of saying thank you for giving me a second chance. Now you have something that no other person in the world has, and *your* libretto was handled by Giacamo Casanova."

Her smile returned and I knew I'd made the right decision in keeping our secret safe. Her remark about Casanova reminded me of the note he had handed me. I opened my mouth to tell her about it, but stopped. Casanova hadn't wanted her to read it, and now that I had time to translate it myself, I could see what it said before sharing.

I examined the libretto. The world wasn't ending from some rift in the time continuum. Maybe it was safe after all.

"I left my pepper spray at the scene. I didn't tell Lawrence," she confessed. "I did some research online early this morning. It doesn't look like it was ever discovered."

"I wouldn't worry about it," I said. "Unless it got buried, the plastic would have disintegrated by now. You might want to replace it in case Lawrence asks about it." Contrary to popular belief, plastics do break down when exposed to sunlight and water. The small pepper spray had probably disappeared within a year or two of the opera.

"I already did," she said.

"So what was it like?"

"What?"

"Hooking up with Casanova? Was it all you hoped it would be?"

Her expression turned angry.

"I'm not trying to make you mad—I'm genuinely interested."

"What do you think I am? I didn't sleep with him." She let out a frustrated groan. "Men can be such idiots. We spent the day together. That's all."

"Oh. Well after you made that remark about Marilyn Monroe, I guess I just assumed—"

"He had syphilis, John. *Jesus,* do you think I would be that stupid? Do you think I would sleep with him just because he was famous—like some groupie?"

"No—I—I'm sorry," I said, "It was a dumb assumption on my

part. I get it. He at least tried, though, right?"

Her anger evaporated and she smiled. "Yes, he tried, but I can handle myself."

"So nothing, huh? No second base? No heavy petting?"

"Shut up."

I laughed. "Maybe *you're* not so bad Lillian Campbell. You're even kind of like a nice person now."

"Thank you," she said. "I didn't thank you properly for saving me from Claude and his thugs."

"Don't mention it, but I think they were coming for me. I just wish I could have nailed Claude before he got your eye."

Her hand reached up to the tender spot, but she stopped short of touching it.

"What was with the old man, Gisçard? He never acted like that before?"

"No," she said. "Like I said, I never even heard him speak until this last trip. It was as if he was holding *you* responsible for something that had gone horribly wrong in his life."

You. America.

"Maybe I'll meet him at the Inauguration. The way he said *America*—I got the impression he had been there before or we had met."

"John, the Inauguration was two years *after* the opera."

"I guess you're right," I said, feeling foolish. "Maybe I just have one of those faces. Anyway, I'm glad I won't have to see him again. He creeped me out."

"Do you mean you won't return to Prague with me to attend the opera?" She smiled.

"I don't think they'd let me." I walked over to the coffee pot and started to get it ready to brew. "Hey, I guess it's my turn to be tour guide," I said, changing the subject. "We're leaving on

Friday."

"So soon?"

"Yeah, something to do with Harrison's aunt not having much time left. He wants her to see Washington with her own eyes."

Lillian's eyes narrowed. "Fantastic. I'm happy for you. Just don't mess things up for yourself like I did."

"Well, I did have my eye on Martha Washington. Do you think she would be up for a roll in the hay? I can be really charming when I want. Ask anyone—well, except Gisçard—and you."

Lillian laughed. "Just prepare for the unexpected. If you feel like things are going bad, just get back into the machine and come back. You can always try again. There's no need to be a hero."

"Thanks, I think we'll be okay. Besides, I've had enough of being a hero. I just want to take in all I can during the experience. Dr. Cohen said we shouldn't have any problems getting into the city. And Mark will be there."

"You're in good hands with Mark," she said. "Just keep your wits."

"I always do."

Lillian leaned in and kissed me on the cheek. "Thanks again. I was wrong about you."

My nerve endings tingled and I felt light-headed. I fought back the urge to wrap my arms around her. "Did you want to stay for coffee?"

"Maybe another time." She turned and left.

I filled my cup and retrieved Casanova's note. It was written in French with impeccable penmanship. I pulled out my laptop and found an online language translator. *People don't write like that anymore,* I thought.

* * *

I spent a few hours browsing the books and materials Dr. Cohen had acquired to aid me. It seemed easy enough. Once we got into the city, we'd have plenty of time to watch the procession and get a good spot for the actual swearing in. The ceremony would take place on the balcony of the second floor of Federal Hall. Getting close enough to hear Washington speak would be difficult. He was known as a fairly soft-spoken public speaker due to his dentures, and he always ran the risk of having them fly out of his mouth if he opened his mouth too wide. I just hoped that the crowd below would be quiet enough for us to hear him.

I met Mark in the cafeteria for lunch, and the first thing he asked about was my knife wound.

"Geez, you sleep through one lousy alarm and everyone already knows what happened," I said. "Who told you?"

"Harrison. He thought it would be best that I knew what happened so I wouldn't have second thoughts about wearing the vest. He's really hell-bent on everyone being safe."

"Well, I'm a believer. The vest saved my life."

"So what happened?" Mark picked up his burger and took a bite.

"I don't know. I guess I offended the sensitivities of a spoiled French noble. I think my going outside during the intermission triggered some reaction in the kid. I didn't even say anything to him to provoke that kind of anger or frustration. I'm guessing his infatuation with Lillian, or a bruised ego, overrode any kind of clear thinking."

"You're just lucky he wasn't aiming for your eye."

"But there was something about that old man, Gisçard. It's possible he was directing things."

"Well, it all worked out. You're back. The past is still the past.

No harm done."

"Maybe he'll think twice before messing with an American again."

* * *

We spent part of Thursday getting fitted for our boots. I took the brown suit I had worn to the opera and pointed out the damage that had been done. The seamstress told me the repairs would be made before we left. She was a little curious as how the tears got there, so I told her it was torn during the fight and that seemed enough to satisfy her.

The entire facility knew about what had transpired by now, though the tale had taken on a life of its own. Mark had heard that I had fought off five men who had assaulted Lillian. I wish that had been true. I don't think I could have even taken all three. Someone even asked Lillian if *I'd* given her the red mark under her eye.

It had become a tradition that prior to every new Observation, the participants would have a sendoff dinner the night before. So, on Thursday, Harrison and Anja, Dr. Cohen, Lawrence, Lillian, Mark, and myself all met for a private dinner in the cafeteria. The food had been helicoptered in from Guy Savoy's in Las Vegas and everyone indulged in a glass or two of wine. It was refreshing to see Lawrence without a lab coat, but he still hadn't managed to keep his hair from sticking up. Lillian seemed to be back to herself and the swelling was starting to subside. Meade led a toast to our success and I left feeling excited and filled with anticipation.

* * *

On Friday morning, I found my repaired clothing, wrapped in plastic and hanging on my trailer door. The stitching was barely noticeable. The undershirt must not have been salvageable because there was a new one included with my suit.

I showered, and after a short deliberation, decided to wear deodorant. Authenticity be damned. My experience with the past taught me that I would have enough trouble dealing with the odors of other people. I wasn't about to deal with my own funk if I could help it.

I put on my Kevlar vest and dressed the same way I did before my opera trip. The only difference was the knee-high riding boots in place of my buckled shoes. A tricorne hat was included with my clothing, but I didn't put it on.

I grabbed a sheet of paper with some handwritten notes I had made about the inauguration and placed it in my pocket. As an afterthought, I grabbed Casanova's note and stuffed it in there as well. I didn't want it lying around in case someone came into my room while I was gone.

Scientists bustled about the computer terminals and around Donna, inspecting for what, I don't know. Mark was in full dress and already wearing his tricorne hat. His suit matched mine in style, but was caramel brown. He carried a small leather purse slung over his shoulder that rested under his opposite arm.

Harrison saw me and walked over to shake my hand. "You're about to witness the birth of our country. I envy you."

"Thank you. You'll see it soon enough. I'll pick out a good seat for you."

He handed me a matching leather purse like the one worn by Mark. "Here's some spending money."

"Thanks," I said. "I'll be sure to pick up a hot dog from one of the New York street vendors the first chance I get."

Lillian hugged us both. "Good luck," she said. "And be careful—Mark, don't let him outside by himself."

"I won't." Mark held up his leather pouch. "I brought a leash in case he gets unruly."

"Nice purse," I said.

Mark rolled his eyes and directed them toward my own haversack. "You too."

Dr. Cohen wheeled next to us, followed by Lawrence.

"Good luck, gentlemen," said Lawrence, shaking hands with both of us. "I look forward to hearing of your experience."

Dr. Cohen looked up. "You may delay, but time will not."

"Benjamin Franklin, right?" I shook his hand. I liked Dr. Cohen, but felt a tinge of guilt. Had he not been in the wheel chair, he would most-likely be leading the Observation instead of me.

"Right you are." He smiled. "Now go witness the birth of our country."

"We'll do our best," I said.

"Well done is better than well said."

Another Franklin quote. I wondered if I would ever get the chance to see Ben Franklin, my favorite founding father.

We climbed into the machine and buckled ourselves in.

"Did you ever think we would be doing something like this?" I asked.

"Oh yeah," Mark answered. "I've been dreaming of this since I was a kid. Thank you for agreeing to come with."

The hatch closed and I heard the buildup of the accelerator.

Whir, whir, whir… The sound intensified. Then, just like before it stopped.

"We're here," said Mark cheerfully. He pushed the button to open the hatch.

"It's too anticlimactic to have this thing travel through time and space and just stop," I said. "You need to add a *ding* or something."

* * *

I wasn't prepared for the darkness in the early morning of April 30, 1789. Some light came from the east, but it took a moment for my eyes to adjust.

"What time is it?" I asked.

"About 4:30," answered Mark. "Listen, I want to show you how to get home in the event something happens to me. Do you see this button? Simply press it and wait. The particle accelerator will take a little longer to activate because we're not at the facility, but it'll get you back."

I looked at the button. Its message was simple enough: *Home.*

"Don't worry," he continued, "I'm planning on coming back with you. This switch here activates the cloaking technology. It's still in its infancy, but should camouflage the machine pretty well while we're gone." He clicked the switch to *"on"* and unbuckled his harness.

The temperature outside was chilly. Just as we planned, we had arrived just outside a small cropping of trees. I climbed down and took in the surroundings. It didn't look like a well-traveled area, but it was hard to tell in the low light.

Mark joined me and pulled out a small remote control from his leather purse.

"I can't lose this," he said, showing me the controller. It was about the size of a cell phone. "In case I do, there's another way to get back in. Watch this."

He pressed a button and the machine began to close. After it was fully sealed, the cloaking material activated, producing a shimmering effect on the surroundings. It was almost impossible to see, but there were areas where light bent around the machine and distorted the background.

"That's pretty cool," I said. "I didn't even know we had the technology for something like this."

"We have a *time machine*."

"True."

"Okay," he began. "In case we get separated or lose the remote, we can enter the machine manually. Place your hand on the machine in this area," He gestured to the area just under where the equator of the machine would be. "Now hold it there for seven seconds."

I held my hand in the area. After a few seconds, the machine appeared.

"It disables the cloaking technology," he said. "Now, press on the hatch there and simply key in the eight-digit code."

I pressed on a small hatch, and it sprung open. "What's the code?"

"07-04-1776," he answered. "We picked an easy one for the historians to remember. I would have chosen 3-1-4-1-5-9-2-6."

"What, do you think I don't know pi?"

"Do you?"

"I guessed it, didn't I? I just don't know what it's used for—the circumference of a circle or something—right?"

"Well, it's—you're messing with me."

My smirk must have given me away. He turned his attention back to the machine.

"You can close the machine the same way you opened it," he said. "Any questions?"

It was reassuring to know we could return to Donna at any time, rather than having to wait at a specific time and place like we did in Prague. I wasn't anticipating trouble, but I hadn't anticipated trouble at the opera either. "No, I think I have it. Let's go see George Washington."

PART 2

"By the all-powerful dispensations of Providence I have been protected beyond all human probability or expectation; for I had four bullets through my coat and two horses shot under me yet escaped unhurt, although death was leveling my companions on every side of me!"

- George Washington in a letter to his brother, 1755

TWELVE

New York, April 30th, 1789

"What do you mean *stuck*?" Stuck as in stuck in a New York where the British won the American Revolution? I stared at the flag again. It had to be a mistake.

Mark's shoulders slumped, and he looked around, as if searching for something. "Remember when we talked about going back in time to kill Hitler—how you couldn't return to a world where Hitler had lived and started World War Two? This is the same thing. We're in a reality where George Washington wasn't president. We're stuck."

"We don't know Washington isn't president. That guy could have been insane. He smelled like stale whiskey."

"You're not understanding." Mark pulled off his hat and ran a hand through his hair. "We both know the British flag didn't fly the day of the inauguration. We're in a reality or alternate universe—whatever you want to call it—where George Washington isn't president. This means a new timeline has started."

"How's that even possible?"

Mark huffed. "Think of it this way, we traveled to the past on a set of train tracks connecting Point A and Point B. Before we reached Point B, we jumped tracks and ended up at Point C—

Point C doesn't connect with Point A. We're on the wrong track. We're *stuck*."

It still didn't make sense to me how we could "jump tracks" and end up in an alternate reality, but I understood the weight of our predicament. "Maybe it isn't as bad as we think," I said. "Maybe it's as simple as your calculations being off."

"No way. I double and triple-checked everything this morning. You realize the world spins at over a thousand miles an hour *and* orbits the sun. This isn't like the movies where you pick a date and magically appear. If the calculations are wrong, you don't end up in the wrong year, you end up in the middle of outer space. Let's find out what's going on. Maybe we can find today's paper."

"Papers were printed on a weekly basis," I said. "It was more like Newsweek."

"Whatever," he said, "Let's just find one."

"Let's head toward the river and see if we can find a place to buy a newspaper."

As we approached the water, I saw the masts of ships and the flags that were flying, mostly British—no American. At the corner of Water Street stood a five-story building. A sign on the first floor read: Merchant's Coffee House. At least we could still get coffee and wouldn't be *stuck* drinking tea.

"Let's go there," I said, pointing.

Ship's captains and businessmen sat at tables drinking coffee—and tea. The large room was almost to capacity, but Mark and I found an empty table with a discarded newspaper.

The title read, "The Royal Gazette." In the top corner was the date: "[NEW-YORK, SATURDAY, April 25, 1789.]" Under that: *TO THE KING'S Most Excellent Majesty.*

The Most Excellent Majesty? Who wrote this? Bill and Ted?

The paper confirmed Mark was right. We definitely weren't where we were supposed to be. "This doesn't look good," I scanned the paper looking for George Washington's name. Nothing. "There should be news of Washington's arrival. He should have already been here for a week."

The paper was one large sheet with print on both sides, folded in half, creating four pages. I found high tide listings, a story about a woman being executed for counterfeiting in London, and a bill being introduced to Parliament allowing the Prince of Wales to act as regent during George III's illness. But no mention of George Washington—or anything uniquely American.

"It's like New York is still a British colony," I said. Could it really be true? Could the Americans have lost the Revolution? It was one of those things in history where so many things had to fall into place for the Americans to defeat the British. There were so many near misses, convenient coincidences, and instances of pure luck that the idea of the Americans losing wasn't so hard to comprehend. The reality was the problem. Did the American Revolution even happen?

"I told you," said Mark. "We've been transported to an alternate reality. I'm just not sure how."

"Is it possible?" I asked.

"No," he said. "We couldn't go back to a past that never happened. It's impossible."

"Well, if it was impossible, we wouldn't be here. Now what?"

"Give me a minute to figure this out," he said, looking around the room.

"This reality we're in," I said. "We went back to our past and found— an alternate reality. What if something earlier in history has been altered that redirected events in such a way that the American Revolution never happened?"

"Then we're stuck here—unless we can fix whatever went wrong."

"How do we know that's how it works—that the path home will be cut-off? You're so positive we're stuck. It's just a theory."

"No, it's not just a theory." Mark's face paled, and he lowered his gaze.

"So this has happened before?" My heart beat heavy as anxiety hit me again.

"Not exactly. We lost a team eight months ago. A tech like me and a historian, Leland Park."

"I know him," I said. "He's a Civil War historian. I've read a few of his books."

"He was the lead historian before Dr. Cohen. They went back to watch the play Lincoln was at when he was assassinated."

"*Our American Cousin*—I'm familiar."

Mark continued looking down as he spoke. "They didn't come back. This was during a time when we controlled the time machine from Nevada so it dropped them off like when you went to the opera. When we sent Donna to retrieve them, it wouldn't work. The path was blocked."

"So, you just left them?"

"There was nothing we could do. It was like trying to pull up a web page with no Internet connection. Dr. Cohen thinks they tried to warn Lincoln. If Lincoln survived the assassination attempt, they couldn't return to our present where Lincoln was killed by John Wilkes Booth. They would have been cut off."

Stuck.

I could understand if we had done something stupid—talked to someone or landed the time machine on George Washington the way Dorothy's house landed on the Wicked Witch of the East. But we didn't—at least not that we were aware of.

"So this reality we're in—it doesn't have an impact on anyone back home? Our United States still exists and all that?"

"Just us."

My daughter, Tabby, would be okay then. New York would still be New York, and the Cubs still couldn't win the World Series. I felt relief that only Mark and I were affected—that we didn't destroy the world with time travel. Well, momentary relief. I still needed to get back home.

After a moment, I spoke, "We need to find out what happened. See if we can pinpoint what event triggered this. I can't stay here. I have a daughter waiting for me."

"I don't want to stay here either," he said. "Where do we start?"

"Books, newspapers—something. Maybe we can talk to someone who can fill us in."

"How about him?" Mark said, pointing to the newspaper, his finger over the name, James Rivington, publisher.

"I've actually heard of him. He was a famous newspaper publisher here in New York, and loyalist to the British Crown. Let's go find him. He might know."

I asked one of the locals to point me toward the offices of The Royal Gazette. "Go to Queen Street and follow it around the corner. You can't miss it."

The Royal Gazette was located in a small building at 1 Queen Street. Under the sign, it listed James Rivington, Publisher.

We opened the door, and a bald man with a dirty, ink-splattered apron stretched across a large midsection looked up.

"What can I do for you?" he asked in a thick, Cockney accent. He was setting type on a printing press.

"Is Mr. Rivington in?" I asked.

"Not here," the man said. "If he offended you with something we printed, he won't listen anyway."

"No, it is nothing like that," I assured. "We just wanted to talk to him. We've been traveling and need to catch up on news we might have missed."

"Well, he still ain't here. Maybe Mr. Hamilton can help you. He's in the back." He dropped what he was doing and walked through a door in the rear of the room.

A moment later the man returned and walked back to his printing press. "He'll be up in a minute," he said, resuming his typesetting.

A man walked through the door and approached us. He was in his early to mid-thirties, thin, and had dark blue eyes that looked almost purple.

"Hello," he said, revealing a slight accent I could not place, "Mr. Rivington is not available. Can I help you?"

My mouth dropped, "Alexander Hamilton?"

THIRTEEN

"Do I know you, sir?" he asked.

I was staring at Alexander Hamilton, a man whose image I had seen thousands of times—hundreds of times—on ten dollar bills. He might have been the most intelligent of all the founding fathers, author of many of the Federalist Papers and architect of the modern American economy. Political rival to Thomas Jefferson —and Aaron Burr, but most importantly, he was one of George Washington's staff members during the Revolution and a trusted cabinet member during Washington's presidency. Stumbling across him was incredibly fortunate. If anyone would know what was going on, it would be Hamilton.

"No," I said recovering from my initial shock, "Not officially. We may have met during your King's College days."

"I don't think so. I would remember if we did. Teeth like yours would have stood out." He gestured toward my mouth. "Yours too," he said to Mark.

I glanced at Hamilton's teeth, but couldn't tell if his were in good shape.

"I don't remember speaking with you either. Maybe we didn't meet," I said. "Anyway, would you be interested in talking to us? We've been traveling abroad for many years and are trying to track down some friends and learn about what happened here while we were gone."

Really? That's the best I could come up with?

He contemplated for a moment. "I could talk for a while. Are you offering to buy my meal?"

"Of course," said Mark, shaking his leather purse.

Hamilton led us to the corner of Broad and Pearl Streets to a three-story brick building with a sign that read: Fraunces Tavern.

The irony was not lost on me. General Washington had addressed his staff in the same tavern after the Revolutionary War—the war that apparently hadn't been won. Or fought.

We were seated at a small table. The early afternoon crowd was sparse. We ordered three plates of duck sausage and boiled potatoes, which seemed preferable to the other option of a leg of roasted lamb. I didn't have much of an appetite anyway.

"Colonel Hamilton, what's going on? Where's General Washington?" I asked, getting right to the point.

Hamilton's face revealed genuine surprise. "Colonel?" he asked, "I think you have me confused with someone else."

"Were you not a Colonel on General Washington's staff during the Revolution?"

"Revolution? Do you mean the disorganized farce of 1776? How long have you been away?"

I needed to change tactics. "Yes, sorry. We've been away for a long time and might have heard conflicting reports. We were under the impression that the Americans won their independence from Great Britain."

Hamilton flinched. "I'm sorry, sirs, but I am afraid you have both been victim to a gross deceit. The *revolution* you speak of was extinguished a long time ago." Hamilton began to rise, apparently finished with us.

Mark slumped further into his chair.

I held up my hand. "I'm sorry, please stay," I pleaded. "We're trying to make sense of this. Could you just tell us what happened? We've lost some friends and would like to know their whereabouts. We could pay you for your time."

Hamilton sat back down.

He looked around the room and spoke in a whisper, "I was never a Colonel, but I did participate. I was a volunteer in the New York militia. Had anyone listened to me, they would have known it was useless to attempt to fight the British head-on. I said as much in a letter I published a year before the buffoonery of 1776. I said, '*Evade a pitched battle and attempt to frustrate the British with frequent skirmishes.*' I said this before any shots were fired. No one listened."

He looked around us to see if anyone was listening. His face was flushed red.

"What happened?" I asked. "Where was General Washington?"

"I don't know who General Washington was," he said. "General Hancock led the Americans at Brooklyn and made the absurd decision to fight face to face. It was over before it started. You can't have politicians leading men into battle. No one stood his ground. Men abandoned their posts in droves. Lines broke without much effort on the part of the British. When Hancock finally ordered the retreat, it was too late. We sat, helplessly engulfed in a thick fog that final morning—waiting for the inevitable. The British surrounded us and mocked us as we laid down our arms."

"So John Hancock led the Americans?" asked Mark.

"Did you know him? Vain, spoiled man." Hamilton's expression morphed into disgust.

If Hancock was appointed commander of the Continental Army, then what happened to George Washington? Why wasn't he there?

"What happened to the army after the surrender?" I asked.

"We were rounded up. Men that could not purchase their freedom—and there were many—were conscripted into the British army or navy as punishment—and as a way to eliminate the possibility of future uprising. I was saved only by the good graces of Mr. Rivington, who felt obliged to me for saving his life when a mob tried to tar and feather him in the early days of the revolt. He purchased my freedom and I went to work for him at the Royal Gazette. It's been fifteen years. I write most of the editorials now and it's not a bad life. I never got to be a lawyer, but I feel indebted to the man. Without him, I would be either dead or serving the British on a ship in some remote corner of the world."

"How about Congress? What happened to them?" I asked.

"Dead, mostly. Hanged as traitors. The King made examples of them. All except John Adams. He was pardoned for defending the British officers after the massacre in Boston. I think one of his boys was conscripted into the army to eliminate any further rabble rousing."

"And Benjamin Franklin?"

"Dr. Franklin was exiled. He was residing in France the last time I heard. I am confounded by your multifarious questions. How were you associated with such a diverse group of men?"

"Acquaintances, mostly," I said. "I didn't really know anyone personally—friends of friends."

Our food arrived, and we ate in relative silence. I hadn't had time to prepare for our meeting with Hamilton. There had to be something I missed. A question I should ask. Countless essays had been written about "What If the Americans had lost the Revolution?" and now I knew. But it didn't help our situation. And it didn't explain why the hell we were here.

Mark sat so quietly, I thought he was in shock, but finally he asked Hamilton, "Is there still unrest in the colonies?"

"No, not anymore," said Hamilton. "The British did finally allow American representation in Parliament, but nothing has changed. The King still does as he pleases, which is unfortunate, because he is completely mad. British soldiers were stationed here for a long time and it fueled resentment, but since we Americans were so soundly defeated in such a short period of time..." He paused, clearly upset with having to rehash the story. "Most Americans are just glad that the soldiers have gone and that we can be left alone."

I found it interesting Hamilton referred to himself as an *American* and referred to the colonists as *we*, but none of that helped us. Even if a second revolution occurred and the Americans gained independence, it wouldn't help us. We couldn't return to our present where it took two American revolutions because in our history, it only took one.

I picked at my food and reflected on what we had learned. One, George Washington was not present during the American Revolution, at least not in a capacity where he gained any notoriety. Two, John Hancock, the President of Congress, was leading troops during the battle for New York. Lexington and Concord probably ignited the Revolution, and the British most likely abandoned Boston and set their sites on New York similar as to what was written in our history books. Three, the Revolution was over so fast the idea of a free, independent country was only a fleeting thought in the minds of most Americans.

We needed to find out what happened to George Washington. He was the key to everything.

We finished eating. I was pretty sure we weren't going to learn much more from him.

I stood and extended a hand to Hamilton. "Thank you very

much for your insight. I do have one more question. Is there a library nearby?"

"Of course," Hamilton replied. "We have the New York Society Library. I could arrange a membership for you."

"We would very much like that," I said. "If you could point us in the right direction we would be grateful."

"It's located at the corner of Wall and Nassau. I'll write you a letter of introduction for the librarian," he said. "It is painful for me to think of those days when I was so young, but I still think fondly of the passion of the people. I am pleased you came to visit today."

We thanked Hamilton and parted ways. Having been to the corner of Nassau and Wall earlier that morning, it wouldn't take us long to find.

* * *

After walking a block in silence, Mark spoke up. "Can you believe we just bought lunch for Alexander Hamilton?"

"I know," I said. "It was almost surreal seeing him in person."

"Is he how you would have pictured him?"

"No, I think we talked to a shell of the man. He was the kind of guy who'd write eighty-thousand-word tirades against things he disagreed with. I mean, he's responsible for our financial system. He *invented* the U.S. economy. He wrote most of the Federalist Papers. To see that talent wasted on being a newspaper editor is sad, but it was probably his only option under British rule after the failed revolution. His fire was gone."

Mark asked, "What are we looking for at the library?"

"We have to find out what happened to Washington. Hamilton said that John Hancock was the commanding general of the

Continental Army. I know Hancock wanted the job, but Congress thought a Virginian leading the American cause would unify the colonies better than a New Englander. That tells me Washington was not there to be nominated or elected."

"What's your theory, history guy?"

History guy. All those years teaching survey courses at community colleges hadn't prepared me for this. Luckily, I read history for enjoyment and had enough working knowledge that I was confident we would be able to pinpoint the event that had thrown the timeline we were in off-track. After that, the ball would be in Mark's court, the *science guy*. He'd have to get us into the time machine and get us home.

"My guess is that something happened earlier in Washington's life that prevented him from participating. That's why I want to have a look in the library. He was a relatively famous American in his day. People would know who George Washington was, but if he died, say at Fort Necessity—it would have happened before Hamilton was born, explaining why Hamilton never heard of him."

"What's Fort Necessity?"

"When Washington was in his early twenties, he was sent by the governor of Virginia to deliver a message to the French telling them to get out of Virginia territory—which was somewhere around Pittsburgh. On the way there, Washington and his troops ran into some French soldiers and ambushed them—basically starting the French and Indian War. The French were pissed and sent an army after Washington. Instead of running away, Washington and his men built a hastily constructed fort that he called Fort Necessity. It wasn't a *good* fort and Washington quickly surrendered after the French attacked. If he was somehow killed during that battle, the name George Washington would just be a footnote in history."

"That doesn't make sense," said Mark. "We both know Washington didn't die at Fort Necessity."

"I don't know, but Hamilton said John Hancock led the Revolution. He never even heard of Washington. You're the one who said we're trapped in an alternate reality."

Part of me wanted to stop and breathe in the surroundings. All history lovers have thought about how awesome it would be to see the past. Now, I was doing just that, but all I could focus on was locating the library and figuring out a way home.

"If we do find out what happened," I said, "what's the possibility we can use the time machine to fix what happened?"

"We have some power, but it's limited, so our travel capabilities are limited. Donna's only designed to have enough juice to return home."

"That's not real efficient."

"It's not designed to be." Mark pulled off his hat and wiped away sweat from his forehead. "It's essentially a cockpit. The particle accelerator does the work. We figured out a way to harness the excess energy and store it to use at another time."

"So if the battery goes dead, we only need 1.21 gigawatts of electricity to get home?"

"It's pronounced *gig*-a-watts, and no, that wouldn't help. We'd need—"

I held up my hand, not wanting him to explain the science. Sometimes Mark was oblivious to sarcasm. "Okay, okay. What's the verdict?"

"If we determine what event caused this rift in our history, it's possible we could travel back to rectify the situation, but if we have any hopes of returning home, we have to do it on the first try. There isn't enough energy to make two trips."

"Then we need to be absolutely sure of what the cause of the rift is."

"Exactly," said Mark. "What's wrong?"

My stare gave me away. Most people probably wouldn't notice, but Mark knew me pretty well. "Just thinking about Washington. He was known for being fearless in battle and had a number of close-calls throughout his life. There's a famous quote of his in a letter to his brother where he said that there was something *charming* in the sound of gunfire. During one battle, he had a couple horses shot out from under him and his jacket was riddled with bullet holes, but he was never injured. There's another story where an Indian guide leading Washington through the wilderness suddenly turned and fired at him at point blank range—and missed."

"It sounds like he was pretty lucky."

"Or protected by divine guidance, like many Americans believe," I said.

"That seems hokey to me," said Mark. "Even if God did exist, I don't think he'd do anything to protect one person from harm."

"Not even with the fate of the free world riding on his shoulders? It's all speculation, anyway. I think we're going to discover that he was killed sometime during his youth. He almost died of smallpox when he was young. Maybe it was something like that."

We arrived at the corner of Nassau and Wall Streets and looked once more at Federal Hall, or what *should* have been Federal Hall. Now, it just looked like an imposing building with a British flag. It represented everything that was wrong with the predicament we were in. It stood three stories with Roman columns spanning the second floor balcony—the balcony where I had expected to see Washington.

We scanned the intersection for any sign of the library, but saw none. I thought of asking a few passersby if they knew where the library was, but by their dress, I concluded that they were probably not literate, let alone members of the library. We investigated Federal Hall and discovered the library was housed on the top floor.

That's ironic.

The same building we traveled to see held the key to our finding a way home.

The librarian eyed us suspiciously when we entered, but his demeanor became affable once we presented Hamilton's letter of introduction.

"We're looking for some information on a person," I said. "Would you be able to help us?"

"It depends on who the person is," the librarian answered. He wore a black suit with white stockings, his gray hair pulled back behind his ears. A dark-brown mole rested on his cheek.

"George Washington," I said. "Have you heard of him?"

'Aye, I have," said the man. "Responsible for starting the Seven Years War. Most people aren't aware."

I heard a sigh of relief from Mark.

"Can you tell us what happened to him?" I asked.

"Killed," he said. "With General Braddock, I believe. You couldn't have known him. You're too young. Why do you ask?"

"We're historians—from Virginia," I said. "Would you have any first-hand accounts as to what happened?"

"Aye," he said, and led us into the library.

* * *

The librarian pulled out some old newspapers that contained accounts of Braddock's campaign and placed them on a large, wooden table. The first two were London newspapers titled the *Public Advertiser*. One was dated August 25, 1755, and the other September 20. He also found an issue of the *Maryland Gazette* dated the 24th of July, and an issue from the *New York Mercury* dated August 4.

"I apologize for our limited selection," he said, "I think you will find what you are looking for. It invigorates my mind to assist a pair following in the footsteps of Montesquieu." He left us with the papers and returned to his desk.

Mark went to work searching the London papers. "Who's Montesquieu?" he asked.

"A French philosopher, but he's considered one of the first modern historians." I opened the *Maryland Gazette* and started skimming. "He argued history could be predicted if viewed in context and minimized the role of chance and the individual. For example, if Caesar hadn't seized power in Rome, someone else would have because Rome was already on the path to empire shying away from being a republic. But he was wrong."

"How so?"

"He underestimated the power of one person to change the world. If the American Revolution was inevitable, someone else would have led the victory. Montesquieu was full of shit."

I got a refresher in history as I glanced through the paper. Braddock's campaign was a disaster for the British army. In an effort to drive the French out of North America, the King sent General Edward Braddock to lead British troops through the American wilderness to Fort Duquesne, near present-day Pittsburgh. Before the troops reached the fort, they were attacked by French and Indian soldiers and defeated soundly. General Braddock was killed.

Evidently, so was George Washington.

"Here it is," I said. "It's a letter from Captain Robert Orme dated July 18, 1755."

"I see it here too," said Mark, referring to one of the issues of the *Public Advertiser*.

I looked at the letter printed in the paper and Mark read the account out loud, "*Mr. Washington had two horses shot under him and his cloaths shot thro in several places behaving the whole time with the greatest courage and resolution until he at last receiv'd a shot thro the chest*—the spelling is atrocious."

Dread surged through me as I heard the account of his death. My fear that Washington had been killed early in life was confirmed.

Another issue of the *Maryland Gazette* dated July 31 that listed all of the soldiers wounded, killed and unharmed during the engagement. Geo. Washington, Esq. was listed under the column "Kill'd."

"At least now we know where we need to go," I said.

"We know the when," Mark said, "but we still will need to locate a good arrival point. We can't just show up in the middle of a battle."

"Plus, we need to figure out what we're going to do when we get there. We can't just walk up to George Washington and say, 'Hey, you might want to take the day off today because you are going to get killed in battle, and we *really* need you to be the father of our country.'"

"What do you suggest?" Mark asked.

"I'm not sure. I've been so focused on studying the inauguration that I'm not prepared for the events of the French and Indian war. I wish I would have read something to refresh my memory."

"Aren't you a history professor? You should know this stuff." said Mark.

"I taught survey courses in American History. I spent about forty-five minutes lecturing on the French and Indian War—mostly surface stuff. Here's what we know: Braddock was defeated at the battle of the Monongahela, near Pittsburgh. The fighting took place in the wilderness, and the British were routed because the French and Indians hid behind trees and shot from cover while the British troops remained exposed. I don't know the terrain well enough to even give an educated guess as to a good place to arrive. The battle happened in the woods."

"Okay, let's assume we figure that part out," said Mark. "Could we talk to him? Ask him to sit the battle out or hide behind a tree during the fighting?"

"I don't think so," I answered. "Part of what made him popular *and* the logical choice to lead the American army during the Revolution was his bravery. If he was accused of being a coward, or if the only memory of him was surrendering Fort Necessity after starting the French and Indian War, we might save his life, but not enough to fix history and get us home."

Mark rested both hands on the table and stared at the papers. "We only have enough power to get one crack at this. Don't mess it up, Mr. Historian."

I smiled confidently. "No problem. Let's learn everything we can."

Don't mess this up.

Most of the information covered the battle specifics. The British engaged the French shortly after crossing the Monongahela River on the afternoon of July 9th. I was unable to find out when the army set out from civilization. I remembered General Braddock's men had actually cut a road through the thick forest to reach the battle site. It would have had to set out at least a month, maybe more, before the actual battle took place.

"Okay," I said, "We don't know enough specifics to try to locate the army before the battle, but do we really need to cut it that close?"

"What do you mean?"

"Why even bother trying to catch up after Washington enlists? Why not just go to Mount Vernon *before* he leaves to join the army? It would also allow us to speak with him privately and warn him or even—"

"Even what?" asked Mark.

"What about these?" I patted my chest, indicating the Kevlar vest I wore. I knew Mark had his on as well.

"We can't do that. That could alter history. We're not even supposed to take anything modern back into the past—"

I raised my eyebrows.

Hello? The past is already screwed up.

Mark understood. "Screw it. Let's give him a vest. So we're going to Mount Vernon?"

"Yeah, I think it would be the safest place to go. We know that battle happened in July and it probably took the army at least a month to get to the battle site. Let's play it safe and try to reach Washington in early May."

"Let's play it even safer and arrive earlier," said Mark. "How about April 25th? It's a nice round number and gives us an extra week."

"Works for me."

* * *

We thanked the librarian for his help and walked back to the street. My first trip to New York, and I couldn't even stick around to enjoy it. Seeing it in this state was a little freaky. Without the famous landmarks, it was hard to believe I was even in New York. There were a few dark-skinned people walking around, but they appeared to be servants or slaves. How would the country evolve after an extended period of being a colony? Was American independence inevitable as Montesquieu would have argued?

We headed back to our entry point, and my feet reminded me that the blisters were still there, alive and well. The walk back to the machine took another two hours. I would never complain about stress at work ever again.

We found Donna safe and sound. No legs stuck out of the bottom so I guess we didn't accidentally land on anyone.

Mark placed his hand on the surface and disarmed the cloak. The machine appeared, and he punched in the code to open it up. We climbed inside and strapped ourselves in. Mark started inputting numbers on the touch screen.

"How do you know where to send us?" I asked.

"I would prefer to have a clean, up-to-date map, but this thing is equipped with most of the known maps the world has ever known. I have an idea as to where to put us."

Mark pulled up a hand-drawn map of Mount Vernon, copied in Washington's own handwriting. It was dated 1760. He cross-referenced it with a modern-day map of Mount Vernon.

"I was thinking here," said Mark, pointing to an area on the Potomac River side of the property.

"It's as good as any," I said. "We won't need to be there long, anyway. We'll get in and out pretty fast, assuming Washington listens to what we have to say. How come this thing doesn't come with Wikipedia or something that could really help us? We need information too."

"Internet access sucks in 1789. That's why."

"You know what I mean. How can this thing have all of those

maps and no encyclopedia?"

"Sorry, I'm doing the best I can."

"Can you do me a favor and hit that home button?" I said. "If this could save us a trip—"

"It's not going to work."

"Please."

To make his point, Mark hit the home button. The machine started up, and the whirring began, building louder and louder. Mark looked at me with his eyebrows raised, surprised by the possibility.

Could it be this simple?

All the stress of the day and learning about Washington's premature death started to evaporate. It was just a bad dream or bad reality, but it didn't matter because we were no longer trapped. We were going to make it home.

The buildup continued and I waited for a crescendo, but none came. The machine simply shut down.

I reached out to give Mark a high-five, but he left me hanging.

Not that simple after all.

Mark's eyes narrowed and lips tightened, forming a pinched expression. "Happy?" He could have said, "See I told you so," but he didn't have to. It was inscribed on his face.

"No. It's the same thing that happens when it works. You really need to add a *ding*."

"As soon as we get back. Can we go to Mount Vernon now?"

I slumped back in my harness. "Make it so."

FOURTEEN

Mount Vernon, VA, April 25, 1755

Thud.

We were both jerked around our seats. The machine teetered, and we began to roll, falling backward and to my right. I held tight to the harness while watching my feet angle over my head. After two or three turns, we came to an abrupt stop complete with an emphatic *bang*.

"What the hell!" I lay on my back, and looked upward at Mark. He was secured in his harness, eyes wide open in surprise.

"I think we just dropped a few feet—and then rolled," he replied. "Now you know why we're wearing these belts."

"You could have given me a heads up."

"I didn't know. The contour of the land may have changed."

He pressed a button on the center console and the hatch began to open revealing a dark sky.

"Four thirty again?"

He nodded. "Safer than when everyone is out and about. No need to freak out the locals. Get out so I can unbuckle."

I undid my harness and slid myself out of the machine. We had rolled down a small hill, our momentum halted by a tree. Through the darkness I saw the house at the top of the hill. Below us lay more trees and a path revealing where the contour of the property dipped toward the black water of the Potomac River.

I heard a small thud and then a curse from Mark. "Is there any damage?" he asked, as he climbed out.

"I don't know. Can't see much out here."

"Come on, help me get this thing turned upright."

Mark closed the machine and we stood on the same side and pushed it so that it stood upright again. It was much lighter than anticipated.

"The bottom's weighted more heavily so it has a tendency to land upright, like a giant Weeble." Mark's hand wiped sweat from his forehead. He took a few steps up the hill toward the house and inspected the ground where we landed. "Damn, I'm good. I'll bet we only landed a few feet above the ground. All from a hand-drawn map."

"Good? Did you enjoy rolling down the hill?"

"No—great. We just navigated through time, space, the Earth spinning really fast while orbiting the sun… And I placed us *feet* from where we wanted to be. A small miscalculation, and we could have dropped four-thousand feet instead of four. I'm the man."

"Yeah, well thanks Magellan."

Mark ignored me, hands on his hips, eyeing the hill. "I'm the man," he repeated.

We found some large branches to prop under it to make sure it didn't start rolling again.

Light streaked the horizon as the orange sun climbed the tree line reflecting in the glistening water. Features of the house started to come into focus. Mount Vernon was much smaller than the pictures I remembered. Washington would have just inherited the house from his brother a few months earlier, and he had not began construction of the estate that most Americans would come to recognize. It was two stories and the front entrance faced east toward the river. In the future, the front entrance would face the road leading in from Alexandria.

"Now what?" said Mark, once the machine seemed stable. He engaged the cloak, and the machine disappeared in a shimmer.

"I guess we wait and then go knock on the door," I said. "Let's head down to the river and then make our way around. We can't make it seem like we've been here all morning."

The ground was soft and still wet from a recent rainfall so we had to be careful making our way down. My steps were slow and precise as I tried not to further irritate the blisters in my boots. Instead of going all the way down to the water, we cut through the trees and made our way around and back up the hill so we could approach the house from the road in case we were observed from someone inside.

We followed the tree line and found a suitable place to enter the road unseen. It was early, but we saw a few slaves emerge from their quarters and pause to watch us move toward the house.

I was aware Washington had owned slaves. All the Virginia gentry did, but to see slavery in context was disturbing. Involuntary labor forced to work the fields of the man responsible for American independence was ironic and discomforting.

We walked around the building to the front entrance, and I knocked on the door.

A house slave answered the door. "Good morning."

"Hello," I answered. "We are here to see Colonel Washington. Is he available?"

"Come inside. Please wait here." He looked down and wouldn't make eye contact as he spoke. The servant disappeared down the hall.

"We're standing in George Washington's house," whispered Mark, a slight smirk on his face.

A few moments later, a figure approached us from down the hallway. "Can I help you?" he asked. He was young, probably in his early twenties and thin. He was not George Washington—too short.

"Good morning," I said, extending my hand. "I'm sorry for the early intrusion, but we've traveled a long way. We're looking for Colonel Washington."

He took my hand, but did not return my smile. "You just missed him. He left to join the army. He is riding to meet with General Braddock at Wills Creek."

Mark and I exchanged brief, troubled looks.

We had purposely traveled back to a point where we thought we had adequate time to locate Washington, and we still missed him.

Not cool.

"Missed him?"

"Two days ago. Did you have a message you wanted me to pass along? I must say I don't expect him to return any time soon, but we will be corresponding by post."

"No," I said. "We will try to locate him at Wills Creek. Thank you for your time."

We turned and left the house.

"Where the hell is Wills Creek?" asked Mark, as we walked back down the road.

"Virginia somewhere," I said. "I don't know how far. I can't believe we miscalculated. Can we go back three more days and try to catch him before he leaves?"

Mark shook his head. "It would take too much power. We'd have no chance of ever getting back home."

"I was afraid of that."

"So we're going to try to find him?"

"Do you have any other ideas?"

Mark squinted. "I can't walk to Wills Creek. My feet are killing me."

"We'd never make it on foot," I said, flinching from the pain in my own boots. "We need to get horses."

"Where?"

"Since D.C. hasn't been conceived yet, we're going to have to find the nearest town. Should we risk looking at one of the maps in the time machine?"

"No. That guy was already suspicious, two strange men showing up on foot in the middle of nowhere. I'm sure someone is watching us now to see which way we go. We can either hide out in the woods all day and return to the machine tonight, or we can follow this road and try to find transportation."

I considered the options. Mark had done his part and we made it to Mount Vernon. It was up to me, the *history guy*, to reach Washington. I couldn't believe we miscalculated—I miscalculated. "It's already been a long day, but I think we need to find Washington sooner than later. He's already got a two-day head start, and we can't afford to let him get further away."

We both took off our boots and stockings and started walking on the dirt road leading away from Mount Vernon. It eased the pain of my blisters, but the bottom of my feet were not accustomed to walking barefoot. About an hour into our walk, a horse-drawn cart pulled up alongside us. It was piloted by a slave, and the man we had spoken to earlier rode shotgun.

The man called out, "Where are your horses?"

"We walked," I said.

The man scrunched his nose. "All through the night?" He

leaned forward, blinking.

"Yes, most of it. We have an important message for Colonel Washington and didn't see any other options."

"Egad," he said. "You two will be *shod in your slippers* by they time you reach Alexandria. Climb into the back."

Mark looked at me and whispered, "What does that mean, shod in your slippers?"

"No idea," I answered. "Some expression." At least I knew where we were headed. Alexandria, Virginia.

Mark and I climbed in. "Thank you," I said, shaking his hand. "I'm John Curry."

"John Augustine," he replied. "Call me Jack."

I knew Washington had a brother, Jack, and assumed this was the man. Mark exchanged pleasantries and we settled in, trying to get comfortable. Uneven wood planks lined the cart making the ride bumpy, but the coarse woodgrain was preferable to walking.

"What takes you to Alexandria?" I asked.

"We are resupplying. George asked me to oversee the renovations of his property while he's gone. My negro, Kit, is a satisfactory carpenter and is assisting in the purchase."

My negro. I felt myself wince.

Mark lay, stretched out on his back, exhausted. Fatigue was catching up with me too. Jack didn't say anything else, and I was soon asleep.

Jack woke us when we reached Alexandria. We thanked him for the lift and set out to find a map and to get transportation to Wills Creek.

Situated on the north side of the Potomac River, Alexandria and was a small river port. A wharf and a few warehouses constituted the harbor. Most of the dwellings were small, wood shacks, but a few brick and stone houses sprung up further from the water's edge. The smell of river water and fish permeated the air.

We found a tavern on a street corner called the "George" and got a much needed meal of heavily salted baked fish and bread.

"Three shillings," said the tavern owner when it was time to pay.

I reached into my leather purse to pay for the meal and discovered I was carrying a lot of coins. Not only did I have the Spanish coins we had discussed, but I also had English pounds, which I wasn't expecting. I pulled out three coins to hand to the tavern owner, not sure the value of each.

"Keep your guineas," he said. "I don't want to make change for that much money. Give me the French crown."

I stared blankly.

"This one." He reached into my hand and pulled out a coin, giving me an incredulous look. "Be right back." He turned to walk away.

"Keep the change," I said.

The man smiled and left.

I turned to Mark. "I thought we agreed that we wouldn't bring British money with us."

"That's right."

"So why am I carrying this?" I pulled out a gold coin embossed with the profile of "Georgius II" and handed it to him. "I'm pretty sure this is a guinea—an English pound."

Mark looked through his own leather carrier and squinted in confusion. "I noticed I was carrying a lot of coins when I paid for our lunch with Hamilton. I thought it was loose change. I didn't really think about it. Is this a lot?"

I eyed the coins in my haversack, careful not to dump them out on the table fearing it would attract attention from the locals. The leather purse was filled with three smaller leather pouches, each filled with gold and silver coins. I pulled out a pie-shaped slice, cut from a Spanish coin—a genuine piece-of-eight.

"I don't know," I said. "*Maybe* not, but this *seems* like a lot of money for a quick sightseeing trip at the inauguration." I knew British pounds were valuable in Colonial times, and I had a lot of them. "How many do you have?"

Mark rifled through his haversack and I grabbed a handful of coins from my own and placed them on the table. Attention be damned. I needed to see how much money we had. There had to be at least a hundred guineas between the three pouches, maybe more. In addition, I had whole Spanish coins that hadn't been cut into wedges, French coins like the one I had given the tavern owner, and a few I couldn't identify.

"How much do we have?" asked Mark.

"It's hard to say." I kept my eyes on the coins in front of me. "The colonial monetary system is hard to determine. I know they were hard up for cash and that's why so many different types of coins are accepted. Most colonies even minted their own coins. I mean, these look genuine. I just can't tell."

"That guy didn't seem to have a problem taking our money." Mark threw a thumb over his shoulder. "What's your best guess?"

"I don't know." I shrugged. "This probably equals thousands of dollars. Maybe tens of thousands of dollars. I'd need to see a price sheet and a conversion table."

Mark's brow furrowed. "Why would Mr. Meade give us so much money?"

"And where'd he get it all? There are a lot of coins here." I lifted my haversack. "No wonder these things are so heavy."

Why would Meade give us so much money for a sightseeing trip to the inauguration? The answer would have to wait. We had more important things to worry about, like trying to catch up with

George Washington at Wills Creek.

FIFTEEN

"Why would anyone want to go to Wills Creek?" asked the owner of the tavern, after I inquired about carriages headed in that direction. "Nothing there but a fort."

"We need to deliver a message." I looked at Mark and back at the man.

"You could join the army." The jowls on his heavy face rose just enough to form a slight smile. "Lord knows they're trying to get every able-bodied man in Alexandria to take up their cause. Been harassing my customers every day since they arrived."

We had already seen some of the British soldiers that lingered in town. I assumed they were waiting for supplies to arrive. I didn't realize they were still trying to build their army.

The man smiled. "Are you sure you don't need lodging for the night?" His eyes focused briefly on my leather haversack.

I guess I did attract attention dumping coins on the table.

"We're just delivering a message," said Mark. "Do you have any other suggestions?"

"Buy a horse."

Funny. I didn't have the slightest idea as to how to ride a horse, and I doubted Mark did either. We would think of something.

We stepped out of the "George," and, as if on cue, were approached by two officers. They wore black tricorne hats and the famous red coats and breeches of the British army.

"You two look like fine candidates for the king's army," said the shorter officer, his skin pockmarked and pale.

"No thank you," I said, trying to walk around them.

The taller one blocked my path. "You're both tall enough. Don't you want to serve your country?" His accent sounded less refined than the smaller man, but maybe it was his teeth, yellow and crooked. I always judged people with poor dental hygiene.

"Maybe some other time," I said. If we joined the army, we would surely cross paths with Washington, but we needed to be able to leave on our own terms and not be shot for desertion.

He pressed. "You ain't Catholic, are you?"

"No."

"Then you'd make a fine soldier."

"So the only qualifications are that you have to be tall and not Catholic?" Mark's face revealed genuine amusement—maybe because he wasn't that tall.

"They's good qualifications if you ask me," answered the taller officer. "We can't have no one having second thoughts about killing a fellow Catholic when we drive the French out of our territory, can we?"

"I guess not," answered Mark. "We're not the right candidates anyway. We don't know how to fight."

The smaller one stepped up and shoved his musket in front of Mark's face. "You see, we'll teach you how. And you even get one of these. What do you say?"

"We have to be going," I said. "We're just passing through and are in a hurry. Good luck to you."

The taller officer relented and moved aside. The shorter man sneered as we passed.

"Maybe we *should* buy some horses," I said after we were safely away from the recruiters.

Mark laughed. "I don't know how to ride a horse. Do you?"

"No," I said. "Maybe someone could teach us."

"You're crazy."

"I don't know if we have any other options."

He thought about it for a second and agreed it would be our best bet. We were wasting time in Alexandria.

We located a livery yard with a hand-written sign that read: *HORSES FOR SALE* and walked over to inquire.

The stable manager was well fed, but dirty. Both his breeches and boots were mud-stained, and he smelled like he slept on a bed of manure.

"We're inquiring about the horses you have for sale," I said. "We need two."

"Have two in the back," he said with a Scottish accent. He set off toward the stockade on other side of the building, and motioned us to follow.

"How much for two horses, saddles, and enough food for a week?"

"Depends on the horse. These two," he pointed toward a black horse and a brown one, "are thirty each. Add saddles and food—fifty each. They ain't much. The army took the good ones."

"Okay," I said, having no idea if this was a good deal or not. "This might sound like a crazy question. Do you give riding lessons?"

The man laughed. "Why would you want riding lessons? You just get off a boat?"

"Something like that," said Mark.

"What are you running from?" The man folded his arms and squinted.

"Nothing," I said. "We just need to get to Wills Creek to deliver a message."

"Why would you want to go there? Nothing but wilderness."

"We need to deliver a message to Colonel Washington. It's not really your concern. So fifty each? Is that in pounds?"

"With riding lessons? Fifty-five each." He smiled, revealing a mouth of yellow and brown teeth.

"Seriously?" I had the distinct feeling we were being ripped off.

He nodded, smug. "But if I were you, I'd go to Frederick Town. That's where Braddock went. Colonel Washington would be with him."

"How would you know that?" Mark asked.

"Army was here for a while. Loose tongues on drunken soldiers. You hear things."

We purchased the two horses and saddles, saddlebags, blankets and feed for the horses. Not trusting us, the man asked for payment up front. He showed us how to mount the horse from the left and laughed as Mark had trouble getting on his dark-brown horse. After a few minutes, we got the hang of walking the horses around the pen. We learned to get the horses moving by pressing our heels into the horses' sides and to get them to stop by pulling back on the reins. It was difficult to feel balanced, but we both got the hang of it after about fifteen minutes. My legs were too long for my stirrups and I couldn't sit comfortably without bending my knees. I hoped it wasn't too far to Wills Creek.

We bought dried beef and fish for our journey and two canteens to hold water. I also purchased a small jug of rum. Mark suggested we buy razors so we could shave and wouldn't look like hillbillies when we met Washington. The blades resembled pocket knives and the prospect of holding one near my throat without a mirror was terrifying.

After some asking around, we learned the army split in two, with half its force going through Virginia towards Fort Cumberland located at Wills Creek, and the other half, including General Braddock, headed north through Maryland in order to gather more supplies for the expedition. The stable manager was probably right. Washington would be with Braddock.

We rode north and passed a few small buildings and tobacco warehouses, finally leaving town by crossing over a small bridge. Our best bet was to go to Frederick Town in Maryland to track down Braddock. If we followed the road, we would be able to catch Hagee's Ferry and cross the Potomac near George Town. We could follow the road running parallel to Rock Creek and turn northwest toward Frederick Town, which was another forty miles.

I was thankful for having a good sense of direction. The highway system wouldn't be developed for another two hundred years and road signs were few and far between. It was hard to get a gauge on how far we were traveling without the reassuring countdown to let us know how many miles were left on our journey.

We found the ferry and paid the man to take us across. Mark estimated it would take us two days to get there. After passing George Town, we followed the road along the creek. Our progress was slow and steady and the horses trotted in a deliberate, practiced pace.

The road wasn't very wide, maybe twelve feet across, consisting of packed dirt and rock. Most times, we were surrounded by trees. Other times, we would emerge into an open meadow only to disappear into a thick forest. Mark hunched over his horse trying to get a feel for riding. As the day progressed, he got better, but if the horse picked up any speed, he immediately lunged forward and clung for dear life, making me laugh.

After a couple of hours, we came across an eighteenth-century motel. It was a small log cabin, about one and a half stories high. A stable connected to the back of the building to shelter horses. We still had enough daylight to push on, so we bought two loaves of bread. Neither of us had a clue as to when horses should eat so we decided to feed them any time we ate.

As late afternoon turned to dusk, we forded a small creek and began looking for a decent campsite. Neither of us was sure how to start a campfire and I complained about the probability of figuring it out in the dark. Mark suggested we press on to until we could find a suitable clearing, and let out a whoop of joy when he spotted a tavern just up the road.

Mark let out a groan as he climbed off. "I can't believe I just rode a horse all day."

My knees and hips were tight from suffering though the short stirrups. My inner thighs had been rubbed raw. I dismounted and stretched out in order to walk without a limp.

The tavern was a wooden cabin with stone chimneys located on either end with a small stable attached to the right side of the building. The owner offered us a room with one bed to spend the night. Not knowing if we would have another opportunity to sleep in a bed before we found Washington, we agreed to rent the room.

The room included a meal consisting of boiled potatoes served in some kind of mystery-meat stew. Neither Mark or myself had the courage to ask about the ingredients. The grimy wooden table and dusty floors would have wrecked my appetite on most occasions, but considering our situation, neither of us complained.

Our room was at the top of a small staircase The tiny space was furnished with one straw mattress the size of a twin. We exchanged looks, but were both too tired to joke about sharing a bed. I hunched my shoulders to avoid hitting my head on the low ceiling as I shuffled around the other side. I lowered myself onto the straw mattress and stretched my legs. The bed was too short and both of my feet hung off the edge.

I envisioned myself spending the night trying to get comfortable on the short mattress. No thanks. I slid off the bed onto the plank floor and formed a makeshift pillow by folding a blanket. I found a comfortable position on my back, my arms folded across my chest. Within minutes, I was out.

Sleep didn't last long. I woke myself up by smacking my right cheek where an insect had just bitten me.

What was that?

I was instantly angry and my heart pounded as I thought of ways to kill every flea in the world.

The increased blood flow got my mind racing and I thought about what lay ahead. What would Washington say? What would *we* say? Were we going to be trapped here for the rest of our lives?

Normally, I would switch on a light and read for a few minutes to clear my mind, but it wasn't an option. The floor felt harder than it had when I first slunk down. The entire building creaked as the wind blew. I heard a shuffling sound on my right that had to be a rodent. If a rat touched me, I would lose my mind. Was the plague around in 1755?

Okay, calm down. You need rest. You have a long day tomorrow. You're just hearing things.

I held my breath for a moment to clear my mind and didn't exhale until I counted five heartbeats. Slowly, I was able to relax and the tension started to lift.

I was drifting when I was bitten again—this time on my hand. I slapped at it hard, but couldn't tell if I got it.

I thought of Casanova and his story of how he escaped prison. Out of all the harshness of prison life, the thing that bothered him most was the incessant attack of fleas. He must have mentioned it four times as he told his story.

Didn't he say that he was imprisoned in 1755? Casanova is probably sitting in his cell at this very moment dealing with the same problem.

At least I could get out of this room. I had a new understanding of "Don't let the bed bugs bite." I would never say that phrase in jest again.

And I would never sleep in an eighteenth-century roadside tavern again either.

SIXTEEN

Light crept into the small room, a welcome relief after a night of misery. I was ready to get back on the road and out of the tavern. I felt like I hadn't slept, but I must have at least had an hour or two. Maybe not.

Stiffness paralyzed my body and it took a moment to sit up.

Mark sat on the edge of the bed, already awake and anxious to continue. "Let's get out of here. We can probably reach Frederick by late afternoon—Oh, my ass." He winced as he swung his legs off the bed. "How was the floor?"

"It sucked. I'm not doing that again. What happened to your face?"

His nose had a huge red welt on it.

"Fleas," he said.

"Me too," I said, pointing to my cheek.

"I left my contacts in overnight. That was stupid," he said as he took them out and put on his glasses. Round, black metal frames were connected by a wide nose bridge, making them rest awkwardly on his face. Both earpieces had round ends half the size of the lenses."You better not say a word about these."

"Aww, you look cute."

We hobbled out of the tavern and limped to the stable. I didn't want to get on my horse. My legs were raw, but the blisters on my feet were worse. Riding was the lesser of two evils.

We mostly rode in silence. Mark seemed a little more comfortable riding on his second day.

After a half hour of riding, he broke the silence. "I'm sorry."

"It's okay. My deodorant wore off too."

"No, about all of this. This quandary we're in. This was my fault. I never should have suggested you. You have a family. You shouldn't be here."

It was upsetting to feel trapped—especially in a place more than two hundred fifty years in the past. I knew Mark felt bad about us being here, but it wouldn't have done either of us any good to be angry about it. We needed to accept our predicament and figure a way out.

"It was my decision," I said. "No one forced me. Anyway, I didn't have *that* much going for me. My contract ran out, and since Amanda took Tabby out of state, it costs me a good chunk to see her. You offered a nice payday. Besides, we're not trapped. I'm treating it like an extended vacation in a third-world country—like we joined the Peace Corps. Why are you bringing this up?"

"I don't know," he said. "I guess it's Mr. Meade. I've been thinking about him constantly since we discovered the money."

"And?"

"Meade did know something," he said. "He *had* to. I didn't put it together until now. A few weeks ago, when we were looking to hire a tour guide for Washington's inauguration, Meade had *everyone* put together a list of suitable candidates—not just Dr. Cohen like we'd done in the past. We mostly came up with historians, authors, historical re-enactors—those kinds of people. I didn't even have you on the list—sorry."

I didn't say a word. I felt the hairs on my arms raise, feeling like I had just been played, but I couldn't figure out why or how.

He continued. "As we went through possibilities, Meade asked us what we knew about each person and then came up with a reason that the person would not be a good fit. 'Too old' or 'Wouldn't be able to keep a secret' were the common ones. Then he asked if we knew of anyone else, for example *friends* or *old college roommates*. That's when I thought of you. When I said I had a friend who taught history at a community college, he perked up and wanted to know more. He said he wanted to meet you and to set up the invitation."

"What are you saying?"

"John, Meade hasn't been hanging around the facility. We never saw the guy—not until you came. For the first time since we began, he started taking an active interest in what we were doing. No one ate a private dinner with him before—except maybe Lawrence—but not at the facility like we did. He certainly didn't barbecue for anyone. He knew something was going to happen. I just don't know what."

I understood what he was saying, but I remained calm. This was not the time to jump to conclusions. We needed to think logically.

"How could he know Washington's inauguration wasn't going to happen? History is history. And why me? I haven't done anything in my career to stand out."

"I'm not sure. It really did come down to three final candidates, but I was under the impression that my knowing you personally was what interested him. I'm sure as hell going to ask him when we get back."

I wasn't buying the idea that Meade knew anything about what might happen to us. Hindsight is always clear. Maybe he just gave us extra money for an emergency. Sometimes the obvious answer is the right answer, but I was bothered by Mark's theory.

He was convinced of some kind of conspiracy—and he wasn't one to jump to conclusions or act overly emotional.

We came to a small stream on the path. The horses waded through easily.

"I think he manipulated your contract," said Mark. "Didn't you say you thought you were getting renewed?"

"Yeah, but what?" It was one thing to lose a job contract. It was another to be manipulated.

"Meade isn't the kind of guy who takes no for an answer. I know he comes across as cool and cultured, but he's got a dark side. You have to be ruthless to be a successful businessman."

"You watch too many movies. He inherited his money. He's just a billion-dollar playboy. I know you're suspicious given our situation, but I like him. He makes good barbecue."

"No, you like the *idea* of him. There's a difference. He threw his money and support into Timeless Arts way too fast. He has some kind of ulterior motive. Don't you think it's a little convenient that you lost your job immediately before I called?"

"I guess it was," I said, recalling the remarkable timing of Mark's job offer only hours after I taught my last course. "Budget cuts." I had only learned of losing my teaching contract two weeks before the end of the semester. Until then, I was under the impression I was being placed on the fast track to tenure. My classes had gone well. I had good relationships with my colleagues. I ran the school's history club. I even chaired a committee to update the curriculum to make student learning outcomes more relevant for the twenty-first century. Then it all ended. The president of the college confessed the school had to tighten its belt due to budget constraints. I had the least amount of seniority and my contract wouldn't be renewed. It was upsetting, but I put it out of my mind once I saw how amazing Mark's job offer was—when one door closes another opens.

"Did you have any inkling there were going to be budget cuts? Was anyone else let go? I'll bet you a thousand dollars that you'll find your old position filled when we get back. I'll take it a step further. The school probably received a huge donation shortly after you were gone—money for research or a new building."

I let that sink in for a second. "Why are you bringing this up now? Where was all of this conspiracy stuff when we were both still safe?" I was doing my best to keep calm. I didn't want to worry about something I couldn't control. It wouldn't help us get home. But Mark's insistance that we both had been deceived was unnerving.

"I had blinders on just like everyone else. Lawrence has been positively giddy. His dreams are coming true on a daily basis. All of ours are—were. Plus, I was looking forward to hanging out. Do you realize that this is the first time we've been together, just the two of us, in over fifteen years?"

"I did. I was looking forward to it too. Just like old times, the two of us, riding our horses—only this time they're real and not part of some role-playing game."

Mark laughed, "Yeah."

"So what do we do about Meade?"

"First we fix the problem—make sure Washington becomes president, then we confront him when we get back. That's all we can do."

"I'm still unsure about Meade's motive," I said. "Assuming he was positive we would run into trouble, he gave us money and protection." I patted my breast, the Kevlar skin firm underneath my coat.

"I'm not sure. I can't work out how he'd know we'd be here."

"*We* chose 1755. It never came up before, did it?"

"No."

A thought hit me, like a slap in the face. I reached into my leather haversack, opened one of the money pouches and pulled out a handful of coins.

"What are you doing?" asked Mark.

"1754." I announced the year minted on the first coin. I read the next one. "1752. 1748. 1732."Anger crept into my voice as I read them off. "The inauguration was in 1789. I haven't found one coin dated later than 1754. How about you?"

Mark thumbed through his own money, his expression determined. "Sonofabich," he said. "This confirms it."

"It isn't proof," I said. "There could be an explanation. Maybe this was all he could get his hands on—someone's Ebay collection or something."

Mark shook his head angrily. "John, we counterfeit most of the stuff we take to the past. Remember the Holy Roman Emperor's seal that got you into Prague with Lillian? Remember the book Lillian gave to that French kid, Claude. She gives him the same book every time. It's not like there are hundreds of copies floating around. Look at your coins. Even though they look old and worn, some of them are old and worn in the same places."

I looked at the coins in my hand. Sure enough, two of the Spanish coins looked almost identical. The only difference was a little discoloration on the back of one, probably caused by acid being poured over it to add authenticity.

I looked at Mark. "How could he have possibly known? What does he know?"

"I don't know."

The forest path opened into a meadow and the sun pelted us with heat. Our hats offered some protection, but my hat mostly made me uncomfortable, itchy and hot. I generally don't wear one. We rode in silence for fifteen minutes until we were back under the protection of the trees in the forest.

"I need a shower," said Mark, breaking the silence.

"I know what you mean," I said. "The Marriott back there was a pit. I'm writing a nasty letter when we get back."

"There is something else I've been meaning to ask."

Uh oh. Now what?

"Go ahead."

"What happened in Prague? I mean what *really happened*? Lillian has seen the premiere four times and never had a problem. You go—and end up getting stabbed."

"I told you. Claude and Gisçard jumped us."

"But why?"

"Claude was pissed at Lillian for giving him the book—the *counterfeit* book." I forced a tight smile. "I went out for air during the opera's intermission and Claude saw me. He waited until after the performance and followed us outside the city gates. If it wasn't for Casanova intervening, Gisçard might have shot me."

"I know you told me this before. It just seems that there is more to the story that you're not sharing—other than not going out for air during intermission."

I thought about Lillian and Casanova, how she looked and spoke of him. Was she in love or was it just infatuation? I remembered my promise not to say anything.

"There is *one* other thing, but I don't think it's related. Casanova asked Lillian if she'd like a private tour of the city. She was curious, so she said yes. They ditched me and I ended up getting drunk with some Germans. They were the ones who came to my rescue during the intermission and saved me from getting beat up."

"What was she thinking? She should know better."

"You or I might have done the same thing. Please don't say anything to her. I promised I wouldn't rat her out."

"I won't. It's just—wow." He pressed his black glasses back in place.

"It's got to get to you, seeing the same person over and over. Even though the experience is brand new for Casanova each time, it's not for Lillian. I think she was initially intrigued by meeting and getting to know him, but every time they meet, she becomes more emotionally attached. Didn't anyone ever consider the psyche of the tour guides? It isn't an easy thing. Maybe if you're only interacting with events or inanimate objects, you can deal with it, but when dealing with people, *real* people, it's different—even if they're two hundred years older."

"So do you think she slept with him?"

I laughed, "I didn't mean to insinuate anything."

Mark tilted his head, skeptical. He saw through my watered-down version of the day.

"I don't know. She denied it—told me Casanova had syphilis, but she *did* give me the double-standard lecture. You know, where guys are allowed to sleep with famous women and it would be awesome, but if she slept with a famous guy, she'd be considered a slut."

"She's right," he said.

"That's what I said. I told her I was going to hook up with Martha Washington."

Mark gave me a steady look. "Well, let's make sure that Martha *becomes* Martha Washington."

* * *

We reached Frederick Town a little after noon. Tents from the army littered the outskirts of town. We found a suitable stable to board our horses, and the stable manager laughed at us for traveling so far with such old horses.

I wonder how much we got ripped off when we bought those horses.

We set out on foot to find Washington. The streets were harder to navigate than the trail we had just traveled. Instead of a worn dirt path, the streets were filled with wagon ruts and mud. The smell of urine wasn't nearly as strong as it had been in New York, but I suspected the wind was in our favor.

We found Braddock's headquarters amongst the log-cabin-lined street situated in a stone tavern. The Union Jack flew proudly outside the door.

I'm tired of seeing that flag everywhere.

"We can't just go in there and ask for him, can we?" Mark asked as we walked past the tavern.

"Probably not. Maybe we can wait around and see if he comes out."

After a few minutes, Mark asked, "Do you know what he looks like?"

I had seen George Washington's portrait thousands of times. His likeness was on the dollar bill, in every American history book I had ever seen, in every documentary about the Revolutionary War, and even on President's Day sale posters. But did I really know what he looked like? How much artistic license did artists use when painting his portrait? Were they trying to be flattering or true to his image?

Washington would be around twenty three. Most young men didn't have their portraits painted when they were that age unless they were rich, but Washington was "new money." He had only recently inherited Mount Vernon.

"I'm not one hundred percent sure," I said. "Don't worry, we'll find him. Look for someone tall."

It turned out Washington never went to Frederick Town.

SEVENTEEN

Frederick Town, MD, April 29th, 1755

"What do you mean Washington isn't here?" I asked.

Mark had just returned from a fact-gathering walk around the town. I was sitting in a second-floor room we had rented from a tavern on the main street. It was small, but clean compared to the room we slept in the previous night. I still couldn't fit my body on the mattress comfortably, but we didn't have to share, and I could lie diagonally to keep my feet from dangling off the edge.

We had already been there two days, and had used the time to rest our sore legs and blistered feet. The search for Washington had taken a lot longer than either of us had hoped, but we didn't have any other options. We should have gone directly to Wills Creek like we initially intended, and I silently cursed myself for putting trust in the word of a stable manager who clearly took advantage of our naiveté and smelled like horse manure.

"He must not have gotten the memo," said Mark, taking his hat off and throwing it on the bed. "Now what?"

"We stay here and shadow the army. We might not know where Washington is *now*, but we know where he will be. The worst-case scenario is that we'll only be here for a few extra days."

A look of disappointment swept over Mark's face. He didn't

say a word. Complaining wouldn't do a thing for either of us. It was an unspoken agreement we had. No whining.

We stayed in Frederick for two more nights trying to adjust to the slower pace, completely opposite of our regular lives dominated by the daily barrage of information from media and smartphone notifications. Information trickled in as travelers and merchants moved in and out of the city. There wasn't a local newspaper so the news we did get was generally a few weeks old by the time it reached us. Not that there was much useful information to us anyway, but it helped pass the time and was a fascinating look into colonial America.

I used the opportunity to soak in as much as possible. Twenty-first century historians could only speculate what language sounded like prior to recordings. All knowledge was based on the written word. People don't speak the way they write. Different accents and dialects flooded the town, some obvious, like Irish and Scottish, others I couldn't place. The people didn't have the benefit of satellite broadcasts to link each other to a common tongue.

Mark and I passed time in a log-built tavern located on the river drinking *flips*. The German bartender prepared the concoction by pouring molasses into a beer, adding a splash of rum, and mixing it with a hot poker to make it foam. We tipped him well the first afternoon and he responded by keeping our cups full.

We learned the army had detoured to Frederick Town in order to gain support and supplies from Maryland. The governor had pledged both and delivered neither. We had only missed Benjamin Franklin and his son, William, by a few days. I lamented to Mark how I wished we could have toasted *flips* with Ben Franklin. Mark's response: No whining.

Franklin promised supplies, and we found the advertisement

he ran in the Pennsylvania papers after it made its way back to Maryland. He had promised good pay for the army's use of the wagons for "light duty." Even though I wasn't exactly sure of the particulars, I knew enough of the terrain to know "light duty" wasn't quite true. Franklin was lying in the advertisements in order to get wagons for the army. More importantly, I knew the outcome of the battle. Most of those wagons would not be returned to their owners.

On Tuesday morning, we learned the army had moved out of Frederick at first light, and now headed northwest. Since the army was on foot and we were on horseback, it wouldn't take us long to catch up. We took our time getting ready to move out. Our horses had received much-needed rest during our stay and we purchased extra blankets to pad our saddles since the thought of riding all day on our sore thighs was still daunting.

Before departing, we learned Braddock was still in Frederick and would most likely stay a few more days. Mark groaned when he heard the news, but caught himself and didn't say a word. It was a letdown for me too. I suggested we stay in town until the General left. We didn't know when or where Braddock would meet Washington so keeping tabs on Braddock seemed to be our best bet. We passed our time by drinking more *flips*.

Braddock departed from Frederick two days later. Both Mark and I were eager to get out of town as we were antsy to find Washington. We followed Braddock's entourage out of town to the northwest in the same direction the army had departed a few days earlier. Since the retinue was traveling on horseback, Braddock riding in a four horse-drawn chariot, we had to push our mounts faster than we ever had. Neither of us was comfortable riding at the swift pace, so we slowed down and lost any trace of the General after a few miles.

The trail was less traveled than the road leading into Frederick, but easy to follow after the recent passage of hundreds of soldiers and thousands of pounds of supplies.

After fifteen miles, we came upon a small cabin located along the foothill of a mountain. We told the owner that we were trying to track down General Braddock to give him a message. We had just missed the general by a few hours and he had turned to the west toward Swearingen's Ferry. Mark gave the man a silver Spanish coin as a thank you and we set off toward the west.

The temperature turned excessively hot as the day progressed, and we both took off our overcoats and tucked them under our saddles. The relief was minimal as we were both wearing Kevlar vests. We feared removing the vests in case we were attacked and to eliminate the possibility of losing them.

We reached the ferry by late afternoon. There was a small cabin located on our side of the river. The ferry operator, presumably Swearingen, told us he was done making crossings for the day.

"Do you have any room for the night?" I asked.

"Nein, no beds." He spoke with a gravely German accent.

I wanted to get across to get an early start and didn't want to wait for him to ferry us in the morning. "We need to get across. Would you ferry us tonight for this?" I held up a silver coin.

Swearingen thought for a moment, then let out a guttural "Yah." He didn't speak to us again.

The previous days of rest in Frederick did us both good, and although we were stiff, we could both manage walking around easily enough. I tied the horses to low tree branches and fed them corn while Mark gathered river stones and firewood. He had purchased flint in Frederick and soon had an impressive fire going. The night was clear but humid, and we watched heat flashes in the sky that looked like lightning. It was eerie watching the clear night sky and not seeing any air travel. The only other time I ever had that sensation was right after 9/11 when all the airports were closed. Thousands upon thousands of stars could be seen without light pollution from electricity. No wonder the ancients spent so much time studying the night sky constructing stories about constellations. It was inspirational and surreal.

Mark sat in front of the fire on a rock the size of a football. I sat with my legs extended trying to stretch them out.

Mark pulled off his glasses and placed them in his leather pouch. "So what's the plan when we meet Washington?"

"You don't think it's practical to walk up and hand him a bulletproof vest?" I had racked my brain almost continuously during our ride trying to come up with the most effective way to approach Washington. The idea of giving the man a Kevlar vest seemed like a good idea while we were at the library, but I wasn't positive it would work. Why would George Washington even speak to us, let alone accept a strange gift? I pictured the newspaper account: *behaving the whole time with the greatest courage and resolution until he at last receiv'd a shot thro the chest.* We would have to convince him to wear the vest.

"You're the history guy. What did you have in mind?"

"I'm not sure yet," I said. "I've been thinking about it. Initially, I thought we could say the vest was a gift from someone Washington would trust, like Sally Fairfax."

"Who?"

"She was Washington's friend's wife. The Fairfax family was one of the most powerful families in Virginia, and Washington was very close to them. Apparently, he was also smitten with Sally, but no one knows for sure if she ever felt the same way about him."

"Juicy, but would giving him a gift from her send the wrong message? We don't want to screw things up any more than they already are."

"I don't know. At this point, I'd be willing to risk anything to make sure Washington becomes president." I crossed my legs in an attempt to get comfortable.

"John, you can't lose sight of the fact that our history must match what happens here, because if it doesn't, there's a good chance our path back home will remain cut off."

"Yeah, because everyone knows Washington had false teeth made of wood and a Kevlar vest. He's what, twenty four? Probably thinks he's bulletproof already. Maybe we could say it's a gift from the King as a token of appreciation."

Mark considered it for a second. "Why wouldn't the king send one to General Braddock then—or any of the other officers?"

I tried to think of a good reason but couldn't come up with one.

The only sound we heard was the rushing of the black river water and the song of the cicadas. Occasional flashes from fireflies glowed within the forest.

"Why couldn't the vest be a gift from us? We're both admirers of Washington—we wouldn't be *lying*, and we could say it's a vest that was manufactured in Europe or somewhere overseas. We could even tell him what the vest was designed to do, but to keep it a secret."

Mark stoked the fire with a long stick. "What would make him keep it a secret?"

"Washington was a principled man. He focused a lot of attention on living an honorable life. If we had him swear to keep it a secret, he would. He was a Freemason. They're known for keeping secrets. Maybe we could say it was from them."

"I don't know about that. We don't want him getting suspicious of us. Plus, I don't know anything about Freemasons. What if they had a secret handshake we didn't know? We'd lose credibility."

Mark had a good point. I agreed that it would be best if we kept everything simple. The sooner we could reach him and give him the vest, the sooner we could get home.

"Maybe we should stick to the idea of saying it's a gift from us. If he balks, we could do a demonstration to show him the value."

"What's the worst that could happen?" Mark asked. "He says no and dies a horrible death from a shot through the heart."

* * *

Mark woke me at dawn. We replenished our canteens in the river, took a quick dip in the water to clean and refresh ourselves, and gave our horses some food and water. We were on the trail within a half hour.

It took two more days until we finally made it to Winchester, a small village comprised of about fifty log cabins. Even though we viewed the previous towns we passed through as primitive, Winchester was the real deal. We were on the edge of the wilderness.

The ruts in the muddy streets sank deeper than they had in Alexandria. Fewer businesses lined the streets, and the local residents seemed less likely to say hello to strangers.

We found a place to board our horses and began our search to find a place to stay for the night. Given Braddock's track record, we would probably be here for a few days. Both of us, and especially our horses, needed rest.

We found a room to rent in a cabin on the edge of town. A hand-painted sign hung next to the door read: ROOM. It had likely been posted when the army started to arrive. The proprietor was a widow, probably in her mid-forties, the equivalent of about seventy in our own time. She didn't talk much but happily accepted our money. She was missing most of her teeth and rarely made eye contact.

The cabin was a tiny, one-room building. It wasn't so much a "room" for rent as it was a "bed" for rent—to share.

Again.

I foresaw another night on the floor with the fleas.

"Let's get out of here," I suggested. "I don't want to spend any more time here than we have to."

Mark didn't need convincing. "Maybe we can find more *flips*." Mark and I had become quite fond of the molasses, rum, and beer concoction we discovered in Frederick Town. The key was the hot poker. A simple stirrer wouldn't do. *Flips* had to be mixed with a hot poker.

"Let's see what we can find."

We trekked up the narrow streets, partially hidden under a cloud of dust from the added foot traffic of soldiers.

Two men approached. The taller man wore a military uniform. "I need this delivered to William Fairfax," he said, handing the other man an envelope.

I stopped and stared. A chill ran the length of my spine and extended to the tips of my fingers. The hair on my arms stood up. The man before us was real and not chiseled out of marble.

I nudged Mark.

George Washington.

He was so young, dressed meticulously in a blue overcoat decorated with gold buttons and gold-embroidered loops. A crimson sash draped over his shoulder. Gold lace emblazoned his black hat. Muscular and well-built, he could have been a professional athlete in our modern world. Reddish-brown hair was pulled into a braid behind his back with the sides of his hair fluffed out like wings. His nose was pockmarked, scarred from a bout with smallpox when he was younger. Surprisingly, though he was tall, I still had him by at least an inch.

He caught me gawking. "Do I know you, sir?"

We had traveled all this way to locate and protect one of the most influential men in history, and had been caught completely off guard trying to locate a tavern. Quickly, I regained my composure. "Colonel Washington?"

"Yes. May I help you?" His voice was softer than I had anticipated, projecting from the back of his throat, yet still confident.

I decided to go for it.

"I'm glad we found you," I said. "We've traveled from your home at Mount Vernon to deliver something to you—a gift."

His brows furrowed. "A gift? All the way from Mount Vernon?"

"Yes, we are boarding down the street and could get it for you now if you have a moment."

"This is quite unusual. I do not have time right now. I have a meeting with the general. You can deliver the gift to Mr. Alton here." He referred to his companion. "I will send him along with you. What is your name?"

"John Curry, sir," I said, extending my hand. His massive hand gripped mine and a bolt of electricity went through me. I was shaking hands with George Washington.

"Mark Shippen," added Mark. "It's a pleasure to meet you, sir."

Washington turned to shake Mark's hand.

"I would ask that we deliver the package to you personally, if that is not a problem," I said.

"It is not convenient," he said, "But since you came all the way from Virginia to deliver it, I owe you the courtesy. Meet me tomorrow morning. Seven o'clock."

"That would be acceptable, sir." I realized my voice was trembling. "Would it be possible to meet somewhere private? The nature of the gift requires discretion."

He stared at us for a moment. "There is an area to the south of town. Seven o'clock."

"Thank you, sir."

* * *

We walked back to the widow's cabin in silence.

Mark finally spoke up, "We just talked to George Washington—and he's a punk kid." He grinned, and in a snooty imitation of Washington's voice said, "You can deliver the gift to my man here, Mr. Alton."

"Don't be a dick," I said. "That's the first President you're talking about."

"Not yet, he isn't. Anyway, I'm just having fun. We've had a crappy trip so far. I've had to ride a horse for the first time in my life and it's killing my legs. I haven't had a shower in what feels like a month, and shaving with a straight blade using ice-cold river water sucks. I'm just blowing off steam. Besides, he *is* a punk kid."

"We can't judge him by our standards. He's playing the part the way he thinks he should act."

Mark put his hand on my shoulder. "Okay, I'll let you have your hero worship. Let's give him the vest and go home."

"That's *George Washington*. Everything we know and feel about America started with him. I think he deserves a little hero worship. Nothing we could do in our lives could ever compare."

"Speak for yourself. I helped invent time travel."

I laughed. "Cool? Yes, but it doesn't compare."

When we got back to the cabin, we both took off our vests. Neither smelled particularly good so we thought it best to wash them.

"So whose vest does he get?" Mark asked as we were wiping the vests down.

"At this point, I don't care."

"Rocks-paper-scissors?"

"Sure."

We did two out of three and Mark won the deciding round by choosing scissors over my paper. He chose the honor of having Washington's life protected by his vest. "Now I can say I invented time travel *and* I saved George Washington's life. Top that, loser."

I should have chosen rock. As I learned from watching Seinfeld: Nothing beats rock.

"Wipe that shit-eating grin off your face. You get to ride unprotected back to Mount Vernon," I said. "If we get ambushed by Indians, you'll be screwed."

"Yeah, but you're the one who's always getting stabbed, so you probably need it more than I do. People tend to like me more. Claude would have never have tried to kill me."

"True, you were always better with people than I was. I tend to mock them *to their faces* while you wait until you're out of ear's reach."

Mark shrugged. He sniffed the vest. It looked cleaner, but the way he scrunched his nose, I could tell he didn't find it a big improvement. "Luckily, this thing smells just like everything else in this century."

We had dinner with the widow. Food was included as part of our room and board and supper was served promptly at 2:00. It was some kind of soup consisting of wild turkey, mushrooms, and Indian corn. Not awful, but not particular good either.

"How long have you lived in Winchester?" I asked her.

"Too long."

"Do you have any family?"

The widow looked at me briefly and then turned her attention to her soup.

She didn't attempt any more small talk and neither did we.

After dinner, we walked around the town to explore a little. Now that we had arranged a meeting with Washington it felt like a great weight had lifted. I was finally relaxed and could take in the surroundings and enjoy the moment. The town was still young—only about ten years old—the edge of civilization for the American colonies. I could still see the saw marks on the edges of the logs.

Most of the army retreated to their tents on the outskirts of the town. Having nothing to do, we retired early in anticipation of our meeting.

EIGHTEEN

Winchester, VA, May 4th, 1755

We met Washington the next morning just south of the village. He'd stood, relaxed next his assistant, Mr. Alton. Mark and I arrived with our package wrapped in cloth we had purchased from the widow.

"Good morning, Colonel," I said as we approached. Washington stood in his full uniform complete with white gloves.

When he saw us, he clasped his arms behind his back and gave a courteous nod.

I had thought about my presentation most of the night. I would speak confident and energetic like any good salesman, focusing on the benefits of the vest. I knew Washington was proud and eager to show off his bravery during battle. I was going to use that to my advantage. Somehow.

I was about to remind Mark to let me do the talking when he stepped toward Washington holding the package and said, "I present to you a bullet-proof vest."

Subtle.

Washington's eyes widened, then narrowed. "A what?"

"Of course," Mark continued while unwrapping the gift, "You can only accept it on condition of complete secrecy."

"We wouldn't want anyone taking head shots at you," I added. What were we doing? This wasn't going the way I had planned. Mark had panicked by being too forward, and I was aiding and abetting our idiocy.

"Gentlemen, you are wasting my time," said Washington, turning to leave.

"No, wait," I said. "It really works. It will stop any bullet—musket ball—fired at it. It's stab proof as well. I've had firsthand experience with mine." I unbuttoned my waistcoat and revealed my matching vest. "I was stabbed while in Prague, and this vest saved my life."

Washington stared. "How can a piece of cloth stop a musket ball? Where did you get this?"

"He invented it," I said, referring to Mark.

"You did?" said Washington. "So, how does it work?"

"It's a synthetic fiber—a special material," said Mark, shooting me a hard look for putting him on the spot. "It's stronger than steel, but it's lightweight so you can wear it under your jacket."

Washington's face remained skeptical.

Mark noticed it too. "I can see you don't believe me. Hang it from that tree over there and shoot it. See what happens."

"No," I said. "We can't draw attention to it. Do either of you have a knife?"

Mr. Alton produced a knife with a five-inch blade.

Mark placed the vest on the ground. He looked up at Alton. "Give it your best shot."

Washington nodded and Alton gave it a few quick jabs.

"Put something into it. Give it a stab like you're in battle." I said.

Alton looked to Washington.

"Go ahead," ordered Washington.

Alton stabbed at the vest again, only harder. After four times, the blade did not penetrate it.

"Let me see that blade," said Washington. He inspected it, bent down, and tried stabbing the vest himself. He thrust the blade into the vest three times. Nothing happened. He looked at us in disbelief. "So you say this vest will protect the wearer from a bayonet or musket shot?"

"Yes," Mark and I both answered at the same time.

"I read your account of the campaign against the French last year and was impressed by your courage under fire," I said. "It would be an honor if you would wear it while you take Fort Duquesne this year. You once said there was something charming in the sound of gunfire. That may be true, but I believe it's more charming to survive and fight another day. It's hard for men to accomplish great things if they die young. The vest won't guarantee your protection, but it will increase your chances of surviving to see old age."

Washington smiled. "The men in my family don't live to see old age. Besides, destiny has complete control over our actions and cannot be resisted by the strongest efforts of human nature."

"Don't be so sure," I said.

"You may believe what you want. The *Grimm King* causes me no distress. I place my trust in Providence to deliver me to whatever destiny holds."

"Now there we can agree," I said. "Think of this gift as Providence."

Washington grinned. "I will accept this gift, gentlemen."

"On a condition of secrecy," Mark added.

"I give you my word," Washington said. He paused for a moment, studying us with gray-blue eyes. "Will you volunteer? I could use good men in the Virginia regiment."

Holy crap. George Washington just asked me to volunteer.

I thought about it for a moment, the opportunity to get to know one of the greatest men in history. Of course, the reality is I would probably be relegated to grunt work and never see him. "No thank you," I said. "We need to return home."

"Where is home?"

"Nevada," said Mark.

"I have not heard of Nevada."

"We have a long way to travel," I said. "In fact, we'll be headed for home today."

"Quite unfortunate," Washington said. "The army can always use good engineers."

"That's him," I said pointing to Mark. "He's the genius. I'm just good at remembering things."

"Mark Shippen and John Curry, right?" asked Washington.

Apparently, he was good at remembering names.

"Yes sir."

"I thank you for the gift. I still do not comprehend why you traveled all this way, but I will honor your wishes and keep it a secret. Mr. Alton will do the same."

Alton nodded.

"I have a busy day," he said. "We leave for Fort Cumberland tomorrow."

"It's been a pleasure, sir. Be safe," I said. "Your country is counting on you."

"God save the king." He tipped his hat and walked away.

* * *

"What do you mean, I invented it?" asked Mark after Washington was out of earshot. "Everyone knows Kevlar was invented by Stephanie Kwolek while working for DuPont in the sixties."

I gave him a crooked look. "Um, no—not everyone knows that. I had to tell him something. If I told him it was manufactured by *DuPont*, he'd think we were French—not necessarily the smartest thing since he's going to fight the French."

"I know. I just want to be known for inventing time travel—not inventing Kevlar. That's so fifty years ago—or two hundred years from now—depending on who you ask."

We gathered our horses and said goodbye to the widow. She grunted something unintelligible which I understood as *Goodbye, have a safe trip and thank you for letting me charge you a lot of extra money for the privilege of sharing a flea-ridden bed with another guy.*

We rode north, retracing our earlier path toward Frederick. About ten miles outside of town, we saw where the British army had cut the road through the forest from the east. We decided to take the more direct route back to Mount Vernon rather than riding north through Maryland again.

Navigating the freshly-cut road was easy enough. March a couple of hundred men, horses, wagons, and cannon through the forest, and a road can be pretty easy to detect. Even if it was nothing more than a trail through the woods.

We took our time, slowed by our horses' lumbering pace. Our moods had lifted. The sun seemed to shine a little brighter. The temperature was a little cooler. We were headed home.

The amount of wildlife was astounding. We saw wild turkeys every couple of hours and even crossed paths with a few deer.

Mark pointed out a tree and said, "That's an American Chestnut tree. They're all but extinct in our time."

"How would you know that?"

"Hey, you're not the only one who's *good at remembering things*," he mocked. "I have my Ph.D. you know."

"In tree spotting? I didn't even know that was a thing."

We opened up the jug of rum that I bought to celebrate our successful mission. I toasted to George Washington's health, and Mark toasted to Kevlar and American Chestnut trees. Before long, we were both a little buzzed, but neither of us cared. It felt like we were kids again, off on another make-believe adventure. We laughed and reminisced about old times, kids from school, ex-girlfriends, teachers, and stupid things we did in college.

"You know, I envy you," said Mark.

"What do you mean?"

"Your family. Your interests. You're more well-rounded than I am. I never made time for a family. I always put everything into research or my work. I sometimes worry that I'm too set in my ways to share my life with anyone else. I've become selfish."

"Man, I've always envied you," I said, taking another pull from the rum jug and passing it to Mark. "You always seemed to have it together. You had your plan and stuck to it. I've always kind of floated along assuming everything is going to work out. Remember when you told me that in the cafeteria?" A floating sensation washed over me as the alcohol worked its way through my system.

Mark pointed out another chestnut tree.

"Why are you saying all this?" I asked.

"I don't know if I'd say anything if I wasn't a little drunk. I just want you to know that even though this trip turned out nothing like we thought it would, I'm glad you're the one with me."

"Me too."

We came to a river and found a ferry. It was starting to get late so we decided to make camp on the east side of the river under the trees at the base of the Blue Ridge Mountains. As the sun set, the wind began to kick up. A storm was on its way.

* * *

It rained the entire next day. Traveling on horseback after wearing the same clothes for two weeks sucks. Doing it in the pouring rain is worse. We spent half the day riding up and down the muddy slopes of the Shenandoah Mountains. We rode silently keeping our misery to ourselves.

Leaves dripped with water and branches littered the ground from the storm. Even the birds took the day off and stayed out of sight, except for the occasional chirp ridiculing us for being out in the rain.

We polished off the jug of rum to help pass the time. The horses were slow and I started to get saddle sore again.

We were able to buy some food from a roadside tavern—or *ordinary* as it was called—after spending most of the day on the mountain. On the menu: a loaf of stale bread and dried beef.

If I never eat beef jerky again, it will be too soon. And we'd overpaid.

We also replenished our food supply for the horses and fed them Indian corn.

We camped under trees but couldn't find any dry wood to make a fire so we spent the night cold and wet.

The next morning brought relief in the form of sunshine and our spirits brightened. The landscape was mostly forest that opened occasionally to settlements where local farmers raised cows and sheep. Corn grew in stalks as high as eight feet, and tobacco plants littered the countryside.

We were road-tested travelers of the eighteenth century wilderness, so we bypassed all the ordinaries and camped. Neither one of us was willing to spend another night in a flea-infested bed.

The next morning began with an unseasonable chill in the air. By ten, it felt unseasonably warm. We rode all day and arrived back in Alexandria late in the afternoon.

Our horses were beat, and we rode to the livery stable to return them and see if we could get some money back.

The stable manager laughed at us. "No one with half a brain would purchase those two old horses."

"Well, you shouldn't have sold them to us. What kind of establishment are you running here?" I knew he had taken advantage of us, but I didn't really care. I was giddy at the prospect of going home. "Can you at least board them for the night?"

"Four pence." He smiled smugly. "I'll give ye' a break for making it to Wills Creek and back."

Screw that guy. By the time the stable manager realized we weren't coming back, we would be safe and sound in the twenty-first century. It wasn't my money anyway. It was Meade's, and it was counterfeit.

"Deal," I said, counting out the money.

Having spent four days on the open road, we decided to spend the night in Alexandria and leave for Mount Vernon in the morning. It was about a ten-mile walk, but we could handle that, especially with the prospect of home waiting at the end. Mark suggested another meal of baked fish at the "George," and we found two rooms with clean beds. After sleeping outside for the past two weeks, the mattress was heaven.

Breakfast consisted of eggs and toast and we were walking on the road to Mount Vernon by eight. It was raining again so we trudged on the side of the road as much as possible to avoid the thick mud in the center. As we approached the house, we could see slaves tending to their chores.

I had once heard a comedian perform a bit where he said if you were white, you could go to any time in history and you'd be fine. If your skin was dark, you probably wouldn't want to travel further back than 1980. It made me laugh when I heard it, but not now. These people—*owned* by George Washington—lived a life in bondage, working from dawn to dusk with no hope for a better life.

It was both awful and ironic. The man who would lead his country to freedom from British tyranny was himself a tyrant of sorts. I knew better than to judge Washington using the standards of my own time, but it was difficult, seeing slavery through the eyes of someone from the twenty-first century. I needed to get away from this place and back to my own time. Life was by no means perfect in our society, but at least people had a chance.

We headed into the woods to avoid being seen. Mark led us down the slope of the hill through the trees toward the river and then turned in the direction of the house where we left the machine.

I couldn't see it, but I could make out the sticks piled where we had left the machine two weeks ago to the day.

"How long does the cloak run?" I asked.

Mark felt around to locate the hull of the machine. "It has an internal voltage meter. The tiles on top act as solar panels, but the energy they absorb is minimal. It'll stay cloaked until its to the point where there's only enough energy left to return to wherever —whenever—*home* is set. I'm actually surprised that it's still engaged. I would have bet it would've run out by now. Is anyone around?"

I scanned the house for any sign of movement. "Coast is clear."

He pulled out the remote and pressed a button until the cloak disengaged. He punched in the key code, and the hatch opened. We both climbed in and started buckling up.

"Let's go home," he said. "The first thing I'm going to do after I shower is order the largest pizza possible with all the toppings. Pepperoni, mushrooms, onions—even anchovies."

"I'm going to call my daughter to tell her I'm moving to Denver to be closer. Then I'm going to have a little talk with Harrison Meade. You're invited to that meeting, of course. Then I'm quitting."

I had enough excitement with this time-travel business. I wasn't cut out for the adventure.

Hey, at least I learned to ride a horse—sort of.

Mark hit the home button on the touchscreen and the time machine came to life. It began its whirring sequence.

The events of the past two weeks flashed through my mind. British New York. Alexander Hamilton. The newspaper accounts of Washington's death. Mount Vernon. Horses. Fleas. Meeting Washington. Slavery.

It didn't seem real. I felt the need to write it all down. I wanted to tell someone and share the experience.

The whirring continued, rising to a crescendo. Then it shut down anticlimactically—like always.

Mark's face turned bright pink, his jaw clenched.

I knew what that look meant.

We were still in 1755.

NINETEEN

"What happened? Don't we have enough juice to get back?" I already knew the answer, but I needed to hear it.

Mark stared at the screen in disbelief.

"Mark?"

"It didn't work. Our path home doesn't exist."

"What do you mean? We gave Washington the vest. There's no way he could get shot in the chest and die. No musket ball could pass through the Kevlar."

"I don't know. If we'd fixed it, we'd be home now." He put his head into his hands and dropped his elbows to his knees. "We did something wrong. Or we changed history too much."

"Can we go back to the library and see what happened?" I asked. "Maybe the vest saved him from that shot in the chest just long enough to get him shot in the head."

"Not enough power. We're stuck."

We both sat in dejected silence.

What had gone wrong? How could Washington have still died in battle? That was a dumb statement. He could have been killed a number of ways. Maybe he was wounded, but the wound became infected. Maybe he was captured by the Indians and scalped. Maybe Washington survived, but giving him the Kevlar vest was too much of a deviation in history and we were stuck.

I had to know. "I guess we have to go back and stay for the battle to make sure he survives."

"I don't know if I can handle that," said Mark. "I'm toast. I don't want to be here anymore. No more horses, no more shitty dried beef, no more uncomfortable clothes, and *no more of these shitty glasses*—" He yanked the glasses off of his face and cocked his arm to throw them, but I grabbed his wrist.

"Don't," I said. "You're going to need them. It sucks. I know—but we have to see this through—one way or another. We can't give up now."

Mark looked at me, dejected, but didn't say a word.

I let go of his wrist. "Let's get back to town. We'll get supplies and make a plan to get back to Washington to set things right. I need you. Don't wig out on me now. You're the smart one with the Ph.D., remember?"

He let out an exasperated sigh. "You're right, sorry. I was just really looking forward to pizza, you know?"

I smiled. "You'll get it."

I hope.

We opened the hatch and looked around. Still no one in sight.

"I don't know how we can camouflage the machine," Mark said. "There's no way the cloak will hold for another two weeks. Even with the solar panels, it will take up too much power."

"Can we roll it deeper into the woods?" I asked. It didn't look good. The trees were dense and we wouldn't make it far before getting it wedged between trees or stuck in undergrowth.

Mark agreed there wasn't anywhere to go with it. "Let's just leave it here and hope for the best. No one will be able to get in even if it is noticed—and it will be. It's gigantic and made of metal."

We worked our way through the woods and back around to

the main road. A few hours later, we were in Alexandria. Our first stop was to the livery stable.

"Didn't expect to see you again," said the stable manager. His smug grin was back.

Mark and I needed transportation to Fort Cumberland, but I wasn't going to be taken advantage of again. I returned his smile. "We've done business a few times now and I don't even know your name. I'm John. What's yours?" I held out my hand.

"Andrew," he said, grasping my hand. He cocked his head slightly, but continued to smile.

"Andrew, after the patron Saint of Scotland. How nice." I stood as upright as I could so I towered over him.

His grin disappeared.

"Andrew, our visit to your fine community has been extended and we're going to need two more horses. Now, I see you have two fine-looking horses for sale, and I thought we could make a deal. What do you think would be a reasonable price?"

He tried to pull his hand away, but I held.

"Since we've done business before, I would say—fifty each."

I smiled. "Andy, Andy, Andy. I know you think me a fool. Perhaps I deserve that, but I didn't step off the boat yesterday—not this time. You took advantage of us last time and I'm— disappointed. I was thinking you'd offer us a better price."

Mark smirked and looked away.

Fear crept into his eyes. "Forty each?"

I let out an exasperated sigh, dramatic as possible, and cocked my head. "We're meeting with our friends, Tony Soprano and Don Corleone. Imagine if I had to tell them we were taken advantage of—not once—but twice, by a two-bit horse jockey? What do you think they'd do?"

Andrew looked around. Mark stood expressionless, arms

folded.

"Did I say forty each?" He smiled. "I meant to say forty for both—because you treated me so fairly before."

I released my grip and smiled. "Andy, you drive a hard bargain. We'll take them."

As we led our new horses away, Mark turned to me. "Really? Don Corleone and Tony Soprano? I didn't think you had it in you."

"I'm tired of getting taken advantage of. The nice-visitor routine wasn't working."

"Well, it only worked because you're tall, Tony Soprano."

I was finally getting the hang of how much things cost. A British pound could buy a lot. Our saddles cost about two pounds. It took twenty shillings to equal one pound, and when we paid for meals, it only cost a shilling or two. Twelve pence equaled one shilling, but if you referred to an individual coin, it was considered a penny. Our experience with Andrew taught me the power of negotiation. I wouldn't get taken advantage of again.

We thought it best to spend the night in Alexandria one more night and get an early start the next day. We picked up food for our trip along with extra canteens. Interestingly enough, the canteens were made of copper and shaped like modern flasks. I expected leather skins like I always saw in movies. Mark was able to buy a dozen or so cucumbers, which were a welcome find.

I thought about my intention to write down our experience when I got home. We weren't sure we would make it back at this point, but it wouldn't be a bad idea to take notes documenting this leg of the journey. I purchased a leather-bound journal, six feather quills, a few jars of ink, and another leather haversack to store everything.

Mark insisted we buy more rum. Since we had enjoyed the

first one so much, I didn't argue.

For the second night in a row, we were able to rent separate rooms. I sat at the small desk with a candle and my new writing instruments. After practicing on a blank sheet of paper, I started to get the hang of writing with a feather quill and ink. I opened up the journal and began to write.

From the Journal of John Curry
Alexandria, VA
May 9th, 1755

I am writing this to document my journey and to record my observations about the Braddock expedition against the French.

I am traveling with my oldest friend, Mark Shippen. We will set out tomorrow in hopes of catching up with the army before they depart Fort Cumberland. We just left Mount Vernon today and have plenty of money, new horses, and enough supplies to get us to Winchester. After that, we're placing our lives in the hands of the British army with hopes of serving under the command of George Washington as volunteers. Neither of us know how to fire a musket or how to be soldiers, but we will do our best.

The worst part of this experience is knowing the outcome of the battle has already been determined. The army is doomed. I guess men have been doing the same thing for millennia— fighting for their country and an ill-fated cause. The difference is the country we're fighting for doesn't exist yet.

* * *

We set off early, feeling much more prepared than our first trip out of Alexandria. Mark was in better spirits, the night's sleep having done him good. We both carried sleeping rolls and extra blankets. Not that we would need them. It was hot, but we were trying to be as prepared as possible.

The sky was clear, but not blue. It was white, indicating high humidity. Mark commented that he never really thought about it when he lived on the east coast, but you don't get blue skies there like you do out west.

Our new horses were much livelier than our previous steeds. They were both brown. Being a history nerd, I named mine Old Bob after Abraham Lincoln's horse he rode while he was a circuit lawyer. Mark named his Kwolek to honor the real inventor of Kevlar. Old Bob's coat had more of a red tint than Kwolek with white patches just above each hoof and on the center of its face.

We followed the same path we used on our return from Winchester. The temperature felt milder and more comfortable than our first trip through the countryside. Maybe it was just my expectation. The weather hadn't really changed. It had only been a day since we returned from Winchester, but our goal this time was more clear-cut: Keep Washington alive by any means necessary. The worst part of our plan was not knowing whether it would really work. What if Washington survived the battle, but we were still trapped?

"Do you think we should have bought guns?" Mark asked as we made our way away from Fairfax Courthouse, located about twenty miles west of Alexandria.

"Neither of us knows how to shoot them. Muskets aren't point and shoot, you know. There's a process."

"I guess I just don't want to be the guy bringing a knife to a gunfight."

"I'm counting on the British to hook us up. I don't even have a knife. If I don't have a gun, I'll have to throw rocks at the French."

We passed a man on horseback, probably a farmer headed to Alexandria. All three of us tipped our hats.

"We can't kill anyone, you know," Mark said. "When we get into this battle, we can't alter history as we know it. I don't want to risk traveling all this way, save Washington—for real this time—and then screw things up by killing an ancestor of Jacques Cousteau."

"I think our priority has to be to protect Washington. Somehow try to watch his back."

"What do you know about the battle?"

"I know the British didn't stand much of a chance. It was called an ambush, but I think the armies just sort of ran into each other in the forest. The British were trying to take Fort Duquesne and didn't anticipate any resistance outside of the fort. The French sent out a small force to meet the British and fought with their Indian allies from the cover of trees. The British fought in their traditional manner, lining up in a straight line and firing on command, but because of the forest and smoke, they couldn't see who they were shooting at. It was a complete rout. Don't you ever watch the History Channel?"

"So can we get Washington to hide behind a tree like the French?"

"I don't think so. The history books tell us he was on horseback throughout the battle trying to rally the troops. Remember the newspaper account said that he had two horses shot out from under him?"

"Yeah, I'm having a hard time trying to figure out how he dies if we already gave him the vest."

"Do you think we altered history too much by giving him the vest?" I know we both had thought about the possibility since our return trip home failed.

"It's possible, but I don't want to believe that," said Mark. "I need hope right now so I can hold it together. I've decided that the first thing I do after we get back and I get my pizza will be to get Lasik so I never have to wear glasses again." He pulled them from his face and wiped the lenses with cloth from his coat.

"Hold on to those thoughts. When we get back, I'll pay for your surgery."

"No way. Meade owes me at least that much."

From the Journal of John Curry
Outside Mr. Coleman's
May 10th, 1755

We just concluded our first day on the road, covering about thirty miles since leaving Alexandria. We camped outside an "ordinary" owned by Mr. Coleman. Ordinaries are fleabag motels located about every fifteen miles. We have learned not to sleep inside them, but do purchase food when we can. The food can be more precarious than the sleeping arrangements so we generally limit our purchases to bread and other recognizable eighteenth-century delicacies.

Today, we talked about volunteering for the army. Mark suggested we seek out Washington and volunteer under his Virginia regiment. It will allow us to keep a closer eye on him and make sure he is protected when the battle happens. Plus, there's the possibility we'll get to know Washington. If we survive... Think of the stories!

We're hoping to receive muskets from the British since we didn't own any. I think the army would be happy to train militia volunteers. We had been promised money and training when we were in Frederick a few weeks ago. I hope the offer still stands.

I estimate it will take four more days at most to reach Winchester if the weather holds. I must confess that roughing it in the wild isn't as bad as I would have thought. Someday, I hope to look back at this journal for fond memories of my days as a soldier.

From the Journal of John Curry
Winchester, VA
May 14th, 1755

The past few days have been uneventful so I decided not to write. The sky has been clear, and we made good time. We crossed back through the Blue Ridge Mountains through Vestal's Gap. We were ferried across the Shenandoah River and made it back to Winchester once again. We're camping here before setting out for Fort Cumberland tomorrow.

I am both excited and apprehensive about joining the British army. I'll admit there is something alluring about the prospect—which is sick —because I know the outcome of the battle. Does our culture place such a premium on military service that I've been conditioned to feel honorable by joining the army and learning how to kill people? What's wrong with me? I never even considered anything like this before.

Of course, I've read about military life, but never experienced any kind of fighting firsthand. Knowing I'm about to witness a battle up close should be a little scary—no—A LOT scary. I used to ask, "Could you imagine fighting like that?" when discussing a scene from a Roman battle or the Civil War. Men will face each other, one-on-one, with the intention of killing. Will I be able to defend myself? Will I keep my head or run for my life? We all like to think that we'd be brave in battle, but I honestly don't know how Mark or I will respond.

Mark says we can't kill anyone and run the risk of changing history. I agree, but it scares me to think it might come down to taking a life or losing my own—or Washington's. It's a lot to think about.

We leave for Fort Cumberland in a few hours and I have this awful feeling that my personal freedom is going to be gone in the next couple of days. My life seems to be spinning out of control.

TWENTY

Wagon ruts and trampled grass pointed the way. While Winchester felt like the edge of civilization, the road to Fort Cumberland felt like we had fallen off. We encountered fewer travelers and sometimes rode for hours without seeing anyone.

During the late afternoon a rider came galloping in our direction. As he got closer, I recognized him by the gold embroidery on his hat and jacket.

"Colonel Washington," I yelled as he approached.

He slowed when he saw us, and we all stopped, facing each other in the middle of the road.

Washington smiled. "John Curry and Mark Shippen. Did you change your mind and decide to volunteer?"

"As a matter of fact, we have," I said. "We decided we couldn't go to Nevada without seeing this campaign through first."

Mark spoke up. "What brings you out this direction? We were riding to meet you."

"I am on an errand for the general to see the quartermaster in Hampton. We need money and supplies. The governors have given this army nothing but promises when it comes to aiding this expedition. I will return as soon as I can. I will give you a letter of introduction to Major Stephen. He is leading the Virginia militia.

Do either of you have paper and a quill?"

"I do," I said as I reached into my leather bag slung around my shoulder and pulled out my leather-bound journal. I opened it to a blank page and handed it to Washington along with a quill and a bottle of ink.

Washington took the journal and scrawled a quick message.

I wonder if it would be bad to ask him for an autograph.

He tore the paper out of the journal and handed everything back. "Give the message to the major and he will see to it that you are taken care of. It will be a glorious day for Britain and Virginia when we drive the French out. I must leave. I hope to reach Winchester by nightfall."

"What about muskets?" asked Mark. "We don't have any."

Annoyance flashed briefly across Washington's face. "I'm sure we can locate something suitable. Major Stephen will see to it."

Washington eyed the jug of rum sticking out of Mark's saddle-bag. "Be careful not to let the general find that," he said pointing. "He is making a great effort to maintain order at the fort. Don't give any to the Indians and do not consume too much or you will find yourself flogged."

"I'll make sure he doesn't see it," said Mark.

Washington tipped his hat and said, "God save the king." Then he rode off at a pace Mark and I could only dream of.

* * *

We traveled a few more hours and came upon another tavern. I guessed it would be our last opportunity to sleep indoors before joining the army. One look inside helped us decide we would be better off taking our chances outside in the elements than we would with the dirt, grime, and fleas.

Mark walked out to make camp about fifty yards from the cabin. He was getting proficient at making campfires.

After securing the horses, I sat next to Mark by the fire. We shared bread I had bought inside as well as rabbit meat too gamey for my tastes. I spat it out and threw the rest into the flame. Mark handed me the jug of rum to rinse the taste from my mouth. I didn't spit out the rum.

"Don't waste your food," chided Mark. "There are starving people *everywhere*."

"I wonder if Major Stephen is Adam Stephen," I said after taking another swig of rum. I handed Mark the jug.

"Who's Adam Stephen?"

"A general in the Revolutionary War. He fought at Trenton and Princeton. Later, he was dismissed for getting drunk and ordering an attack on friendly soldiers."

"Really? Never heard of him."

"I guess Americans don't like to highlight the dumb things their generals do by putting them in history books. I could be wrong, though. I imagine Stephen could be a popular name."

"I guess we'll find out tomorrow." Mark took another swig and raised the jug in toast. "To our last night of freedom."

I hoped he was wrong.

* * *

We set off early the next morning knowing it was the final stretch before reaching Fort Cumberland. It was amazing Washington made it so far in one day. The topography of the land grew hillier, forcing us to summit two mountains. The views were incredible, with forest so dense I couldn't pick out individual trees. Purple mountains circled the horizon offering a glimpse of the vast land of America. In a little over two hundred years, the greenest trees I'd ever seen would succumb to the sprawl of civilization complete with strip malls and HOAs.

We crossed a small river and looked at the exposed grayish purple rocks on the bank.

"It makes you want to have a camera doesn't it?" said Mark as we crossed the shallow water.

"It's so—pristine," I said. "We need to come back and hike this area when we get home. It would be cool to see firsthand how much everything will change."

"We're probably walking through someone's garage or maybe a gas station."

We trotted through a long, narrow valley and passed another outpost. The road conditions worsened and I could make out deep ruts cut into the mud. The army had been through here recently. The path transitioned to a road looking like a strip of corduroy laid on the forest floor. The road, made of logs laid side by side and end to end, were to aid the army in moving artillery over muddy ground.

Our horses didn't like the feel of walking on wood, so we steered clear of the log road when possible. The log road extended for miles, and I wondered how long it took the army to assemble. The road ended at a trading post fortified with a stockade.

"Let's check it out," I said. "This is our last opportunity to buy anything before we reach Fort Cumberland."

Mark tied his horse to a wooden post at the entrance to the stockade. I stepped down and tied Old Bob. I bent over to stretch and try to alleviate some of the stiffness in my legs. The door was ajar so we walked in.

The trading post consisted of a small building made of stacked logs packed with mud. A hand-painted sign hung next to an open door that read: Cresap's.

As we walked inside, a weather-worn man with gray hair greeted us. His accent was English. "Don't have much," he said. "Army took most of my supplies. Have some furs to trade or sell."

"No thanks, we're headed for Fort Cumberland," I said. "We were looking for fresh food if you have it."

"Not today," he said. "Have corn liquor. Home brewed. Mighty powerful. Better than the watered-down grog you'll get from that cheap bastard Braddock."

"Maybe another time," I said. "How far to Fort Cumberland from here?"

"Couple of hours. You sure you don't want anything? Better get it before the Indians trade for all of it. Gets them riled up something fierce."

We left without buying anything and headed up the road. We followed the bank of a river and arrived at Fort Cumberland in the afternoon.

* * *

Fort Cumberland sat at the top of a hill overlooking the confluence of two rivers: Wills Creek and the Potomac. It was laid out like a large Indian arrowhead with the pointy end facing Wills Creek. The stockade walls consisted of 12-foot high, green-tinted logs stripped of their bark. They looked like a cluster of sharpened pencils driven into the ground, pointy side up. Outside the fort were hundreds of white army tents.

We tied our horses outside the main gate and gave our letter of introduction to the sentries posted outside. They admitted us without a word. Inside the fort, men moved artillery and supplies. Lieutenant Colonel Thomas Gage had just arrived earlier in the day with artillery from Alexandria.

There were also groups of Indians spread throughout the fort, not only men, but women and children too. A group of Indian warriors passed in front of us, the sides of their heads freshly shaved, with feathers threaded on top. Their faces and bodies were painted a shade of burnt sienna with streaks of black and yellow. One turned his head toward us, staring through dark eyes. A string of bear claws hung around his neck. His gaze only lasted a moment, then he continued with his group.

The fort was built in two sections. The larger section at the tip of the "arrow" housed barracks while the front section was heavily fortified with cannon. The entire fort was probably about 250 feet in diameter. The British Union Jack flew proudly from a pole in the center.

We were ignored by the soldiers, who clustered in groups based on their regiment. British Regulars wore the traditional red uniforms. The Colonial volunteers could be spotted by their tricorne hats and leather breeches. We approached a group of Colonials and asked the whereabouts of Major Stephen.

"Excuse me, sir," I said to the closest man. He was inspecting his musket. "Could you tell us where we might find Major Stephen?" The man looked up and pointed toward an officer in a blue overcoat speaking to a colonial about ten yards away.

"Thank you," I said, and we headed over to introduce ourselves.

We waited at a polite distance until the conversation was over. Stephen turned toward us.

"What's this?" he asked in a Scottish brogue. His eyes were large and brown, his face weather-worn. Around his neck hung a gleaming gold gorget engraved with the British royal crest.

"Two more volunteers, sir. Colonel Washington gave us this." I handed him the letter of introduction.

"Good, good," he said reading it. "I see that you have already found some of the men. I will introduce you." He led us back to the original group of men we first encountered.

"Men, this is John Curry and Mark Shippen. They will be joining us. Please show them around."

"Major Stephen," I said. "I'm not sure what capacity you'd like to use us, but I wanted to let you know that neither of us has a weapon or experience with muskets."

He smiled and some of the men started to laugh. "Patterson. Perry. See to it that these two are given muskets and take them over to Lieutenant Allen so we can get them on the rolls for morning exercises."

That was it. We were officially soldiers.

* * *

Walter Patterson and Charles Perry were volunteers from the Tidewater region of Virginia. Eager to please Major Stephen, they hurried to lead us to find Lieutenant Allen.

Lieutenant James Allen was the British officer in charge of training the colonials to fight in the traditional, *English way*. He was cut from the mold of the stereotypical hardass and looked us up and down as we approached his desk.

"Sir, these men have volunteered and we were ordered to bring them to you to get on the rolls," said Patterson.

"More colonials," he said with a heavy Irish inflection, disdain in his voice. "All right then, I expect to see you for exercises at five tomorrow morning. You're going to drill until you learn to fight like proper soldiers of the King." He dismissed us with a wave of his hand.

"Don't you think that was a little too fast?" asked Mark as we returned to the group of Virginia volunteers. "We just walked into camp, and now we're—in. No interviews, no inspections, no questions—"

"Were you worried about don't ask, don't tell?"

"Shut up. You know what I mean. We didn't even have to sign our names."

"I guess they're desperate for volunteers, or maybe Washington's letter carried some weight."

We met two of the other men in our group, Boyce and Nicholson, and followed them outside the fort to camp where there was more of a breeze and easier access to water. Since there was no well within the fort, water was obtained by carrying a bucket down the slope of the hill to Wills Creek and filling it there.

It took us a half hour to gather firewood as the forest around the fort was being cleared daily by soldiers gathering wood for their own fires. Mark lit the fire and I took care of our horses and grabbed what was left of our rum to share with our new mates.

We were the oldest of the group. Richard Boyce was probably in his early twenties. Originally from Scotland, he came to America at the age of fourteen as an indentured servant to a rope maker. After a few years, he escaped from his servitude in South Carolina to head north because his master was a bastard and a drunk who treated him "no better than a slave."

Charles Perry and Walter Patterson were boyhood friends from Alexandria. Perry's father was a candle maker, and Patterson's father helped unload the ships that came up the Potomac. Young and illiterate, neither wanted to share in the lives their fathers had built. When the army came through, they signed up, eager to get out of Alexandria.

William Nicholson was the youngest and most handsome of

the group. Locks of brown hair partially covered his eyes and high cheekbones.

"Where are you from, William?" I asked.

He looked up from the fire. "It's not important." He returned his gaze to the flames.

"Come on, Willie boy," said Perry, raising the jug of rum and trying to hand it to William. "Empty the bag. Where are you from?"

William ignored him and squinted at the flames.

"Leave him be," said Patterson, taking the jug. "I want to know more about our rum bearers." He raised a toast toward Mark and me, and took a long pull.

"Pass it around before you give the bottle a black eye," scolded Perry, taking the bottle back. He swigged the rum and handed the bottle to me.

"West," I said. "Nevada. Although we've been traveling for many years."

Mark cleared his throat. I knew he wanted us to say as little as possible, but I didn't see any harm in mentioning Nevada. It meant as much to these guys as it would had I mentioned Sydney or Beijing. I winked and handed him the bottle.

Patterson pressed. "Why did you join up with the rest of us caterpillars?"

"It's important to protect your country, don't you think?"

"I suppose so." He stood up, momentary losing his balance. "I've got to piss."

"Keep it away from us," said Boyce. "We don't want to smell it all night."

"You should talk, Sandy. I've been smelling you all week." Patterson sauntered off toward the river.

"What's a Sandy?" I asked.

William Nicholson looked up from the flames. "A Scotsman."

"So what's it like here?" Mark finally spoke. "We volunteered and they placed us with you without telling us much."

"We're under Dunbar's 48th," said Perry. "But stay away from the gentlemen in red, especially if they're mauled. Surly bastards think they're better than us, but they're mostly here to avoid the repository."

"Fucking Paddywhacks," added Boyce. Evidently, the colonials felt the same way about their British counterparts.

Perry shifted so he lay on his side. "They feel they've been banished to the colonies and resent fighting our battles. Even our officers are treated as inferior. British officers outrank American officers no matter what their rank. Just keep away from them and you'll get along well enough."

Of course, I already knew how the British felt about American volunteers. This was a frustrating annoyance for Washington too—and one of the reasons he had volunteered to be a consultant for Braddock's campaign. His dream was to be a commissioned officer in the British army, and Braddock had insinuated that an officer's commission lay at the conclusion of the offensive. Unfortunately, or fortunately for Americans, Braddock would not survive the battle and Washington's own aspirations of a career in the British army would die with him.

Patterson returned. "I'm baked," he announced. "Time for sleep."

Drills were to begin early so we all lay down to get a good night's rest. We were going to learn how to be soldiers the next day. It was hard to sleep. We could hear sounds from the Indian camp down by the river. I sat and watched them for a while as they danced around their fire and chanted their songs.

"Wish they'd be quiet. They do this every night." Perry sat up with a look of contempt. "Damn savages."

TWENTY-ONE

What did I get myself into? Sleeping outdoors exposed to the sounds of cicadas and crickets was demanding enough. Factor in the cacophony of hundreds of men farting and snoring, and it was almost impossible to get good rest. I didn't blame the Indians for wanting to separate from the main army.

I felt like I had just fallen asleep when the morning drums signaled it was time to rise. I ate the last of the cucumbers from my pack and headed to the training grounds with Mark and the other Virginia volunteers. After roll call, Mark and I were sent to pick up our muskets.

"Don't go shooting your face off," said the Quartermaster, handing me a five-foot long musket.

Having no experience with guns, its weight felt foreign to me, almost too heavy. I wondered how the hell I was going to handle the weapon. Weren't eighteenth-century weapons prone to overheating and exploding in the face of the soldier firing them?

Mark was inspecting his own "Brown Bess," the endearing nickname given to the British musket. He looked as unsure as I felt.

"Off you go now," said the Quartermaster, dismissing us with a wave.

Mark and I exchanged looks and headed back to the other

volunteers.

"Do you ever get a feeling you're making a mistake?" Mark's face had gone pale.

"Were you reading my mind?"

"I can't do this," he said. "I'm a pacifist. I can't shoot a gun."

"Do your best. It'll be okay—like playing video games."

I hope.

"We can't kill people," he stressed for at least the thirtieth time since we arrived.

"I know, I know. Just make it look good."

Giving Mark a pep talk helped calm me. The thought of standing upright and firing our new muskets against an enemy army trying to kill us was nerve-wracking. No, it was foolish. No way was I going to be able to do that. Neither would Mark. We would have to do our best to fit in with the army, but once the firing started, we would take cover.

We caught up with our platoon, already in the midst of drilling. The men stood shoulder to shoulder, marching carefully to the beat of a drum.

"Get in line, you bastards," roared the drill sergeant. "Bloody hell. I'm going to stick a bayonet up your arse, God help me, if you don't keep your position." He aimed his fury at a colonial who didn't look older than sixteen. Poking the boy's buttocks with his saber, he shouted, "Move!"

Tears streamed down the lad's face as he tried to keep up with the group. I felt sorry for him. He had no rhythm. Couple that with the fear choking his body, and it was going to take him a long time to get it—assuming the drill sergeant didn't skewer him first.

The boy looked around, helplessly. We made eye contact and I gave him a reassuring nod. The boy stared ahead, trying to concentrate.

Mark and I took places in the back of the line. I didn't want to draw the ire of the sergeant and his bayonet so I focused hard on what the other soldiers were doing. Drilling consisted of lining up in two even lines and advancing shoulder to shoulder to the beat of a drum, since drum sounds carried better than men's voices during battle. The point was for the unit to act as one. The British regulars were much more efficient than we were, having had more practice, but the volunteers were catching on. The first few minutes consisted of frantically trying to keep up and not look out of place. It was that feeling you get at a wedding when everyone is performing a new dance move you don't know, but by the end of the song, you have it. Within fifteen minutes, Mark and I could march in-time, but we drilled for the rest of the morning because it wasn't easy for some of the others.

After a brief lunch of hard bread and a hunk of borderline-rotten beef, we moved on to the firing range. The Brown Bess was a flintlock muzzle loader, which meant firing the weapon wasn't as simple as pointing and squeezing the trigger. It was a precise process to load and fire, and the men were continually yelled at until they got it right.

Most of the men had a rudimentary knowledge on how to load the musket. Mark and I—not so much.

I lifted my musket and lined up the target, holding the butt of the rifle against my right cheek. There was no escaping the wrath of the sergeant this time.

"Haven't you never fired a musket before? You'll shoot off your bloody face if you hold it that way." The sergeant stood as close as he could. I was grateful he was at least seven inches shorter. I fought to control my gag-reflex when I smelled his breath, which reeked of rancid meat and whiskey.

"No, sir. First time."

"What are they sending me? A bunch of *Peter Gunners*." He looked around to the other soldiers and pointed his thumb at me. "This one's never fired a gun before, he tells me."

A few of the soldiers laughed. Others looked down in an effort to avoid attention. They probably couldn't shoot a musket either.

"I'm willing to learn, sir, if you'll teach me." I tried to sound subordinate. I didn't want to get on his bad side. I'm not sure what my response would be if he tried to stick me in the ass with his sword, but I knew it wouldn't end well.

"Me too, sir," added Mark.

"Ah, two of you. All right then. Bloody hell. I'm only going to show you once, so you better pay attention." He jerked the musket from my grip and held it up.

A few other soldiers stopped what they were doing and watched.

He clutched the musket with his right hand. "First, you half-cock the *frizzen* like so," He opened a metal latch on the top of the gun, then grabbed a paper cartridge from his pack. "Next you bite off the top of the paper and hold the ball in your mouth." He did as he said and poured a little powder into the pan and snapped the frizzen closed. He dropped the butt of the gun to the ground and poured the remaining powder down the muzzle. He spit the musket ball down the shaft and pressed the remaining paper into the barrel.

"Next you take your ramrod and push everything in nice and tight." The ramrod was a metal shaft located under the muzzle of the gun. He pulled it out and thrust it down the barrel of the gun four or five times before returning the ramrod to its place.

"You present your musket." The sergeant aimed at one of the targets by holding the musket against his shoulder and looking down the barrel. "Lock it." He cocked the hammer.

"Prepare to fire!" he yelled.

Bang.

The musket ball had found its target. The sergeant handed me the musket. "See, there's nothing to it. Now, you try."

I tentatively held up the gun and went through the procedure as I remembered. Mark did the same.

I bit the top off the paper cartridge and kept the lead ball in my mouth. There was residual gunpowder on the musket ball. It tasted metallic, seasoned with pepper. It was nasty. I half-cocked the frizzen and poured powder into the pan.

"Not so much powder," corrected the sergeant. "Just enough to make a spark."

After I spit the ball into the barrel, I pulled out the ramrod and forced the contents of the ammunition down to the bottom of the gun barrel. I tried feeding the ramrod back through its metal housing, but couldn't quite get it through the hole.

"I hope you don't fuck like you load a weapon," screamed the sergeant. "Just put it in the bloody hole."

This prompted nervous laughter from the soldiers gathered around. One harsh look from the sergeant sobered their expressions.

I finally got the ramrod replaced and looked up. My hands trembled.

Mark was already ready to fire.

"You first," he said, looking at me. "Present your weapon!"

I took aim at the target, a hand-drawn bullseye on a piece of paper attached to a bail of hay.

"Fire!"

My body tensed and I pulled the trigger. The gun gave more of a kick than I was expecting, and I reflexively closed my eyes. I opened them slowly to look at the target. White smoke wafted away from where I had fired and started to clear.

I missed.

"Bloody hell! Open your eyes!" The sergeant's hand reached for the handle of his saber and he took an aggressive step toward me. I stepped back to prepare to defend myself, but he caught his temper and turned to Mark. "Your turn—and keep your fucking eyes open."

For a second, I thought Mark was going to point his gun toward the sergeant. Instead, he aimed at the target and waited for the order.

"Fire!"

There was no hesitation.

Bulls-eye.

"Bloody hell," said the sergeant. The contempt in his voice was replaced suspicion. "Where'd you learn to shoot? Tell me or I'll spill your guts myself." He moved toward Mark, hand on his saber again.

Mark held his ground. "Duck Hunt."

"So you're a hunter. Why'd you lie and say you never fired a weapon?"

"I haven't. It's a game we used to play," said Mark. "He used to play too." Mark raised his finger and pointed at me.

Funny. Firing a gun conjured up feelings of being completely out of my element. Could it be as simple as playing a video game? And wasn't that the advice I had just given Mark?

"Can I try that again?" I asked the sergeant.

"Let's see."

I loaded my weapon again, careful not to put too much powder in the pan. This time, the ramrod slid easily back into place.

"Present your weapon!"

I took aim.

Just like a video game.

"Fire!"

This time, I kept my eyes open and steeled myself for the recoil. I didn't need to wait for the smoke to clear to know I had hit the target.

"Bloody hell," said the sergeant, dumbfounded. "Right in the middle." He looked at me and then at Mark. "Duck hunting, eh?"

Mark shrugged.

We spent the rest of the afternoon perfecting the twenty-one specific motions required to hold and fire the weapon. The idea was that soldiers in line should coordinate their movements to reduce the risk of poking each other's eyes out. It was a good idea considering most of the soldiers in the British army were serving in lieu of going to prison or the hangman's noose. Discipline had to literally be beaten into many of them. It was hard to believe those recruiting practices would produce the best-fighting army in the world—almost invincible until the Americans learned how to fight against it during the Revolution.

Better soldiers could fire three rounds a minute. Expert soldiers could fire three rounds in forty seconds. Neither Mark nor myself were very fast, but we demonstrated definite improvement between our first and final shots of the day.

Accuracy was another thing. Muskets were accurate within about eighty yards, but we were taught not to fire until our target was inside fifty yards and to fire only when ordered. Mark didn't miss a bullseye all day. *Mr. Pacifist* was a natural.

* * *

Mark and I spent the evening around the campfire with Perry, Patterson, Boyce, and Nicholson. Mark and I had each been given an extra ration of rum after our display of marksmanship on the first day. Everyone received a daily alcohol ration of watered-down rum. It was very weak—probably one part rum to three parts water. The reason was twofold: it helped build morale within the camp. Army life was of a lot of tedious drilling and even more *hurry up and wait*. Alcohol helped the men unwind. It also combated sickness and dysentery since water supplies around armies could be unreliable. Alcohol was strictly forbidden to be given or sold to Indians at camp. Anyone caught giving the Indians liquor could expect a severe punishment or court martial.

"Did you hear about the Captain that died today?" Perry held a cup, nursing his rum ration.

"What happened?" asked Boyce. His Scottish accent became more prominent when he was agitated. "Did one of his soldiers get tired of being abused and slit his throat?"

"Nothin' like that," answered Perry. "Fever. There's gonna be a funeral tomorrow."

"It was probably something he ate or drank," said Mark.

"Probably barrel fever from drinking this rag water." Patterson made a face at his cup, but did not pour out its contents.

Mark ignored him. "We need to be careful. Boil the water before you put it in your canteens."

"Boil water? Why the hell would we want to do that?" said Perry. "It's already hot enough. I don't want to be drinking no boiling water."

"No, you boil it before you put it in your canteen. You don't drink it while it's boiling."

"You beef-head!" said Patterson.

This brought laughter from all around, all except William Nicholson, who maintained his usual, pensive look. "What does boiling the water do?" he asked.

"It helps kill the germs," answered Mark. The blank stares told him no one had heard of germs, so he explained. "Germs are really small bugs that live in the food we eat and the water we drink. If you eat them, you can get sick. If we boil the water, we have less of a chance of getting sick."

"There ain't bugs in the water," asserted Perry. "It's clean."

Mark sighed, exasperated. "The bugs are really small—too small for you to see. You'll have to take my word for it."

I decided to take a different tact. "Perry, do you eat raw pork?"

"Eeew—no."

"Why not?"

"It's disgusting, that's why."

"Any other reason?"

"It can make you sick." I saw the lightbulb go off in his head as he finally started to understand. He thought about it for a moment and his brow furrowed. "But I never heard of nobody getting sick from drinking water."

Mark jumped back in to the conversation. "Perry, would you drink water out of a pond with a dead cow floating in it?"

The group let out a collective *Eeew*.

Mark continued. "You wouldn't because you'd get sick, right? Same thing here. We have men relieving themselves upstream into the same water that you are filling your canteens in downstream. We're essentially filling our canteens with piss. You don't want to drink piss, do you?"

Perry shook his head.

"We boil the water to make sure we don't get sick from drinking other people's piss."

"Another thing," I added. "We need to listen to the General's orders and stay clean. Bathe at least every other day." Reasonable grooming was expected of all soldiers, not just for cleanliness but to help maintain discipline.

"I'm not taking a bath just because some *knob* thinks I should," said Boyce. "And not because *you* told me either."

"Boyce," said Mark. "If you have such a problem with authority, you shouldn't have joined the army." Boyce just looked at him.

The rest of the night was spent telling stories. The men mostly told us lies about female conquests. As the night progressed, we got bolder and bolder. I recounted my experience at the opera in Prague. Only Nicholson had heard of Mozart, so the story wasn't as impressive as I thought it would be.

I asked if anyone had ever heard of Casanova, and since none of them did, I retold the story of Casanova's escape from prison in Venice. I don't think any of them really believed it happened, but they seemed to enjoy it. Afterward, Mark asked me about it.

"Did Casanova really tell you that entire story?"

"Yes, didn't you get to hear any of it?" I said.

"No, Lillian and I met him at a coffee house and then we toured Prague all day. I didn't understand two words he said."

"I didn't either. Lillian translated the story. We must have been in that coffee house for three hours."

We listened to the Indians for the next hour, and I fell asleep thinking about Casanova and Venice.

* * *

The next morning began with more drilling. Mark and I were getting more efficient with loading and firing our muskets. Secretly, I pushed myself to try to get off three shots in a minute—just like the elite British soldiers. So far, I could only fire two rounds, but I'd only had a musket for two days.

At ten, the officers had to attend the funeral of the captain who had died the previous day. Mark and I tended to the horses and cleaned up in the river water. We had to keep a careful watch on our horses as there was a recurring problem of horses disappearing every night. The British liked to blame the Indians. Most of the colonials thought it was deserters. It was likely a combination of the two.

After the funeral, we gathered to listen to Braddock's articles of war being read to us. We lined up by company and a junior officer read the rules. His voice was high pitched, but projected well.

"Any soldier who shall desert, though he return again, shall be hanged without mercy. Every man will be allowed every day as much fresh or salt provision and bread or flour—as it would be possible to provide them—unless any man should be found drunk, negligent, or disobedient. In such case, this gratuity shall be stopped."

The officer cleared his voice and continued, "Every officer leaving his company upon a march will be answerable for the men of his company left behind. And the commanding officers of each regiment are to order to be punished with the utmost severity any soldier who shall leave his line without leave, sickness, or disability. Officers of companies are to have their arms in constant good order and every man to be provided with a brush and picker and two spare flints and twenty-four cartridges. The roll of each company will be called by an officer morning, noon, and night."

The articles were straightforward enough. It was a way for the General to maintain discipline and order. We would hear the articles read multiple times over the coming weeks.

I got a glimpse of General Braddock for the first time. I didn't know much about him other than what I had been told by the other soldiers. He was supposedly crude and boisterous and didn't think much of the colonial militia. Gray hair covered his head, resting on a short and burly frame. He remained silent while the articles were read. After the message was delivered, he turned away and headed toward his quarters.

* * *

Days were spent marching and drilling. Nights were spent around the campfire telling stories and listening to each other's lies.

The camp was filled with a veritable who's who of the American Revolution. The French and Indian War would be a training ground for the American Revolution in the same way the war with Mexico in the 1840s prepared Union and Confederate generals for the Civil War. Lieutenant Colonel Thomas Gage would be the British commander in Boston at the outbreak of the American Revolution—the general who would order the march on Lexington and Concord. Horatio Gates and Charles Lee, both future American Generals, were currently British officers. Our own commander, Major Stephen, was the same General Adam Stephen I had mentioned to Mark earlier—the one relieved of duty for being drunk during battle and ordering his men to fire on other Continental soldiers.

It was overwhelming to see living, breathing men I had only read about in history books. The emotion wasn't quite as powerful as the moment I made eye contact with Mozart or the first time I met George Washington, but it still felt like seeing a painting come to life. I made a mental note to look up these men when I got home, to see if history had been kind—or unkind—to them. Mark wasn't as impressed. He treated our circumstances as a means to get home.

The most surprising thing about camp life was the number of women. There were at least fifty. I never knew colonial armies had so many women around. I had always assumed armies to be made up entirely of men. I was especially amazed to see so many women this far out in the middle of nowhere. Many were soldiers' wives who were paid to cook and clean. Others were from the *oldest* profession and performed *alternative* services for the men. Prostitution was just like every other business—it abided by the laws of supply and demand. Out in the wilderness, the demand was great, and plenty of women, referred to by Patterson as *pintle merchants*, seemed willing to satisfy that demand. General Braddock was aware of the camp followers and had them regularly inspected for venereal diseases.

Prostitutes weren't the only ones taking care of the soldiers. The Indians had a curious tradition where a squaw would dance for a man that she had her eye on. If he reciprocated—soldiers always did—she'd spend a week in his tent before returning to her actual mate. This custom was not lost on the soldiers who enticed the Indian women with extra rations, even though the soldiers were expressly forbidden to fraternize with the Indians.

I found myself adapting to army life, but wished Washington would return from his mission for General Braddock. I needed to figure out a way to keep him alive.

From the Journal of John Curry
Fort Cumberland
May 21st, 1755

Most of our days consist of drilling, drilling, and more drilling. That's okay. Mark and I are both becoming excellent marksmen and have quickly earned the respect of our company.

There was a rumor General Braddock was going to cancel the expedition due to a lack of support from the governors of the colonies. He was fully prepared to pack up and go home—of course, Mark and I knew better—when five Quakers from Pennsylvania rode in at the last minute. They had been delayed while cutting their own road through the wilderness. Eighty wagons with fresh supplies are on their way. The unexpected supplies were courtesy of Benjamin Franklin. I guess his newspaper advertisements paid off. This helped the morale in the fort tremendously as most of the soldiers are eager to go meet the French and push them out of North America.

Most of the Indians have left. Braddock convinced them to send their families home and recruit more warriors to take up the hatchet against the French. There was a huge celebration last night after the Indians agreed to help. They oiled up their bodies and danced around a huge bonfire while performing a symbolic scalping of an imaginary Frenchman. It was quite a sight, but I have a feeling we won't see most of them return to the army.

The much needed supplies have ignited a flurry of activity. Preparations are being made to build a bridge over Wills Creek. Blacksmiths have been busy fabricating tools for our march through the forest to Fort Duquesne.

The weather has been remained hot and humid, but I have been careful to continuously wear my vest. I don't want it lost or stolen, so I am sacrificing comfort in order to preserve history. I hope this pays off.

From the Journal of John Curry
Fort Cumberland
May 27th, 1755

Still drilling every day, but not a lot of new activity to report. Military life has become very tedious. I am becoming quite the marksman, if I do say so myself, but I am nowhere close to the shot Mark is.

We witnessed our first public flogging. Two men had been caught deserting, and even though Braddock's articles clearly state that deserters will be hanged, the punishment for these two was one thousand lashes each. Colonel Gage conducted the court martial and doled out the punishment. The lashes were spread out over a few days because a thousand at one time would probably have killed them—and the army needs every man it can get. We lined up to watch a soldier bear two hundred blows, but I turned away after a handful because the sight sickened me. I can't begin to describe the awful sound. All I can say is I will do everything possible to avoid something like that happening to me.

One man was tried for murdering another soldier when hunting, but he was acquitted.

Braddock had to send thirty wagons back to Winchester and Conococheague to get more supplies. The barrels of salted meat that had been supplied by Colonel Cresap (the last trading post we stopped before reaching Fort Cumberland) were spoiled. Braddock wants Cresap arrested, but I have a feeling he won't be easy to track down. One British officer referred to him as the "Rattlesnake Colonel." I'm glad we didn't do business with him. Most of the food we get is borderline-rotten to begin with. When meat is deemed not edible enough for an eighteenth-century army, it's in another league of spoiled.

The weather continues to be hot, and even though we are in the midst of a drought, the mosquitos by the river have been out in full force. Mark has made a crude insect repellant by boiling cedar leaves and bark. It's not perfect, but it helps.

An Indian messenger came into camp yesterday and told Braddock that Fort Duquesne is severely undermanned and has only fifty soldiers. The rumor isn't true, but I know the soldiers are ready to attack the fort and earn glory. I am just eager to get out of Fort Cumberland. We've been here two weeks and I want to get this march over with. We have each been given ten flints and twenty-four rounds of ammunition, which tells me we will start marching any day.

Washington still hasn't returned.

From the Journal of John Curry
Fort Cumberland
June 6th, 1755

We're still sitting in Fort Cumberland, but the army has finally begun its March west. Braddock gave the order to march almost a week ago. It's going to be a slow process because a road has to be cut wide enough for the wagons and artillery to pass through. The first group to march were the engineers who will cut down the trees and use explosives to blow up the remaining tree trunks. I think we'll be ordered to march in the next day or two—whenever the 44th gets its orders, as we will be marching with them.

Given the terrain and mountains that we need to cross, I can't imagine we can travel more than ten miles in a given day. Most of the men are on foot.

Washington returned a few days ago. We didn't get to speak to him right away, but have since crossed paths. He was worn out from his long ride and pushed his horses hard to make it back. He was impressed with our marksmanship and received praise from Major Stephen for finding such "fine soldiers" as us. I don't know if I should feel proud or disheartened to realize it only took a few weeks to transform from a novice into a "fine soldier." The results would be quite different if we had joined the Marines back home.

Recent thunderstorms have finally brought an end to the awful drought that has been plaguing this region. It rained constantly the past few days and nights forcing us to sleep inside the barracks. At least I have a dry space to write, although it's stuffy and humid. The ceiling has sprung leaks in at least seven places that I can tell. I thought it was tough falling asleep outside. This is much worse.

We witnessed more court-martials—mostly for desertion, but one was for theft and he got sentenced with five hundred lashes. Wanting to desert is understandable, but the penalty for getting caught would be too much of a deterrent for me.

The flux has started working its way through the camp. It's a bacterial infection caused by drinking bad water that punishes its victims with painful stomach cramps and bloody diarrhea. Mark and I have been fine so far due to our daily regimen of boiling our drinking water, but we still need to be careful. I have seen its crippling effects and want no part of it. So far, our warnings to a few of the Virginia volunteers have paid off. We're all healthy for now.

I hope this is my last entry from Fort Cumberland.

TWENTY-TWO

June 7th, 1755

I've always felt excitement at the beginning of a trip—even if it's for business or something I'm not excited to do. It was no different when we received our orders to march. Finally. Even though many of the men would not be returning, it was the final leg of our journey. We would either succeed and make it home or—well, I didn't want to consider the alternative.

We set off at daybreak on a dreary morning. It had rained all night and was still drizzling as Mark and I mounted our horses and made our trek westward. With twenty-five hundred men walking in front of us, we couldn't push the horses to make good time. The exhilaration of the moment wore of fast as I realized it was going to be a long, slow march.

We had approximately one hundred and fifteen miles to cover through thick forest. Braddock was under the impression that Fort Duquesne was only fifteen miles from Cumberland when he got the assignment. I guess the joke was on him. Maybe if he'd known that our little *walk* would take over a month, he would have retired rather than make the trip across the Atlantic. In the twenty-first century, we take access to information for granted. It was unnerving to think how much every army prior to the twentieth century stumbled around in the dark. Lack of information was going to decimate this army, and there was nothing we could do about it.

Our companions from the Virginia volunteers did not have horses and were forced to walk. As we trotted past them, I wished them well. "Enjoy your walk, boys," I taunted.

Perry turned to Patterson. "Who put that monkey on horseback without tying his tail?"

"I'd rather be a riding monkey than a walking baboon." I winked at him and waved goodbye.

Perry waved back, dismissively. "Arse upward, you belly guts."

Patterson and Boyce laughed. William was William and appeared unfazed.

I turned to Mark. "I understand about twenty percent of what comes out of Perry's mouth."

Acquiring horses was fortunate for us. The Virginia militia's mounted troops rode in the same segment of the line as General Braddock and his military *family*, so Washington was always close. He rode alongside us as we started the climb of what would be the first of seven mountains to summit.

"Good morning," he said. "What a glorious day for a march." His eyes beamed. He lived for this life.

"Glorious," I said sarcastically, holding my hand out to catch rain. Thunder rumbled in the distance.

"How are the men?" he asked. "Will the Virginians represent themselves when the fighting starts?"

"The men are fine," answered Mark. "We all are."

"I am of the same mind," he said. "The general does not think much of colonial soldiers. He feels we are too undisciplined and will run at the first sign of danger. I fear he underestimates the abilities of the Indians as well. I have seen them in battle, and they are fierce warriors."

"The men will be fine," I assured him. "Major Stephen shares your assessment of the Indians and their fighting methods. He said we should take the battle to them using their own methods."

Washington smiled. "We served together last year. He has seen their tactics firsthand. You would do well to listen to his commands."

"So would the general," I said.

"I have time to change his mind. This is going to be a long march. He respects my experience in this land."

I couldn't tell if he was trying to convince us or himself.

* * *

Standard practice was to begin marching at six and travel all day until six or seven in the evening. Every three days, the army would camp for an entire day to rest. It gave time for the road crews ahead of the army to clear more forest. The army was long and bloated. Braddock ordered all non-essential baggage sent back to Cumberland to lighten the load. We traveled maybe eight miles on a good day. After traveling almost thirty miles a day on our trip to Fort Cumberland, the pace was maddening. It was like being stuck in a traffic jam—all day, every day—for a month.

Thunderstorms rolled through, finally relenting to oppressive heat and humidity—and mosquitoes. The soldiers shed their overcoats and marched with as little clothing as possible. I draped my overcoat over my horse pinning it under my saddle pad so I could sit on it, but left on the vest.

The mountains were covered in early summer blooms of sycamores, willows, and occasional oak trees that wreaked havoc on Mark's allergies. He was constantly sneezing and blowing his nose into the few handkerchiefs he had.

He was doing his best not to complain. "Do you think we could stop at the next Walgreen's?" he asked. "I need to pick up an antihistamine."

"Yeah, I'll go let the general know."

* * *

On Friday the 13th, we began our march at 4 a.m., traveled five miles to a plantation situated at the base of a mountain, and camped for the night. Pickets were posted outside of our flanks on either side keeping watch for hostile Indians. We were reminded to not let our horses eat any of the laurel bushes growing in the area because they would cause certain death.

Mark and I camped with our four companions who were exhausted after marching all day.

"How can you be tired? We only went five miles." I said, kidding them.

"Why don't we trade places tomorrow, stiff rump?" replied Perry. "You walk. I'll ride."

I laughed.

Our position was too close to the artillery's ammunition to allow us to build a campfire. No fires were allowed within one hundred yards of the artillery wagons. It was muggy and uncomfortable, and a fire would have only made it worse—especially since I still wore my vest. It itched and stank, but I dared not remove it.

We were in the process of deciding where we were all going to sleep when I noticed my overcoat was missing. It must have fallen off my horse at some point during the day. It wasn't so much a source of warmth as it was a comforting connection to home. I'd also planned on making it my pillow for the night.

My disappointment was interrupted as a commotion rippled through the camp. Four North Carolina volunteers had been caught in a desertion ploy. We were summoned to the edge of the plantation where four men were tied to the backs of wagons with their shirts off.

A British officer read the verdicts ranging from five hundred lashes to a thousand. A burly British officer removed his red coat and was handed a leather cat-o'-nine-tails, a thick whip with nine smaller strands attached. The man sentenced to a thousand lashes turned his head, giving an icy stare to a colonial volunteer, apparently the man who informed his superiors about the desertion. The colonial looked away.

"One. Two. Three…" Each lash was announced with the slapping sound of leather on flesh.

At first, each blow made me flinch. I couldn't help it. I diverted my attention to the former conspirator. He watched in horror as his former friends shrieked with each strike. After a few minutes, I was numb to the sound and was left with the image of shredded skin and blood. My stomach gagged, and I held back an urge to vomit.

"It'll be too soon if I never have to see a man get whipped again," said Mark as we headed back to our camp.

"No kidding. That sound. It will take me hours to get it off my mind."

The flogging dampened our spirits and we fell asleep listening to songs of the cicadas interrupted only by the rhythmic flogging sound of leather on flesh as it replayed in my mind.

A few hours later, something jarred me from sleep. I woke to find George Washington standing over me, pointing a pistol at my head.

* * *

"Get up," he said.

I was disoriented having been in a deep sleep, and for a moment couldn't make sense of time or place. The sky was almost pitch black and the only light came from a small lantern held by Mr. Alton. Some of the soldiers around me started to stir, but no one woke.

"Get up," he said again, pulling me by the arm. "Him too." He pointed to Mark.

Mr. Alton moved to wake up Mark.

"What's this about?" I said. "What's going on?"

"You can explain yourself in a moment." His arms were flexed and his movements sharp. I had heard of Washington's famous temper and now I found myself on the business end of it. I didn't know why.

"Okay, okay," I said.

"Huh?" exclaimed Mark as he was woken from his slumber. The rest of the party woke up with Mark, as well as a few others sleeping around us. Perry, who always had something to say, said nothing. William sat up, staring vacant at us being hauled away.

"That way," Washington said, pointing to the trees ahead of us.

I could barely see. The only light came from the lantern Alton was carrying. Mark was behind me, followed by Washington and Alton.

"I can't lead the way in the dark," I said, irritated.

Alton moved up front and led us away from the camp. In the hand not carrying the lantern, he carried a rolled up blanket.

There was a man waiting for us about thirty feet away, an Indian from what I could see in the low light. He held a lantern in one hand.

"Mister Montour. Thank you for meeting us," said Washington. "I apologize for having you walk all this way through the dark. I did not want to alert any of the officers as to what we found until we were sure."

"What's happening?" asked Mark.

"This was found today along the side of the road," said Washington. He took the blanket from Alton and held it up. It wasn't a blanket. It was my overcoat.

"My jacket?" I said.

"Yes, it was discovered by one of the grenadiers during today's march. I happened to see it and recognized it as being yours. I took it from him with the intention of returning it to you when I noticed this." He reached in the inside pocket and pulled out folded pieces of paper.

Shit. My notes on the inauguration and Casanova's letter.

The paper looked old and worn. He unfolded them and held them up to the light so Montour could see. Ink had run where it had gotten wet, but the hand-drawn map of New York was still clear.

"You two are French spies," he said.

"No, no, no," I said. "It's a note from a friend."

"Who? Your French contact? I cannot read this one. It is written in French. These are plans for New York. Are the French planning an invasion of New York? There are times listed for an inauguration and a church service. I am not sure of the meaning yet."

"No, Giacomo Casanova. The note is from Casanova."

"Casanova?" said Mark.

"Yes, he wrote me a message when we were in Prague. I put it in my jacket pocket and forgot about it. It's written in French—I don't even know what it says. I haven't translated it yet."

"You brought something—back?" Mark's tone was incredulous. The cords on his neck strained as he stiffened.

"We shall see what it says momentarily." Washington handed the message to Montour.

The Indian took the note. His features looked European—probably inherited from a white-skinned father or mother. He read the note slowly, *"Hatred kills the unhappy wretch who delights in nursing it in his bosom. Do not let this happen to you or hate me. Tell her how you feel. Submit to her without trying to conquer. Someday you will understand. – Casanova."*

Everyone was silent for a moment.

"What does it mean?" asked Washington.

"It means we're not spies," I said, embarrassed and irritated. "The map of New York and the times listed are for an event we planned on attending. The French would never be stupid—or brave—enough to invade."

"Do you love her? Was this worth it?" asked Mark.

We had just been woken up in the middle of the night by George Washington himself, and Mark was worried that I was in love with Lillian. What the hell?

"No," I said softly. "Maybe under different circumstances. Not now. I just want to make it though this and get back home."

"Who?" asked Washington.

"A mutual friend," said Mark. "Someone he should *not* be thinking about in that manner."

"Can we go now?" I asked.

"I suppose it was all a misunderstanding," said Washington, finally calming down. "I apologize for doubting you. After last year's experience, I have no trust for the French. Please accept my sincere apologies." He handed me the jacket and the note.

Alton led us back to our campsite and left us to face our companions and explain what happened. Washington walked back with Montour.

"Washington found an inappropriate note in John's jacket written in French. He thought we were spies," said Mark.

"How inappropriate?" asked Patterson.

"It was advice, really," I said.

"About a girl," added Mark. The anger had not left his voice.

"Ooh," said everyone all at once. The tension lifted, but I was still a little frazzled. I know Mark was angry—I'm guessing he had *inappropriate* feelings too, but I was irritated with myself for even bringing the note and for not taking the time to read it in the privacy of my own room.

"You buggering the same girl?" said Perry.

Leave it to Perry to say something crude. "No," I said.

We laid down to try to get some sleep. Mark moved his blanket further from mine onto the outskirts of our campsite.

I tossed and turned the rest of the night, thinking about Washington and Casanova—and Mark and Lillian. What if Washington had been a *shoot first, ask questions later* kind of guy? We would have been screwed. Maybe my journal wasn't such a good idea after all. *What if my bringing Casanova's letter was the reason we were stuck in this reality in the first place?* Crap. I would have to ask Mark after he calmed down. Maybe that was the source of his anger. Relief finally came when dawn broke.

I was tired and grumpy. I was sick of the army-issued bread and needed a long shower and a shave. Washington approached as I sat in our campsite, staring at the trees in the distance. Mark had wandered off somewhere and I sat alone.

"I am regretful for last night," he said. "I truly am. I feel foolish for coming to a conclusion before gathering evidence. It will not happen again."

"It's okay," I said. "Anyone would have done the same thing. Thanks for not shooting first and asking questions later."

He smiled and handed me his canteen. It was filled with rum —real rum—strong, not watered down like the stuff the soldiers were given every day.

"I understand how it feels to yearn for one who is unattainable. Someone you want to hold close more than anyone else, but cannot—because of duty or moral virtue. Feelings you wish you could obliterate, but are painfully revived because you know deep in your heart her feelings are reciprocated."

"Sally Fairfax?" I blurted out.

Shit.

"How would you know that?" he asked in a defensive tone.

"I'm sorry. Lucky guess."

"There is no luck involved, sir. There is no way for you to possibly know. Have you been reading my correspondence? I demand to know—"

I held up my hand to slow him down. "There is no need for you to worry. I wouldn't tell a soul. I know a lot of things about you—about this place. Just know that I am going to do everything in my power to make sure you return to her—to at least see her with your own eyes again. Even if you can never truly be together."

That seemed to depress him and his shoulders slumped.

"What is it about you? You appear at the edge of civilization and give me a vest that you say cannot be penetrated by blade or musket ball. Now you know things about my personal life that *not a soul* knows. Who are you?"

"Maybe you're not as discreet as you think you are." I had said too much already and was in jeopardy of blowing our only chance to return home if I hadn't already.

He bailed me out. "Maybe you are correct. I will be watching you, John Curry." He smiled. "Excuse me, nature calls."

He walked away without looking back. I had just had a heart-to-heart with George Washington—not the old, reserved in-control one—the young, passionate 23 year-old who almost shot me last night.

Mark avoided me for much of the day and the next. He wouldn't even sleep near me. When we started marching again, he started off without me, forcing me to catch up.

"Okay, spill it." I said. "Why the cold shoulder?"

"Do I really have to explain it to you?"

"Listen, there is nothing and I mean *nothing* going on between Lillian and me. I'll admit it. I was a little jealous in the carriage when Claude was hitting on her—and when I saw the way she melted into Casanova's arms, but it was more like a simple crush. I'm over it. Casanova must've noticed something and written the note. I didn't even know you liked her."

"You're an idiot. That has nothing to do with it. You jeopardized everything by bringing something back from the past. What else did you bring back?"

"Nothing—well, a playbill from the opera, but *that* was Lillian. She brought it for me."

"Why the hell would she do that? She should know better. Do you not understand that making stupid emotional decisions like that could be the difference in whether or not you have the ability to return home?" Mark's face reddened.

"I forgot about the note. I told Lillian *not* to bring back the playbill while we were at the opera. She's the one who didn't listen."

We made our way around an artillery piece that had broken a wheel and turned over. The wheel had already been repaired and eight sailors were trying to pull it back up and get it moving again. The British army used sailors from the Royal Navy to help move the heavy artillery through the wilderness and over the mountains. We ducked under some low-hanging branches on the edge of the road. Mark remained silent.

"So what we're doing now? Is this going to work?" I asked. "I mean, we already tried to go back once thinking we fixed the problem. What if Washington survives and history happens the way we think it's going to happen? Are we still stuck here? I mean —George Washington *didn't* wear a bullet-proof vest."

"I've been thinking about it *a lot,* and I don't know," he said.

"Was my bringing the note from Casanova the cause of all this?"

"I don't think so. I can't see how the events would be related. It has to be something else."

"Well, you're the genius. What does your gut tell you?"

"It tells me to keep pushing on. Maybe there's some variable we haven't considered. That's all we can do."

"Then let's keep pushing on. I promise not to try to take anything back from here that I shouldn't. You promise not to give me the cold shoulder anymore."

He didn't reply, and we rode in silence for a few minutes.

Mark finally spoke. "I love her."

Finally, the truth comes out. Now I know where the "womanizer" comment came from when we ate with Lillian.

I had been through Mark's crushes before. He was a genius when it came to academic or abstract thinking, but when it came to women, not so much. Melinda Fairfax—no relation to Sally that

I'm aware. He was in love with her in the fifth or sixth grade. He bought this silly little necklace and carried it to school with the intention of giving it to her. Every day, he chickened out for some reason or another. I don't think she ever knew how he felt.

"Does she know?"

His eyes were focused on the trail before us. "I've known her four years. She's never been anything but professional toward me. Do you know how many times I've wanted to ask her out, but didn't because I thought it would wreck our friendship? You come along, and she goes out of her way to treat you like crap—like she's in junior high or something. I *know* she likes you and it pisses me off."

She likes me?

I remained silent waiting for more. After nothing came, I said, "Look, I didn't know you liked her. I wouldn't mess up our friendship over a girl. She was a bitch to me, remember? She wasn't even *remotely* approachable until we were in Prague, and even then, she didn't show any interest. She wanted Casanova. Remember?"

"Casanova's an old man."

"Maybe she has daddy issues."

Mark laughed.

"Tell her how you feel when we get back," I said. "It's the only way you'll ever know. Maybe Casanova knew what he was talking about. *Hatred kills the unhappy wretch,* remember? That's advice from *freaking* Casanova. He's the top of the food chain when it comes to love. Tell her how you feel."

"I will, thanks." He looked me in the eye for the first time in two days. "I'm sorry I've been acting like I'm 14. All the stuff that's going on, and I get mad for this. It's stupid."

"There's rarely any logic in our emotions," I said. "I forgive you."

"Wow, now who's the genius?"

I smiled.

"I have one more confession," he said. He looked stressed again.

"Uh-oh. What?"

"It's about Casanova. I think I may have messed up. We didn't know how we were going to get into the opera. Lillian and I went weeks in advance of opening night to try to purchase tickets from the box office, but with no luck. That's when we ran into Casanova—it was unexpected, but cool, you know?"

I understood.

"He was in Prague to help with the production of the opera, so we had our *in* since we couldn't get tickets. Anyway, on the next scouting trip, we knew where we'd find Casanova and planned on running into him again. He was obviously interested in Lillian—who wouldn't be—and we spent the day talking. I couldn't understand anything he said, so the conversation centered on him and Lillian with an occasional attempt to include me."

I *really* understood that.

Mark reached back and rubbed his neck. "By the end of the day, I was starting to get frustrated. Partly, because of the obvious chemistry between Casanova and Lillian, and partly because we still hadn't been invited to opening night. I mean, that was the *point* of the trip. I started talking about things from the future: flying passengers across the continent, televisions—stuff like that. He couldn't understand English, so what would it matter? He stared at me, indifferent to anything I said—"

"It was you?" I said. "Lillian and I got questioned about clueing in Casanova on things from the future. I didn't know what Lawrence was talking about. He wrote a book or something—"

"Yes, I think I might have been the inspiration for the book. I could be wrong, but I don't think so. I never heard of it before we met him, but I looked it up after we got back, and sure enough, Casanova wrote a book about a futuristic society. It's called *Icosameron*."

"So he *did* speak English? That sneaky bastard."

"I guess he spoke enough. I thought we would have to go back and try the day over because we hadn't been invited to the opera, but sure enough, he invited Lillian at the end of the night. We never went back to repeat the day so—"

"That's messed up." A nervous laugh escaped my mouth. "You need to be off my case about changing the past from now on. Even I know better than to—"

"I get it," he said abruptly. "Listen, no one knows more than I how seemingly insignificant things can snowball. I just needed you to know—so we don't screw up anything else."

I thought about my conversation with Washington. I had just confessed my knowledge about his relationship—or at least his infatuation—with Sally Fairfax. What if I had just created my own snowball that would radically change history? What if Washington survived the war only to return home and consummate his relationship with his forbidden love? It would create a scandal that would ruin his reputation and eliminate any chance he had of leading the Revolution. More importantly, it would completely remove any possibility Mark and I had of returning home.

I kept this revelation to myself.

From the Journal of John Curry
Little Meadows
June 17th, 1755

We reached the Little Meadows yesterday after a long day of riding. We passed over Allegheny Mountain and forded the Savage Creek. It was one of the more difficult legs of the journey so far. When we reached the tops of the mountain passes, the views were spectacular. It's hard to fathom the need to attack and drive the French from a tiny fort in the middle of this wilderness because they're infringing on our space. There seems to be room for everyone.

I know it is technically not "my" space and there isn't really an "our" that I'm a part of, but having been in this army for so long now, it is hard not to adopt the "us against them" attitude.

It isn't hard to know where the army procession is at all times. Even if you can't see the long line of men, you can see buzzards circling overhead, slowly following the path of the army waiting for scraps left behind.

Mark and I both stopped shaving. We have no regular water supply and simply don't care anymore. Most of the soldiers have done the same and some have even discarded their overcoats so they don't have to carry them through the heat. The meticulous order that was so prevalent at Fort Duquesne is dissipating. The wilderness is assimilating its new residents, and only a few of us know it. You don't have to listen hard to know that many of the men in the ranks are unhappy.

Some of the officers are not helping. One admonished a group for looking like "undisciplined sand diggers." I watched another officer berate a wagon driver for not moving fast enough. There was nowhere for the wagon to go. He was in line like the rest of us. The driver apologized, but the officer wouldn't let up calling him a "lazy colonial laggard." Finally the man jumped down from the wagon and got in the officer's face telling him to "piss off." The driver was young, huge and angry. The officer lost his mind and swung his saber at the man—hitting him with the flat of the blade. The man defended himself by lashing the officer with his horsewhip. Then he jumped on the officer and started pummeling him. They were separated and the driver was immediately sentenced to 500 lashes. He stood there eyeing the officer during his punishment until he finally passed out. I don't know if he lived or not, but something like that should never have happened. What a waste. It is this kind of mentality that is going to cost the British their colonies.

Well, maybe.

We have been told that we will camp here for three days to allow the crew clearing the trees to make some headway. I just hope order is maintained around here before the men start killing each other.

* * *

Washington woke us at four a.m. to let us know we'd been transferred to the Virginia light cavalry regiment under the command of Captain Stewart. The officers feared the army was moving too slow, and the men were growing restless. Following Washington's advice, the army was dividing and creating a *Flying Column* to move more swiftly to Duquesne. Washington was visibly excited that his counsel was being followed, but he didn't look well. Even in the low light, I could tell he was uncomfortable.

"Are you okay?" I asked.

"I'm fine," he said. "Just having minor stomach problems. I'll survive."

Mark and I exchanged troubled looks.

"See you on the road," he said, then got on his horse and galloped off.

"What do you think?" I asked Mark.

"I think he hasn't been boiling his water like we have. He's made this journey before. He's young and strong. Probably thinks he's bulletproof."

"He is—he's wearing your vest."

"Let's hope so."

We said a quick goodbye to our friends before riding to join our new troop.

"Don't get *snabbed*," advised Perry.

"I don't think the French will be using swords," I said.

"Not stabbed, you beef-head. *Snabbed*. Killed." Perry rolled his eyes.

"Save a few French for us," called Boyce as we rode away.

There would be plenty.

Captain Stewart was a Scotsman who told us we were Braddock's bodyguard and to act accordingly as gentlemen and soldiers. We were given twenty-four rounds of ammunition and told to travel light. Given that we had already been on the road for almost two weeks, I wasn't sure how much lighter we could get. At least we were still on horseback.

We moved faster, but not by much. The crews were still clearing trees in front of us. Our troop headed the flying column with riders in the front and on either side. Behind the horses was a detachment of thirty sailors who's job it was to help move the cannon over the mountains and rough terrain. Then came the long wagon train containing 550 of the best soldiers, along with Braddock and his *military family,* including Washington, riding at the center. Then more of our Virginia troop. Mark and I were part of the rear guard.

At night, the layout of the column was the same except for pickets placed in a perimeter around the camp to prevent any kind of sneak attack.

After two days of travel, our *flying* column made only minor progress to an area known as Bear Camp and paused for two days to wait for the road to be cleared. Washington looked terrible. He lay face-down on a blanket on the ground outside his tent. His face was pale and he looked haggard. Beads of sweat collected on his forehead.

"Are you okay?" I asked as Mark and I entered his tent.

"It's the flux," he said. "I've had it a few days now. Alton has it too. Can't kick this fever. It hurts to sit down."

"Here," said Mark handing him his canteen. "Drink this. You need to get water into your system."

"I have rum," said Washington.

"No, you need water."

"He's right," I added. "The alcohol isn't going to help you. It will only make you weaker."

Washington took the canteen and drank from it.

"Keep it," said Mark. "The water is safe to drink."

Washington closed his eyes and dozed off.

* * *

"He looks bad," I said to Mark as we walked away.

"Smells bad too. I hope the doctors don't try to do anything stupid like bleeding him. It will only make him weaker."

"At least we know he'll survive — at least long enough to see the battle. We don't have to worry too much."

From the Journal of John Curry
Fort Necessity
June 26th, 1755

We're getting closer now. We've encountered more signs of Indians. Two days ago, we came across an abandoned camp that must have slept close to 200 Indians. They'd stripped the bark off the trees and painted warnings on them in an effort to frighten us—stick-figure drawings in red depicting Indians scalping British soldiers. I kept looking for a sign that said, "I'd turn back if I were you," or "Haunted Forest: Witches Castle: 1 mile," but I couldn't find one.

Some men laughed at the drawings. I did not. I knew what was coming.

We rode on without Washington. He was too sick to move. The doctor told him if he kept going, it would kill him. Of course, that only made him want to go more. It took a direct intervention from Braddock himself to keep Washington back. The general promised he would bring Washington up before the assault on Duquesne. This placated Washington enough to stay.

Yesterday, a wagon driver was ambushed by hostile Indians and shot in the stomach while tending to his horses. He was able to escape and make it back to the main body, but he died shortly after. Four other wagon drivers were also killed in various attacks when they strayed from the main body or from the safety of our pickets.

The few Indian guides the army has reported seeing hostile Indians everywhere in the forest. Speaking of Indians, we don't have many on our side. All of those Indians that were at Cumberland when we arrived have deserted. They took their families home and promised to return, but none did. I don't know if it's nerves, but I continuously have the feeling I'm being watched. The suspense of waiting for the unknown is the hardest part of this march. I know the army will reach the battlefield, but I don't know who will get killed along the way.

We're currently camped at the ruins of Fort Necessity where Washington surrendered to the French last year. Human bones and disabled guns are located all around the site. I wish he was here for me to talk to him about it. I will have to remember to ask him when I see him again.

From the Journal of John Curry
Northeast of the Youghiogheny River
June 29th, 1755

At least it's dry today. We spent yesterday crossing the Youghiogheny River in the pouring rain. The river was only three feet deep, but it was very broad—about two football fields wide. During the crossing, men swore they saw Indians waiting to ambush us and started shooting wildly into the trees. There may or may not have been Indians. Mark and I didn't see any.

We're deep into enemy territory—even though we're making this march to drive the French out of lands claimed by the British. The forest and undergrowth is very thick. Even on horseback, it's hard to see the line of men right in front of you. We passed a second Indian camp recently abandoned with the campfires still burning. More images were painted on the trees along with the names Rochefort, Chauraudray and Picauday. No one laughed this time. I don't know what the names mean, but the French names have added weight to the threats.

Everyone is on edge. It is amazing how the mood of the army can swing from one extreme to the other. Three days ago, we crossed the last ridge, Chestnut, before we reach Duquesne. Everyone was relieved—especially the sailors whose job it is to move the heavy cannon. To celebrate, Colonel Halkett ordered extra rum rations and everyone was in high spirits. I couldn't help but think that it might have been one of the last moments of happiness some of the men would ever experience—myself included. We camped at Christopher Gist's plantation ruins. I have read about him—I know he's friends with Washington, but I don't know if he's a part of this expedition.

Our sentries are being fired on every night—not a real attack, but enough to cause men to lose sleep, and I think that's the point. I haven't had a good night's sleep in two months, but this is worse. We camped in the same spot all day to give the men rest and to give the road crew time to clear more trees. Bread is being baked for the last leg of the journey and smells fantastic. Even though we're mostly sleep deprived, the overall spirit of the army is strong—for the moment.

TWENTY-THREE

July 6th, 1755

We were less than twenty miles from Fort Duquesne, but Mark and I knew we'd never see the fort.

Many of the men spoke of how we were just a few days from spending the night at Duquesne. Our old commander, Major Stephen, was just called up to support the main column so we were reunited with our friends Perry, Nicholson, Patterson and Boyce. They brought much needed supplies of flour and beef, which was good, because we were down to three-quarters rations.

We got to talk to them briefly in the morning before setting out.

"We thought we'd be hearing the cannon leveling Fort Duquesne when they finally called up," said Patterson. "Thanks for saving some French for us to kill."

"Just be careful when the fighting starts. It will probably happen in the next three days. The French and Indians aren't going to play nice," I warned.

Mark gave me a stern look.

Screw it. We already have. We don't have any guarantees that we're going to make it home anyway, so if I can save another couple of lives—especially of my friends, I'm going to do it.

"We aren't afraid of any Indians," said Patterson. "They tried harassing us the whole time we were bringing the supplies up, and our pickets always saw them and shot first. They are cowards and always run at the first sign of trouble."

"Just keep your head down when the real shooting starts. Listen to Major Stephen and find a tree for cover."

"There's no way we're gonna die dunghill," said Perry. "We'll leave that to you and glass-eyes."

Mark swore under his breath.

I eyed Perry. "Just keep your head down, *beef-head*."

* * *

Around eleven, we heard shots coming from just in front of us. We saw smoke rising where Indians had shot at the part of the column near where the cattle were being herded. It was a quick, guerilla-type attack, but in a matter of minutes a soldier and a woman were both scalped, and another man shot in the shoulder.

I watched the soldiers escort him past us. The man held his shoulder, his face plastered in a painful wince. Given the limited skills of the army physicians, his wound could be a death sentence. I hoped the shot was clean.

Two hours later we heard shots fired near the front of the column. Men all around us started to panic. The army's blood was up.

"Don't worry," I said to Mark, and to anyone in our immediate vicinity. "It isn't happening today."

"I know, but people are still dying. I mean, they just scalped—a woman."

"We're invading their territory—not the other way around."

"Are you justifying what they just did?"

"No, but I can understand it. People do shitty things to other people. It's the way of the world."

That night we learned that during the confusion of the attack, a British soldier accidentally shot one of our remaining Indian guides who happened to be the son of Chief Monacatuca. Not good. Braddock thought it would be prudent to give a full military funeral for Monacatuca's son, as the Chief was one of the few Indians that still supported the army. I heard two soldiers joking that all it meant was that we'd have one less Indian to kill.

We were to the rear of the column, so we didn't have to attend the funeral.

Shitty things do happen, especially during wartime.

From the Journal of John Curry
South Bank of the Monongahela River
July 8th, 1755

I'm starting to freak out. It's one thing to talk about and prepare for an upcoming battle. It is a quite another to actually fight. Mark and I know what is coming tomorrow and none of the men around us do. I don't think it's fair. I feel somehow responsible for sending these men to their deaths. The British soldiers were mostly drafted into the army against their will or because there were no other options. The American volunteers are seeking glory or a better station in life so maybe they know the risk they're taking. To top it off, my horse, Old Bob, gave out today and died. I didn't have the heart to shoot him, so one of the other riders in our troop did it. It was a pretty emotional experience for me, but the result is I'm walking now. At least I can keep some of my belongings on Mark's horse, who seems to be keeping up okay. We marched eight miles today. I had to walk about half of them after Old Bob gave out sometime after noon.

The British officers are entirely too overconfident and we can hear them encouraging their soldiers, saying things like, "Don't worry boys. Once they see us on the battlefield, they will run away like rabbits through the trees." Only the colonial officers are trying to talk sense into their men. Major Stephen saw Mark and me today and told us to remember our training and find a tree to aid our cover while fighting.

Washington was called up today. We didn't see him, but we saw the covered wagon that brought him to the front. If someone is so sick that they cannot ride or walk, what business do they have on the battlefield? I guess it's the same thing athletes do when they insist on playing while injured. People do stupid things for glory and to stroke their ego.

The past two days have been long and frustrating. Two days ago, we started following a route along a ridge that would lead us directly to Duquesne. Braddock felt that the path was too dangerous and open to ambush so we turned back. It was a nightmare of confusion, and at the end of the day, we made little progress. It was a total waste. What if we continued? Would the outcome be any different?

Mark and I are going to try to visit Washington tonight to see how he's holding up. I know the fate that awaits most of these men, and my stomach is in knots. Is Washington going to make it? Has all of this sacrifice been worth it? Will Mark survive? Will I?

I miss my little girl. If this doesn't work, will she even be conceived? I know Mark would try to make me feel better by explaining about parallel universes, but I still feel like the weight of the world is on me. I have to keep Washington alive.

* * *

Mark and I found Washington resting in his tent, surprisingly in good spirits.

"How are you feeling?" I asked.

"Better, I feel I am fit for duty now," he said. His color was much better than it had been the last time we saw him. "The fever is finally gone and my stomach is returning to normal. The doctor gave me one of the best medicines in the world to aid my recovery. I would highly recommend it." He held up a small glass jar. The label read: DR. JAMES'S POWDER.

There were no ingredients listed, only a London address. I could only imagine what was inside. Hopefully, something more suitable than dragon scales and unicorn horn. Washington looked better, and that was enough for me.

"Riding is a different matter. I'll have to strap pillows to my saddle to ride. The flux caused me some painful hemorrhoids." Washington displayed an embarrassed smile. "I am afraid Mr. Alton is still recovering."

Mark spoke up. "Do you have your vest? I think we will find the French tomorrow."

The look on Washington's face revealed he did not have it with him.

"No, I regret I left it with my baggage. During my sickness, I completely forgot about it until it was too late to turn back. I am sorry."

"You need protection," I said. "You can have mine." I took off my shirt and vest and handed it to him. The feeling of danger enveloped me immediately. "Please put this on tonight. You're going to need this tomorrow."

"How can you be so sure?" he asked. "We probably won't reach Duquesne until tomorrow evening. There will be no engagement tomorrow—maybe not for two days or maybe not at all if the French capitulate."

I decided to throw caution into the wind. "Remember when I told you that I know a lot of things about this place?"

He nodded. Through my peripheral vision, I noticed Mark tense up.

"I have a pretty good feeling that we're going to meet the French tomorrow."

He didn't argue with me—the strange man with the perfect teeth who had brought him a musket ball-proof vest and knew about his secret infatuation with a married woman. Maybe he didn't need any more convincing. He simply nodded and accepted the vest.

He sat up and removed his shirt. He was muscular with a broad chest. He had the physique of a professional athlete, built like a tight end in football. He slid on the vest and it fit him well.

"Be careful tomorrow," I said.

"Godspeed to you," he said to us as we left his tent.

* * *

As we walked back to our camp, Mark turned to me. "You just lost your protection."

"Now we're even. Besides, the French and Indians will be targeting officers—not colonials wearing brown coats. Maybe I'll blend in. I'm just glad I wasn't given a bright pink coat to wear to the opera."

Mark smiled. "Hey, we still have a chance to make this right. Washington left his vest back with his baggage. That means he wouldn't have been wearing it during the battle which explains why the time machine didn't work when we went back for it. I think we might be able to make it home after all."

A blanket of stress lifted away. My body felt lighter. "That's the best news I've heard in weeks. Let's make a strong effort not to get killed."

Mark laughed. "I'm riding with the cavalry tomorrow."

Bam! The stress returned. I turned toward him. "You're not marching with us?"

"I'll camp with you, but I want to make sure we clear the way for everyone. Once contact is made, I'll move closer to Washington. When the gunfire starts, try to make your way to us."

I didn't like the idea of splitting up, not this close to the defining moments of this campaign—and our lives. "Are you sure it's a good idea to split up? Now?"

"I'll be okay. There's going to be a lot of confusion. I think it's best knowing at least one of us will be there when the fighting starts. You'd do the same if you were in my shoes."

Maybe I would—maybe I wouldn't. I had been counting on the vest protecting Washington, not Mark or myself. As far as I was concerned, we had done our part. It might even be a good idea to go home now. Sneak off in the dark and get out of Dodge.

I had a vision of being caught by British pickets trying to sneak out of camp and the subsequent flogging in front of the army before the morning's march. I could hear the officer's voice ringing out as the cat-o'-nine-tails thwacked my bare back. *One... Two... Three...*

No thanks. I would see this through.

"Okay, I'll head for Washington the first sign of trouble."

* * *

We camped with the members of Major Stephen's Virginia volunteers. Since I no longer had a horse, I was no good to the cavalry.

Fires were prohibited so we wouldn't give our position away, but that was silly. The enemy had been dogging our movements constantly for the past week and a half. They knew exactly where we were. All of the men knew this.

When we returned, Patterson was boasting to the rest. "I'm going to show those Indians that we're the ones to fear. They think that pictures and warnings painted on trees are going to scare us. We will see who gets scared when they face the might of the British Empire tomorrow."

The men nodded and boasted in agreement—all except Nicholson.

"Have you ever killed a man?" asked William. He had a brooding, far-away look in his eyes.

It was the most I'd heard him speak since we met. Mark and I sat down and made ourselves comfortable.

"No," said Patterson after a brief hesitation. "But I will tomorrow." He smiled and looked around hoping his friends would agree with him.

Nicholson held his gaze. "I have. There's nothing glorious in killing a man."

"Bollocks," said Perry. "Let him boast, Willie boy. Why'd you join up if you didn't want to kill the French and their savages?"

Boyce chimed in. "Yeah, Nicholson. We're going to be heroes tomorrow."

Nicholson turned his attention to Boyce. "My name isn't Nicholson. It's Charles. William Charles."

We all looked at each other.

"I didn't sign up to kill the *French and their savages*. I signed up because it was either that or get shipped to the Caribbean doing forced labor."

"What'd you do?" asked Boyce.

"I killed a man. A slave overseer of a plantation. I lived in George Town. I was caught with the daughter of the plantation owner and her father sent his overseer to teach me a lesson. Well, I taught him a lesson and smashed his head with a wagon spoke. I didn't know what to do, so I fled south to Alexandria, but was caught. I could either go back to George Town and face sentencing, or the sheriff gave me the option of joining up with the army. He would take my bounty for signing on, which was more than the reward Peggy's father would have paid. I don't know why I changed my name. It just happened when I signed on. I told the officer Nicholson instead of Charles."

We all sat for a moment in silence.

"Do your duty," he continued, "Just don't pretend that it is glorious killing someone. It's not."

Mark spoke up. "Just listen to Major Stephen tomorrow. He knows how to fight the Indians—and make sure you take cover. The British are going to line up and give the French a nice big, red target to aim for. Don't get caught standing your ground like that."

"Mark's right. Don't try to be a hero," I said. "The world is full of dead heroes. You might think there's glory or honor acting brave, but it won't keep you alive."

"You just want to get back to your woman," said Patterson. "Maybe you should stick to writing her love letters—in French."

Everyone laughed and that was okay. I just hoped they would listen to Mark's advice. Tomorrow was going to be hell.

TWENTY-FOUR

July 9th, 1755

You would think that knowing you're going to walk into a hornet's nest in the morning would keep you awake at night, but I slept soundly. In fact, it was the best night's sleep I had since the whole adventure started. Maybe it was my body telling me, "You're going to die tomorrow. I thought I would give you one more night of peace."

I hoped not.

They woke us at dawn to prepare to march, but like so much of this expedition, we got ready and waited—and waited—for the order. I could already hear the chopping sounds from the road crew clearing a path for the army and artillery. Braddock expected to encounter some resistance this morning and sent Colonel Gage with a detachment of infantry to provide cover for the army crossing the Monongahela.

Mark had already left. No note. No goodbye. Maybe it was better this way. I would catch up with him as soon as I heard the first shots.

It was hot and most of the men didn't have time for breakfast, causing some grumbling. The only thing keeping the men from openly rebelling was the prospect of this expedition being concluded in a matter of hours. Courtesy of Mark, I found one of my saddlebags next to where I slept. I ate a piece of stale bread and some dried beef and gave the rest to William—*Charles*—and Perry, who were close by. There wasn't enough left for everyone.

The army had begun marching at two in the morning. Our orders were to cross the Monongahela River, follow a parallel path next to the river for about two miles and then cross back over the river at a former trading post that had been abandoned and burned.

By eight, our unit of Virginia volunteers finally marched across the first ford. The water was only knee high due to the drought that had lingered most of the summer. The cool water offered modest relief countering the effects of the scorching sun above us.

Around noon, we came to the second crossing. We were part of the rear guard, but I could see Braddock and Washington crossing the river. General Braddock rode in full military dress, complete with a bright-red sash. A leopard-skin saddle pad was prominently displayed, putting on a show for the men and the French, who no doubt watched.

Washington looked much better, the only sign of his sickness was the pillow strapped between himself and his saddle.

Surrounding the general on all sides was the Virginia cavalry. Mark rode confidently on his horse, Kwolek. Gone was the frightened, first-time rider hunched over holding on for dear life. Mark had learned to ride—well.

The British regulars marched in battle formation with their regimental flags waving high while the fifers and drummers performed the "Grenadiers' March." If the French had somehow forgotten to set their alarms, this would surely wake them up. The sound would carry for miles.

The rear guard finished crossing a half hour later. The men

reformed on the bank, and the procession moved forward through a clearing in the forest.

"It will be an easy March to Duquesne now," said Patterson to no one in particular. "If they wouldn't attack us in the river, they wont dare attack us here—"

A volley of shots rang out ahead, about a half a mile away. The battle had begun.

* * *

Major Stephen sprang into action giving orders to the Virginians. "Move up boys!" He shouted in his thick, Scottish accent. "Double time!"

A few volunteers replied with a "Huzzah," and we followed the Major up the trail listening to the increasing frequency of musket shots as the battle heated up.

My mouth dried out instantly, and my heart started to pound. I checked my ammunition as we moved forward. I had twenty-four rounds.

After another four-hundred yards, we were no longer in the clearing—we were in dense forest. British regulars formed up in battle lines, facing both sides of the road, firing their weapons aimlessly at the trees. The right side of the road sloped upward, and I saw puffs of smoke from French and Indian muskets as bullets rained down on the redcoats in the road. British soldiers dropped every second in groups of two and three.

Soldiers retreating from the front of the line crashed into the reinforcements trying to hold the line.

Stephens called out, "This way!" and darted off into the trees heading up the slope. The Virginians let out another "Huzzah" and followed him.

I ignored them and pressed forward toward the main body of the army in search of Washington. I raced along the side of the main road, keeping my head down.

It was almost impossible to see through the trees, undergrowth and smoke. Injured soldiers cried out in pain only to be drowned out by the primal war whoops of the Indian attackers. I found Washington after about fifty yards yelling at the men, trying to rally them.

Musket balls flew everywhere, destroying branches and shattering bones. I was within ten feet of Washington when his horse let out a scream, lifted up on its hind legs, and collapsed to the ground. Washington tumbled down with it.

The battle seemed to play out in slow motion. I could make out the beads of sweat on his forehead, and the look of surprise on his face. He lay on the ground— momentarily stunned.

Oh no. I'm too late. He's been killed.

Slowly, his head turned and he inspected his surroundings. He leapt to his feet, injury free. He yelled to one of the attendants for another horse. The speed of the battle returned to normal.

I let out an audible sigh of relief.

Braddock was close, a white handkerchief tied to his hat and saber raised, yelling at the men. "Reform! Reform!" he screamed. "Reform, damn you!" He swung the flat of his blade at a soldier running from the fray and knocked him to the ground. "Back to the line!"

I recognized soldiers from the cavalry rallying around the general. Many of them off their horses firing from cover whenever possible. Robert Stewart, my old commander, stood there, yelling something unintelligible. I couldn't see Mark.

Where is he? He's supposed to be watching Washington's back.

Braddock's horse was hit and slumped down. He calmly

dismounted and waited for an aid to bring him another mount. He screamed at the retreating troops rallying them to, "Form up and fight like the King's soldiers!"

It occurred to me that I hadn't seen one Indian or French soldier yet. All I saw was smoke. I heard the war cries, but had yet to see anyone. A muzzle flash and its accompanying puff of smoke interrupted my thought. I saw an Indian dart from a tree and take refuge behind another up the ridge.

Men continued to fall around me. Groups of British regulars formed their lines and fired in the direction of the trees, following the steady staccato orders issued from drummers and the hoarse shrieks of officers. No sooner would an officer scream an order than he would be cut down. Drummers were also targets. They huddled together in clusters, five and six deep, seeking safety in numbers and relying on their training. All they did was provide a large, red bullseye for the Frenchmen and Indians firing upon them.

"Take cover, you idiots," I screamed, but no one heard—or they wouldn't listen.

Washington sat atop another horse, riding back and forth barking orders at the men impervious to the musket balls whizzing all around him. I made my way closer, intent on protecting him. I saw a French soldier behind a tree line up Washington in his sights and pull the trigger. He missed.

Or did he?

My eyes followed the Frenchman as he inspected his rifle with a quizzical expression. His hesitation was brief and he reloaded to take another shot.

Not on my watch.

I held up my musket, determined to take him out before he got off another shot. The hours of drilling came to me like second nature, and I flawlessly loaded my gun. Major Stephen would have been proud.

The Frenchman was still reloading. He peered around the tree to take aim, and I fired. Bark exploded around his face, and he dropped his weapon. His hands immediately covered his eyes. After a moment, he bent down and picked up his gun. Within seconds, he had run off into the trees intent on finding another target.

"Did you get him?" Washington's piercing gaze caught my attention. He was smiling.

"Almost," I said, picking up my ramrod and reloading my weapon. "Keep your head down."

Washington laughed and resumed his command, yelling at the British troops and telling them to keep their heads.

I scanned the area for Mark expecting to see him any minute, but he was nowhere to be found.

Where is he? He should be here by now.

Braddock had another horse shot out from under him. He swore loudly and called for another horse. Men in full retreat ran past him. "Fucking cowards," he yelled, taking lethal swings at them with his saber.

One man dodged his swing and ran to take cover under a tree. Braddock took a few heavy steps toward the man and ran him through with his sword.

Jesus. He's one of ours.

No hesitation. No remorse. He calmly re-sheathed his sword and returned to his command.

The British officers repeatedly tried to reform their ranks. After a flurry of fire and smoke, the line would be decimated and panic would resume.

Men started to shoot anywhere there was smoke or

movement. I watched a group of Virginians move up the rise to take the high ground from the enemy. Quickly, they cleared out the Indians who had no intentions of standing head to head in a fair fight. A regiment of British soldiers mistook the smoke from the Virginian guns as enemy musket fire.

"To the trees," yelled their British officer. "Make ready!"

"No, those are Virginians," I yelled. The officer didn't hear me. I ran toward them, shouting, "No! No!"

I'm here to protect Washington. I stopped and returned to where Washington was. The Virginians were soon annihilated by their own army.

I stayed as close to Washington as I could. Changing history be damned, I was looking for someone to shoot—someone to kill. I have heard stories of soldiers having their blood up during battle and losing rational thought. This is what I felt now. Washington had once said that there was something charming about the sound of bullets during battle. I barely noticed anything other than trying to seek out a target. I started to do the same thing as the panic-stricken soldiers. I started firing at any puff of smoke I saw—and it was frustrating, because I couldn't see anything but smoke.

I felt a musket ball whiz by my head. It hit the tree behind me. I scanned the forest to see who fired the shot. Nothing. Just smoke and—then I saw him. The same Frenchman I had encountered earlier. He was reloading.

Motherfucker.

I ducked down and moved up the ridge through the bushes toward where the Frenchman had fired. I emerged a few feet from where I thought he would be, but he had moved. I looked around the ridge and saw nothing but trees and smoke. Another musket ball passed over my head. I held up my rifle but found no target.

I continued to crawl toward the smoke and it dawned on me that I was sitting in no-man's land, directly in the crossfire between the attacking French and Indians and the British army firing up the hill toward where I was.

This is stupid. I need to get out of here.

I turned to head down the hill when I heard a scream. The Frenchman lunged at me, swinging his musket. I dove out of the way and turned my own musket toward him and fired.

And missed.

Of course. All the training and good marksmanship went out the door as soon as I was faced with a living target, trying to kill me.

He came at me again, swinging violently with his weapon. I jumped back and plunged down the hill, rolling about ten yards, and landed in a small clearing. There was no tree nearby to hide behind, so I grabbed my gun and braced myself for the next attack.

The Frenchman stood at the spot where I had just fallen. He glared at me and started to reload. Blood covered the right side of his face, probably caused by splinters from my own shot at him. He had a dark-brown, bushy unibrow that formed a V-shaped scowl over his eyes.

Gisçard? Holy shit. He did know me.

I grabbed a fresh cartridge and bit off the top of the paper, spitting the excess to the ground.

Poured powder into the priming pan…

Half-cocked the trigger…

Set the gun down and poured the remaining powder down the barrel of the muzzle…

Spit the musket ball down the shaft…

Pulled out my ramrod and shoved the rest of the wadding

down the barrel and rammed it in. The ramrod refused to slide back into place, so I dropped it to the ground and took aim.

Gisçard had raised his musket to fire.

I pulled my trigger.

A flash of smoke erupted from his gun as he fired. He let out a scream and dropped his weapon. He stood there, bent over, looking at his hand. Blood poured from stumps where his fingers used to be.

I pictured him in Prague, revealing his mangled hand, aiming his pistol at my head.

America. You.

A hail of gunfire erupted around him. The British soldiers finally had a target. Remarkably, Gisçard was untouched. Maybe it wasn't all that remarkable. I knew where he would be in thirty years. He gained his composure and darted off into the trees without looking back.

I slumped down to the ground, stunned by what had happened. I had just come incredibly close to being killed by the younger version of the man who tried to kill me during my trip to Prague.

That's really messed up.

Since I still found myself in the middle of the kill zone, I crawled my way back toward Washington. It was difficult navigating through the smoke and thick brush, but I eventually found him.

Washington sat on his horse, cool and calm, providing an excellent target to any ambitious Frenchman or Indian.

God damn it. Get down!

His eyes scanned the trees for men to direct or for an enemy to shoot. He located a group of Virginian volunteers and yelled words of encouragement. "Take the battle to them, boys!"

Officers ran to Braddock trying to receive orders in an attempt to turn the tide of a battle they were clearly losing. One officer approached and pleaded with Braddock to let them take the high ground, but Braddock ignored him.

"Form up!" he kept yelling, looking at no one in particular. "God save the King!"

Washington rode to the general and cried out, "Let me post my Virginians behind those trees and take the fight to the Indians in their own way."

Braddock barked at him, "I've a mind to run you through the body! We'll sup today in Fort Duquesne or else in Hell. Form up!"

Idiot.

Bodies lay everywhere. Retreating soldiers reached down to pull unused ammunition from the dead. Others fired their last musket ball and took off toward the river as fast as their feet would take them.

It went on like this for three hours.

Slowly, we retreated back toward the river. A wounded officer staggered toward Braddock and started babbling an incoherent report that sounded like Italian. Finally, he pointed up toward the ground above us and yelled out, "For God's sake, the rising on our right!"

Braddock looked up and nodded his head. "Burton, the clearing," he called out, and pointed in the same direction.

The British officer acknowledged him and led his men up the slope. Minutes later, Burton's men were cut down in a hail of gunfire. The advance turned into a hurried retreat as soldiers ignored the imploring cries for order from the remaining officers. It was too little, too late.

Braddock had another horse shot out from under him. He swore once more and got up a little more slowly this time, the effects of prolonged battle and depleted adrenaline finally kicking in. Another horse was brought to him. As he climbed up, he let out a scream and fell back to the ground. I looked around in an attempt to see where the shot came from. A colonial volunteer, unfamiliar to me, gave an icy stare for a moment and then moved in the direction of his company.

I ran toward Washington to tell him what I saw, and who did it, but he had already leapt off his horse to go to the general's side. One of Braddock's attendants was also there.

"Help me," Washington commanded as I reached him. Braddock had been shot in the side. All of the other officers had been wounded or killed. Only Washington remained unhurt. The ground all around us was soaked red from the blood of the dead.

Washington and I picked up the general by his large red sash. "We need to get him to the back of the line."

I helped Washington drag Braddock back toward the river. Captain Stewart tried to help. The injured general groaned in pain as we pulled him past the bodies, tree branches, and discarded muskets. As the grenadiers and soldiers watched us struggle past with the general, the fight drained from them. Many simply dropped their weapons and started running, shedding as much extra weight as possible, never breaking pace.

The Indians kept coming warning us with their shrill war whoops. Panicked soldiers tried to outrun them, but were easily caught and tomahawked.

We found a two-wheeled wagon to place the ailing general in. Another officer saw us and rushed over. Braddock looked at him and spoke, "Your pistol, sir. So I can die like an old Roman." The officer considered the request but ignored him.

A procession of British wagons sped across the river, trying to catch up with the others already in full retreat on the other side.

"The wagons are running away," exclaimed an officer. "Bloody bastards are leaving us to die."

Washington mounted a horse and headed toward the river to find a place to rally the men. I attempted to follow on foot, but he returned quickly and informed us that Colonel Gage was already there.

We were just pulling the general through the water when my left shoulder exploded in a sudden and violent burst. I saw stars and fell face-first into the knee-deep water—stunned.

What happened? I had just been shot—my shoulder, I think. Strangely, it didn't hurt. I tried to put my arms in front of me to push myself up, but they wouldn't move. I focused, willing any kind of movement, knowing I would drown in the shallow stream if I couldn't get my head above the water. Nothing happened. A surge of panic bolted through me. One of my greatest fears was coming true, and I couldn't do anything about it.

My face rested on a smooth stone, and my senses had been reduced to the cool sensation of rushing water and the low warble of the Monongahela. I could no longer hear gunshots or cannon. No more blood-curdling screams from savage tomahawk attacks. No more cries for help from injured soldiers. It was serene.

And I was going to die.

Tabby, I thought. *I'm sorry I couldn't come home.*

I clenched my eyes. *Move, Goddammit!* I wouldn't let myself die like this. Not here. Not now.

Strong hands yanked me out of the water and helped me to my feet. Captain Stewart. I coughed out a mouthful of water and control of my body returned. I mumbled my thanks and lumbered across the water to the other side. The pain hadn't kicked in yet.

When we got across, I turned to Stewart. "Shippen?" I asked.

He shook his head.

I froze. "Did he die?"

"I don't know," he said. "I don't know."

* * *

The army regrouped on the other side of the river about a quarter mile from the water's edge. We prepared for the inevitable pursuit from the French and Indians.

I heard the general summon Washington to his side and order him to ride to Colonel Dunbar's camp. Dunbar was to prepare wagons and medical supplies for the retreating army and to rendezvous at Gist's plantation or somewhere closer. Washington agreed and rode off.

But where the hell was Mark?

It was getting late. The battle had lasted three or four hours and exhaustion was setting in for most of the men. We could hear the screams of fallen soldiers as the Indians fell upon them and took their scalps. Cries for mercy went unanswered.

We readied ourselves for the next French attack eager to exact revenge. We waited.

The expected attack never came.

I was no longer worried for Washington's health. He had survived the battle. We had prevented him from being shot through the heart as the newspaper account said. Now Mark and I could go home.

I just had to find him. Where the hell was he?

Fatigue was setting in. I was more tired than I had been in my entire life, but there was no time for rest. I felt unbalanced and lightheaded and needed to sit down, but I had to find Mark.

"I'm going back," I said to a black-faced soldier with a vacant stare.

The world went black.

TWENTY-FIVE

I heard the wagon wheels rotating over the rough road and realized the army must be getting ready to move out. I wondered why no one bothered to wake me. Someone was nestled close to me—either Mark or Patterson. I had to get up. If I was caught snuggling in camp, I would never live it down. We hadn't been late for a march yet and there would be hell to pay if the officers caught us oversleeping and we missed morning roll call.

Wait. The march is over.

We've already had the battle.

My eyes flew open. I found myself staring up at the tops of trees. My body jostled, in motion. Men lay all around me, most of them groaning or passed out. We were crammed in the back of a slow-moving wagon. The events of the battle flooded my memory. The sun had already set behind the trees. It was late afternoon.

Shit! I've lost a few hours. I have to find Mark.

I tried to sit up, but the pain in my shoulder prevented me from moving. I lay motionless for a minute and then used my good arm to force myself up.

"Where are we?" I asked.

"Retreating, almost to Gist's." The soldier sat with his back against the wall of the wagon. His head was wrapped in a white cloth that was stained red over his right ear. He had another bandage on his leg.

"Gist's? How long have I been asleep? I can't stay here. I have to find Mark."

He just looked at me.

"How long have we been traveling?"

"All day. They say the General's gonna die."

Oh God, I must have slept for over twenty-four hours.

"Where's Washington?"

"Don't know."

We arrived at the remains of Gist's plantation an hour or so after dark. It was mass confusion. We had just been though here a few days ago with so much anticipation. Now it was a nightmare.

The army had retreated though the night and all the next day in an effort to put distance between itself and the French attack that was expected at any time. A rumor pervaded throughout the camp that the French would be upon us within the hour.

When we stopped, I wandered to find Mark, but to no avail. Most of the horses were lost in the battle, and if he was wounded, he would be part of the long trail of injured soldiers trickling into the camp. I decided to seek out Washington to see if he knew anything.

I found him coming out of Braddock's tent. The general was still alive, giving orders and trying to reinstate the discipline that had completely disappeared during the battle. Regiments were formed in case the French came up the road and attacked.

"Have you heard anything about Mark? I haven't seen him since before the battle."

He shook his head. "I'm sorry," he said. "He might come in with the stragglers. We lost a lot of men yesterday. General Braddock has ordered we deposit flour and water on the side of the road so any men that miss the initial retreat will be able to survive until they reach Fort Cumberland. If he is alive, we will find him."

Despite his reassurance, I needed to do something.

"I need to go find him," I said. "I can't leave him behind."

"You are in no condition to go back," he said, glancing at my shoulder. "I'm sorry. I truly am. I owe you both much thanks, but we have to push forward and return to Fort Cumberland." He placed his hand on his coat over his heart. When he removed it, I saw the hole where the musket ball tore through the cloth.

The vest saved his life.

"Just give me a horse and I'll go alone."

"I cannot allow that. All of the horses are being used to transport the injured. I am sorry."

The weight of the moment hit me like a sledge hammer. My oldest friend was lost. I couldn't leave him behind. Not like this.

"You ungrateful bastard. How could you be so heartless? We risked our lives to save yours. All I'm asking for is a *fucking horse*."

Washington looked at me thoughtfully. "I am sorry," he said. Then he turned and walked away.

I took a step forward and grabbed him by the arm.

He spun on his heel and shook off my grip. His stare stopped me in my tracks.

He didn't say a word.

I dropped my arm down to my side and looked down at the ground. It was my turn to walk away.

I wandered back to the wagon that had transported me, not sure what to do. It was close to the entrance of the camp, and I could at least watch the stragglers as they came in.

The procession of the wounded arrived every few minutes, but their numbers dwindled as each hour passed. Soon, soldiers only wandered in every few hours. It was dark and difficult to see who was coming in, but no one fit Mark's description.

I spent the night waiting for Mark to arrive, but he never did. We headed out at first light.

My shoulder burned, but I felt that walking would help me try to focus on something else so I gave up my space on the wagon to someone who needed it more than I did.

I followed the trail of the army in a daze and ignored pleas from exhausted and injured soldiers who littered both sides of the road and asked for help. I had nothing to offer and I refused to make eye contact with any of them.

We met up with Colonel Dunbar's troops after a long day of walking. Almost immediately, efforts were made to disable the cannons in order to free up wagons and horses to transport the wounded. Ammunition was also destroyed or buried to prevent it from falling into the hands of the French. At least a hundred wagons were burned because there weren't enough horses left to pull them. The smell of smoke choked the air adding more dread to the already-anxious camp.

My thoughts again turned to Mark. For about the thousandth time that day, I wondered if he was even alive. I sat and watched the road all night waiting for him to appear. He never did.

From the Journal of John Curry
Great Meadows near Fort Necessity
July 13th or 14th, 1755

I'm not sure what day it is. I have heard two conflicting dates. One soldier told me it was the 12th of July. Another told me it was the 14th. I'm not even sure exactly where we are, but I recognize this area as being similar to the area around Fort Necessity so I am guessing we are close to there.

The battle was every bit the disaster I thought it would be. The soldiers panicked, and most of the officers were either killed or wounded. All except Washington. Thankfully, he has survived.

Mark is missing. I lost track of him early in the battle and no one has seen him since.

I remember falling asleep watching the road waiting for Mark after the army had met up with Colonel Dunbar's troops. The next thing I know, I was being carried with the wounded in the back of a wagon. I feel extremely weak. I remember bits and pieces of things that have happened, but most of my memories have been a blur. I frequently pass out. I feel alert now, so I'm attempting to write down everything I know before it's lost.

There is a rumor throughout the camp that Braddock has died. His last words were: "We shall know better how to deal with them the next time." I don't know if he really said that or not. There are so many conflicting reports floating around. Someone told me the army buried all of our pay in one of the muzzles of a cannon to prevent it from falling in the hands of the French. I find that hard to believe.

I tried to locate our companions from the Virginia volunteers, but I haven't been able to find out what happened to them either. I hope they made it.

My journal has mostly survived the battle. There was spilled ink from a shattered ink bottle that got on some of the pages, but I have two undamaged quills left. I will try to write to keep my mind sharp.

My leather pouch that holds my journal has been punctured by a musket ball. The bullet didn't make it all the way through, and I wonder if it saved my life.

From the Journal of John Curry
Fort Cumberland
July 18th, 1755

I know the date for sure now. It's July 18th and we have returned to Fort Cumberland. I was surprised to find the wagon driver that transported me back to this place is the same one who I saw whipped for beating the British officer during our march toward Fort Duquesne. He recovered from his flogging much faster than I thought possible.

He said he's had enough of "the fucking pompous" British orders. "Stupid buggars just stood there trying to block bullets with their bodies and got their hats handed to them by savages behind trees." I asked him how his wounds were healing and he said he'd be fine. He's young and strong and arrogant enough that I think he will survive. He told me his name is Daniel Morgan. If he is who I think he is, he will someday be a General during the Revolution. Revelations like this don't even faze me anymore.

I hear screams constantly from the soldiers having slugs being pulled out of their bodies by the surgeons. I have heard that most of the musket balls removed came from British muskets. Were we so incompetent that we killed each other?

I only have strength for short moments of clarity so I write when I can. I have lost the use of my left arm and have given up any hope of finding Mark. I need to locate Washington to see if he can get me back to Mount Vernon. I don't know if I can survive the trip. For the first time, I think I might actually die.

I'm not frightened. Just tired.

From the Journal of John Curry

July 21st

I don't know where we are. I am traveling with Washington and his man Alton. I think his name is John because Washington keeps saying my name, but when I look, he isn't talking to me.

Washington agreed to take me back to Mount Vernon although he isn't sure what to do with me when we get there. I am tied to a horse to keep me from falling off. Washington rides fast, much faster than Mark and I did.

Mark, where are you?

I have decided to tell Washington about the time machine in hopes that he will help me get in it and get home. I don't think I can do it by myself.

From the Journal of John Curry
No date given

I told Washington to remember the Fourth of July. You should be able to remember it. It's what made you famous.

He replied that the Fourth of July was a dark day in the history of his country as it was the day he surrendered Fort Necessity.

No, no <illegible> Press the rectangle. Push the numbers: 07041776

TWENTY-SIX

Gliding over trees. That is the way to travel. Thick forest blanketed the landscape as far as I could see.

Why didn't we just fly to Fort Duquesne? It would have been so much faster.

I slowed and sank to the ground, landing softly. I was at Mount Vernon again. That was so much faster than before.

"We need to go around the road so no one can see us," I explained, but I didn't move. I couldn't see the house. Mark would have to explain.

Eventually, we came across a large, round coffin.

Why would anyone build a round coffin? I was placed inside and could see it closing around me.

"No," I screamed. "I'm not dead yet. I'm not dead!"

Go home.

Darkness started to envelop me. I wanted to scream more, but I was too tired.

Home.

TWENTY-SEVEN

When you wake up, which comes first? Conscious thought or light? For me, it was light.

I opened my eyes. The room was bright. White. It took a second for my eyes to adjust. I was in a bed—a real bed.

"John?" a voice said. It was female. "Oh my God. John?"

Lillian.

I watched as she ran from the room. I was in a hospital.

A moment later a doctor walked in, trailed by Lillian—and my daughter, Tabitha.

"Tabby?" I gasped, choking on the lump in my throat. Tears ran down my cheek. Tabby ran over and hugged me tight. My shoulder screamed in pain, but it was worth it.

"We flew her in the moment you got back," said Lillian. "Her mother too."

Amanda's here. How bad must I be for Amanda to be here?

"What happened? Where am I? Where's Mark?"

Lillian paled. "You're back in Las Vegas—Sunrise Hospital. We don't know where Mark is. He wasn't with you when you returned. We were hoping you could explain."

"I don't know," I said. "After the battle—"

"Battle? What battle? Where'd you go?"

"We had to save Washington. I don't know. I can't remember

—"

"You must be tired." She grabbed my hand and bent down to kiss my forehead. "Get some rest, and we can talk about it later. I need to let Lawrence know you're awake."

I reached to grab her hand, but it hurt too much to move. I blurted out, "Gisçard."

She stopped at the door and turned.

"Gisçard. He was there. The same guy from Prague—only younger. I shot him in the hand and took his fingers."

She walked back over to me. "Where were you?"

"Not at the Inauguration. We were in the middle of the French and Indian War."

She considered what I just told her. "I'm going to get the doctor and call Lawrence. You rest. I'll be right back."

Tabby hugged me tight again and everything felt right with the world. Well, almost everything.

* * *

The doctor entered my room and tried to make Tabby leave, but I pleaded for her to stay and he allowed her to sit quietly as he went through his examination. I had tubes hooked up to me and my shoulder was bandaged and wrapped, but at least I was clean-shaven.

"What happened to you?" he asked.

"I think I was shot."

"You were, but I haven't seen a bullet wound like this. It looks like you were shot by a musket ball."

"Yeah, I think I was."

"Who shot you?"

"I don't know."

I spent some time with Tabby. We didn't say much. I lay there savoring the moment. Just being near her did me better than any medicine. Amanda came in and checked on us. After half an hour she told Tabby she should let me rest and they could come back tomorrow. I drifted off into a dreamless sleep.

* * *

A few hours later, Lawrence arrived. He looked like he had aged ten years. Maybe he had. I had no idea *when* I was anymore. He came into the room with Lillian.

"John, thank God you're alive," he said walking over to the bed. "I'm so sorry. We sent you and Mark off in the time machine and six hours later only *you* returned—but in this condition." Tears welled up in his eyes.

Six hours.

We had been gone for months, and to everyone back home we were gone only six hours. I couldn't wrap my head around something like that.

"How long have I been back?" I asked.

"Three days," answered Lillian. "The doctors said we almost lost you."

"I know it's soon," said Lawrence. "But can you tell us what happened? Do you have any idea where Mark is? We have to try to locate him."

The events of the past few months washed over me in complete clarity. I explained how Mark and I arrived in New York, but no one had heard of Washington. I told how we met Alexander Hamilton at the newspaper printer and he directed us to the library where we learned Washington had been killed during the French and Indian War while under the command of General

Braddock.

I described how we came to the conclusion to go back further in time to Mount Vernon and gave him one of the Kevlar vests we were wearing. It seemed the best course of action.

Lawrence hadn't known about the vests and was visibly bothered when I mentioned them, but he didn't say anything.

I recounted our meeting with Washington at Winchester where we gave him the vest and tried to return, but the machine didn't work, so we had to go back and volunteer for the army to ensure Washington survived. I described our march through the wilderness and how we learned to ride horses, and build campfires, and fire muskets, and we were good at shooting—especially Mark.

I described the battle and how Mark rode ahead with the cavalry to act as the general's bodyguard—and I never saw him again.

I explained how I was shot in the shoulder while trying to get Braddock back across the river and how I wasn't allowed to go back in search of Mark. I gave my account of the retreat back to Fort Cumberland, what I remembered of it at least, and how Washington agreed to take me back to Mount Vernon.

"I don't remember much of the ride back to Mount Vernon," I said. "I have no idea how I got into the time machine or how I returned home. I think there might be some details in my journal."

He stared at me and then looked at Lillian. "There's no journal, John."

Lillian spoke, "We have to find out what happened to Mark—"

"And then we shut this down. The entire operation," said Lawrence. "We're dabbling in something we can't control. I told Mr. Meade that everything was happening too fast. If we can't find Mark, he'll be the third one we've lost."

"I can start scouring history books for the lists of wounded and killed," said Lillian. "Dr. Cohen can help me." She was already standing up to go make a call.

"I'm so sorry, John. It was never supposed to work this way," said Lawrence.

"There's more," I said after Lillian had left. "I think Meade knew something was up."

I explained the theory Mark and I had formed after we discovered how much money we had for our *short* trip to New York, how none of those coins had been dated later than 1754, and how he *insisted* we wear protective vests. I came clean about my wearing the vest in Prague when I had been attacked by Claude and Gisçard.

He contemplated his next words, "We can ask him when he gets here. I called him the moment I heard you woke up. He's flying in from California." He stood. "For now, get some rest. We'll get this all straightened out. Don't worry."

* * *

I didn't see Meade until the next day. He was clean-shaven when he walked in, wearing an expensive suit but no tie. Under his arm, he carried a large, black portfolio—the kind art students carry at universities. Lawrence followed him and closed the door.

"John, how are you feeling?" He smiled as he approached. He extended his hand. I remained still.

He ignored my slight and pulled up a chair. Lawrence was doing the same thing, but Meade put up his hand. "Lawrence, can John and I have a few minutes?"

Lawrence began to protest, "Mr. Meade, we have a lot to—"

"Please, Lawrence." Meade cut him off. "Just a few minutes."

"But—"

Meade's stare halted his objection. It was the same look Washington gave me when I grabbed his arm. Lawrence stepped back and retreated out the door, closing it behind him.

"You son of a bitch," I said. "You knew this was going to happen."

"That's not entirely true," he said. He was relaxed. "Was I entirely forthcoming about my knowledge? No, but I want to explain everything to you."

"Mark's gone—probably dead," I said. "You weren't *entirely forthcoming*, and now Mark is gone. I even bought into that bullshit about your aunt." I wanted to stand up and deck him, but after a slight shift on the bed, I knew I didn't have the strength.

"Please. I have something for you."

He opened the black portfolio and removed a large envelope that looked very old. He also took out a Kevlar vest. It was no longer white. Time—and sweat—had yellowed it.

MY Kevlar vest.

"Yes, I knew about the vests before you left," he said, acknowledging my surprise. "Of course, we have the other one too. We couldn't just tell you what we had speculated about for generations—we didn't even understand *how* Washington got possession of them until Lawrence contacted me to get funding for his experiments."

"Who is *we*?" I asked.

Meade showed me a small titanium ring on his finger. Its insignia featured a symbol made up of a square and compass.

"Freemasons?"

"Yes, but don't draw the wrong conclusions. This isn't some worldwide conspiracy. It's simply a secret about one of our members that we've kept for over two hundred years. Washington was a prominent member of our organization—along with your friend

Casanova, *and* Mozart, *and* Benjamin Franklin. I could go on."

I knew he could.

"You see, after Washington died, the Masons from his lodge were the first people to go through his belongings, and they found *this*—" He held up the Kevlar vest, "And this—"

Pulled out a large envelope sealed with wax. The letters GW were embossed in the wax.

Washington's seal.

Written on the front in large, carefully written letters, probably in Washington's own handwriting, was my name: John Curry.

My heart began to pound. Goosebumps worked their way down both my arms—even the bad one.

My name. George Washington sent me a letter.

"This has never been opened," said Meade. "Washington left explicit instructions that the only person who should ever open this letter is *John Curry*. You will be the first person to view the contents since it was sealed. Maybe you can start to understand why I couldn't tell you everything before you departed, and why it was so important that *you* were the one who had to go."

I held it in my hand for a moment. I felt the shape and familiar weight. I already knew what was inside.

"Now?" I asked. The contempt had left my voice. I was curious. George Washington, the father of his country—*my country*—had left me a message not to be read until over two hundred years after his death.

It was almost a shame to break the seal and open the envelope. It had been preserved so well.

Almost a shame.

I tore the top of the envelope off and pulled out my journal. He must have taken it from me sometime during our ride back to Mount Vernon. Maybe I gave it to him. That explained *how* I got home. *George Washington* had put me in the time machine. *He* had the code to open it up because I had given it to him. I remembered writing it in the journal.

Meade's eyes were wide and curious. He sat forward, his arms resting on his knees. He had never seen this before.

"My journal," I said. "When we decided to join the army, I thought it would be cool to keep a journal to help remember the experience. I guess it saved my life."

Twice, I thought. The hole from the musket ball was still there.

Meade just looked at me. I hadn't told him what happened. I assumed Lawrence filled him in.

I opened the front cover. Out dropped two more sealed envelopes—both with my name written on the front. I recognized the handwriting on both. One was Washington's. The other—Mark's tiny chicken scratch.

A sob escaped me when I saw it. He survived.

"What is it?" asked Meade.

"Mark," I said. "This one is from Mark. He made it—and he met with Washington." I held both letters in my hand. My entire body was trembling. "Which one should I read first?"

"Read Mark's."

I carefully opened the top of the envelope and pulled out the letter.

May 18, 1792

Dear John,

If you're reading this, then you made it back safe and our mission was a success. I suppose you are wondering what happened to me.

At the start of the battle, we heard gunshots and rushed forward with Braddock and Washington. Not three minutes into the fight, my horse, Kwolek, was shot and I was thrown. I woke up hours later at the base of a tree surrounded by the dead. I was partially covered by the carcass of a dead horse (not Kwolek) and pulled myself up. I was disoriented and had no idea if we had won or lost. The battlefield was deserted except for the dead and wounded. I wandered around in the dark looking for you or any sign of the army, but found nothing. I heard gunshots and Indian war cries so I ran away from the sounds. When I reached the banks of the river, I didn't know what I would find on the other side, so I avoided the road and tried to work my way back through the dense forest.

I was lost for two days until finally locating our road. Thankfully, the army had discarded some supplies and water. I was able to survive long enough to work my way back to Fort Cumberland. When I got there, I ran into William and learned that you had left with Washington for Mount Vernon, but he thought you were going to die.

I had no horse to follow you, and no way to reach Mount Vernon, so I waited with the army until Colonel Dunbar decided to retreat to

Philadelphia. Thankfully, I still had a considerable amount of Meade's money so I bought a horse as soon as the army reached civilization. I rode hard to Mount Vernon. The time machine was gone so I figured that you were gone too. At that point, I didn't want to contact Washington. There was nothing more he could do for me, and I didn't want to be around to influence any more of his actions or decisions.

I made my way north and settled in Philadelphia. I had money and spent some time trying to figure out a way to get home. I spent months thinking of ways to try to send a message to you, in hopes that you could arrange a rescue, but came up with nothing I thought would work. After a year or so, I concluded that I actually liked it here and decided to stay. I bought a small farm near Pottsgrove Manor west of Philadelphia and built a small blacksmith business where I specialized in shoeing horses. I married and had six children and am proud to say they all survived to adulthood. Who knows? Maybe I am your great-great grandfather!

I changed my name so that you won't be able to easily track me down. My life is here, and I am an old man. By the standards of the eighteenth century, I am ancient.

I saw Washington three more times after our expedition with General Braddock. Once, while he was camped at Valley Forge I delivered a wagon full of supplies and horseshoes for the army. We made brief eye contact, but he didn't recognize me from what I could tell. I was too old to fight in the Revolution (I was almost 60), but two of my boys did, and they fought bravely and survived. I taught them how to shoot AND keep their heads down.

The second time was at his first presidential inauguration. I figured the inauguration was the whole reason my life ended up the way it did, so why not? We made the trip to New York, and I was able to find a great spot to listen to his speech. Tell Dr. Cohen, he didn't say it—"So help me God." He'll appreciate that.

The final time was today when I traveled to New York to see if he could help me deliver a message to you. My wife has long been gone and now my children are old and starting to die off too. I don't know what keeps me breathing. Maybe this is the closure I need so I can finally cash in my chips. Washington remembered me when I introduced myself. It's amazing how easy it is to get a meeting with the President in 1792! We talked for hours reminiscing about the old days—and the hero who made all of this possible, John Curry.

I know you're probably thinking you can track me down and bring me back, but I don't want you to. I have had a happy life. What more could anyone want? I once told you I envied you because you made time to have a family. After experiencing both the joy and heartache of family life, I can say in all sincerity that I couldn't bear to be without the memory of my wife and children.

PLEASE DON'T COME. *If you do, I will hide and will not acknowledge you—I decided that a long time ago. But, since I have no recollection of your coming, I know that you won't try, so* THANK YOU. *I did leave a gift for you to track down from your* present *location. It's in Pottsgrove, and you'll have to dig deep. I hope you make time to find it one day.*

I'm not sure how much time has passed since you returned home. You may or may not have had time to process what happened. I have spent hours and hours thinking about our experience and the reasons that caused it. I have come to only one conclusion that makes sense: WE DID NOT ALTER HISTORY. *We played a role in it. It was always destined—our traveling to New York and discovering that we had travel back further to give Washington the vest. That's what Meade knew, and that's what Washington believed. What's destined is destined. You can't control it. The vest has always been a part of the secret history of the United States, but maybe no one knew exactly why or how until we went. Don't be angry with Meade. He's as much of a hero as you and I. If you think about it, we're Founding Fathers. You, of all people, can appreciate that.*

We will always be friends no matter how much space or time sepa-

rates us. Follow your gut and you will always end up okay. Give my best to Lawrence and Lillian and even Meade who made this all possible.

Warm regards,
Mark Shippen

* * *

"What does it say?" asked Meade.

I handed him the letter and wiped the tears from my eyes. "He says thank you."

As he read Mark's letter, I opened the other letter addressed to me from George Washington.

* * *

Mount Vernon, July 4, 1799

My dear Sir: Four and forty years, nearly, have passed since I last enjoyed your company. During this period, so many important events have occurred, and such changes in myself have taken place, as the compass of a letter would give you but an inadequate idea of. It is unnecessary for me to apologize to you for my long silence as it appears you embarked from this country in a matter as such that no letters of mine cou'd have arrived. It has always been my intention to pay my respects to you.

A few years ago, I had the pleasure to receive a visit from our mutual friend, Mr. Shippen. In a word, I was lost in amazement to be reacquainted with the good company of Mark. After taking time to reminisce, he placed himself in the study composing to you a letter he is positive will reach your hand. I am inclined to believe his conviction that the letter will arrive as intended.

The sacrifice you made for your country must entitle you to all possible gratitude and affection. At the same time that it endears your Name to this Country. No one owes more appreciation to you than myself.

A sincere apology must be made for not returning your journal. You handed it to me while in a delirium brought on by fever. You spoke of things of which I had no practical knowledge, and I treated your words as nothing more than an affect of the disorder. As we approached Mount Vernon, my brother, Jack brought to my attention the great, round object that had simply appeared on the property. Upon this revelation, I opened your journal and followed your instructions. After placing you inside, the vessel closed. Moments later, you were gone.

I make no attempt to make sense of things I do not understand. I confess to you sincerely it is so much beyond any thing we had a right to imagine or expect these forty years, that it will demonstrate as visibly the finger of Providence, as any possible event in the course of human affairs can ever designate it.

Free as I am now from the toil, the cares and responsibility of public occupations and engaged in rural and Agricultural pursuits, I hope aided by the reflection of having contributed my best endeavors to promote the happiness and welfare of that Country which gave me, and my Ancestors, birth. My dear John, you by hand of Providence have also supplied no small part.

It is only appropriate that I compose this letter on the Anniversary of the Declaration of Independence, a date on which you correctly prophesied I would build my own reputation.

My most earnest wishes for your happiness, and that your successes and glory may always be equal to your Merits. You may assure yourself of the sincere esteem, regard and friendship of, dear Sir, your affectionate, &c.

G. Washington

* * *

I looked up at Meade who wept openly. When he was finished, he looked at me. "Lawrence needs to read this."

After Lawrence returned and read both letters, we sat in silence reflecting on what we read.

I looked at Lawrence. "Was Mark correct? That we didn't really change anything—that our actions were simply part of the historical record of 1755?"

"It's possible," he said.

"Of course he's correct," said Meade, holding up the vest. "Here's the proof. Just because it didn't come out of a book doesn't mean it didn't happen."

We all looked at the vest. It stood the test of time fairly well.

After a moment, Meade said, "There's one more thing."

He opened up the black portfolio and pulled out an 8"x10" picture. "This is a print. The original is safe."

I looked at the picture. It was a painting of George Washington. He stood in front of a full-length, oval-shaped mirror. The perspective was from behind Washington, but you could make out his features reflected in the mirror. It was a military pose I had seen a thousand times where Washington's arm was bent. Instead of the hand being tucked into his jacket, it was busy buttoning a waistcoat. Four buttons from the top were already clasped, but the bottom revealed a white vest. A Kevlar vest.

It was proof that Washington had always had it in his possession.

"It was painted by Charles Willson Peale, another Mason,"

said Meade. "I thought you deserved a copy of it. Few people—even members—have ever seen this."

"Thank you," I said. "Thank you."

EPILOGUE

I stood at the top of a ridge overlooking farmland in southeastern Pennsylvania and double-checked the map printed from the online archives. After a brief indecision, I made my way down to the banks of the Schuylkill River. I walked for fifteen minutes and looked at the map displaying the topography of Pottsgrove.

The undergrowth was thick and hard to navigate, but eventually opened to a clearing. My arm was still sore, but it worked.

This has to be the place.

I searched around until I found the remains of a stone foundation laid sometime in the eighteenth century. Weeds, rocks, and a few rusted beer cans littered the site, but nothing interesting caught my attention.

Maybe I should have grabbed the metal detector from the trunk.

I decided against returning to the car and widened my perimeter. About thirty feet from the main site, I came upon the remains of a small, eight-foot section of stone wall hidden beneath the tall grass.

I paced back and forth trying to figure out where the outside of the foundation originally stood.

Nothing. I never do things the easy way.

Frustrated, I returned to the car to grab the metal detector and shovel. Knowing my destination made the return trip a little faster, but I still lost a half-hour of the remaining daylight.

With the sensitivity set to maximum, I surveyed the secondary area first, walking up and down an imaginary grid. I used a sweeping motion to the right and left as I walked, listening for hopeful beeps. During my fifth pass, the detector alerted me that I found something large. The depth looked to be around nine or ten inches. I started digging.

Inside the hole was a large metal cylinder, the end-cap about ten inches in diameter. It was heavy and I used the shovel to pry it out of the ground. It was sealed tight so I worked the blade of my pocketknife into the seam. After a moment, it finally budged.

I popped the lid off to find a wooden box the size of a shoebox. I pried it open.

Found you.

Inside were two packages wrapped in leather oilskins. The first contained a pair of black spectacles—Mark's spectacles. The ones he hated. The second wrap revealed the time machine's remote control. A small note was attached.

It read: *The batteries have died. You will need to replace them.*

Classic Mark.

I placed the remote inside the cylinder so I could carry it back to the car and my hand brushed against a third wrap. I pulled it out. The material was canvas, rather than leather—probably taken from an old sail and soaked in linseed oil. It was about the size of a small book.

Too heavy to be a book.

I peeled back the canvas and exposed an envelope. It was addressed to me and written in handwriting I didn't recognize. Behind the envelope was a photograph of three men on an old daguerrotype.

Photographs weren't around in Mark's time.

I examined it not quite believing what I saw. The man on the right was unfamiliar. He had a handsome face and wore a dark suit with a high, white collar. Dark eyes stared into the camera.

The man in the middle was easy enough to place. Tall, with a slight smirk on his face.

Oh my God.

That's me.

How would a photograph of me end up in Mark's box?

That only means one thing—

And who's that third guy?

I had seen him before, but couldn't place where. Dark hair, thick eyebrows, bags under his eyes. His mustache covered his entire lip.

Where have I seen him before?

"Oh shit," I said. "That's—"

Edgar Allen Poe.

Author's Note

When I sat down to write this book, I had no idea where it would end up, or if I would even finish. I had never written anything before—not novel-length at least. I remember sitting in my living room thinking, "What if you traveled to the past and history wasn't what you anticipated? What if it had completely changed, and the *real* history had been manipulated by someone from the future?" I know I'm not the first person to come up with an idea like this. Fiction is full of far-out questions needing to be answered. I thought about the idea for three days, then placed it in the recess of my mind. Three years later, while driving on a long-distance trip, I listened to Richard Brookhiser's *Washington on Leadership* and was inspired to revisit the idea.

I love history. I love reading it and watching documentaries on television, so I was already familiar with the close-calls George Washington had in his lifetime. For the rest of you history lovers, I tried to incorporate as much of the real history as as possible.

I stumbled across Casanova while researching *Don Giovanni*. He really was in Prague for the premiere, and his hand-written notes detailing his suggested changes for the libretto were found with his papers following his death. He was friends with Mozart's lyricisist—and fellow libertine—Da Ponte, so the idea that Casanova helped with the production of a story based on the fictional Don Juan is both compelling and plausible.

I would encourage everyone to read Casanova's autobiography. You can download it for free on most e-readers. His writing is both engaging and conversational, and you can easily picture him narrating his tale to a captivated audience. There was so much more to him than his reputation as a lover. My first draft of this novel had Casanova detailing his escape from prison, but I felt it was too much of a detour from the main story. Maybe I can revisit his tale in a future book.

The hardest part of writing this novel was the science. I read (and tried to understand) two books on physics and countless web sites to make sure the science behind time-travel was at least plausible. I will, no doubt, receive emails explaining why I'm wrong, but please understand I did make an effort. Be nice sci-fi nerds! I know most readers won't care, but again, I was shooting for accuracy. Plus, I'm a nerd too, and *I care*, so there.

A number of books were instrumental in helping me get the history as accurate as possible. I would like to especially thank historians David McCullough and Joseph Ellis for triggering inspiration and feeding my love for the historical narrative. The following books were invaluable in making the details of my own story come alive: both *Washington* and *Hamilton* by Ron Chernow, *George Washington's First War* by David Clary, Thomas Crocker's work on *Braddock's March*, Ian Kelly's biography on Casanova, *Braddock at the Monongahela* by Paul E. Kopperman, *Realistic Visionary by* Peter Henriques, and finally, Andrew Wahll's excellent *Braddock Road Chronicles*. I am also indebted to the University of Virginia's online database containing the Writings of George Washington edited by John C. Fitzpatrick. There were many more sources, but these were especially helpful.

If you're more of a visual learner, please check out Robert

Matzen's fantastic trilogy detailing the events of the French and Indian War. Footage from *When the Forest Ran Red* can be seen in the *Washington's Providence* book trailer.

I want to take a moment to thank everyone who supported me in getting this book completed. Corrine Heyeck, Detta Penna, Beth Luedke, Ken Gunter, Erik Heyeck, the writers at Rocky Mountain Fiction, Wendy Terrien and Terri Spesock from my coal-fired critique group, Lorin Oberweger of Free Expressions, and novelist Kevin J. Anderson who made the point: if he could write eight novels in year, I could complete one.

Last, but not least, I would like to thank my wife, Molly. Had it not been for her love and support, I would still be writing at a snail's pace.

I'd also like to extend my personal thanks to the Freemasons for keeping the secret.

July 30th, 2012

Reading Group Guide

Washington's Providence

A Timeless Arts Novel

Chris LaFata

Questions and topics for discussion

*** Chris is available for "author chats" with your book club. Arrangements can be made for both in-person and virtual meetings. To schedule, please email chris@chrislafata.com.**

1. In Chapter One, John travels to Las Vegas for the *job of his dreams*, but has no idea what the opportunity is—only that the offer came from his childhood friend, Mark. What does this tell you about John and his feelings toward his friend?
2. When John is shown the video for prospective clients in Chapter Two, it's revealed that Timeless Arts' mission is to observe historical and artistic events of the past. If you were given the choice of visiting any event in the past, where would you go and why?
3. Lillian explains that prior arrangements must be made for each Observation, and the arrangements could change depending on the number of clients traveling to an event. In her preparations for *Don Giovanni*, Lillian had met Casanova multiple times, but Casanova only met Lillian twice. What are the potential dangers this kind of arrangement?
4. How does the story deal with the problem of time-travel paradoxes?
5. Timeless Arts employees are reminded multiple times not to time travel with any modern items, yet all of them break this rule. Why is it not strictly enforced?
6. After meeting Alexander Hamilton, John laments Hamilton was the "shell of the man" he expected—presumably because Hamilton's chance for distinction never materialized. Do you feel talent will always rise, or are we shaped by the circumstances surrounding us?
7. In order to save George Washington's life, John and Mark face the prospect of joining the British army they know will be decimated in battle. Were there better options that might have been safer than subjecting themselves to the dangers associated with the battle?

8. Mark reminds John not to befriend any of the other soldiers because of the temptation to protect their lives and possibly change history. What was John's response? How would you respond in a similar situation?
9. When John returns to his own time, Harrison Meade acknowledges he's always known about Washington's vest prompting John's realization that his experience was always part of history. Had Meade told John beforehand, do you think John would have made the trip to the past?
10. John encounters Gisçard twice during his travels. What might have happened if they had never crossed paths?

"Flip" recipe that would make John and Mark happy

1/2 oz. molasses (feel free to substitute maple syrup)

1 1/2 oz. rum

1 hot poker heated in fireplace

pewter mug

12 oz. stout beer

1. Stir molasses and rum in pewter mug.
2. Fill remaining space with beer.
3. Insert poker into mug. Drink will foam.
4. Raise your cup and toast Ben Franklin.

* Recipe adapted from: http://harmonioushomestead.com/2013/03/12/rum-flip-cocktail/

If you liked Washington's Providence, please post an online review on Amazon or Goodreads and share it on Facebook. For Indie authors, nothing is more helpful than an honest reader's opinion.

If you didn't like it, please send me an email telling me why: chris@chrislafata.com.

Subscribe to my newsletter on my website, and I'll keep you posted on the sequel.

Please visit my website: http://www.chrislafata.com

"Like" Washington's Providence on Facebook

https://www.facebook.com/WashingtonsProvidence